This is a work of fiction. Any similarity between the names and characters in this book and any real persons, living or dead, is purely coincidental.

FIRST EDITION

All rights reserved, including the right of reproduction in whole or in part in any form.

Copyright © 2005 by Nicholas A. Clemente

Published by Vantage Press, Inc.
419 Park Ave. South, New York, NY 10016

Manufactured in the United States of America
ISBN: 0-533-15018-3

Library of Congress Catalog Card No.: 2004096076

0 9 8 7 6 5 4 3 2 1

BROKEN GAVEL

A Novel

Nicholas A. Clemente

VANTAGE PRESS
New York

For Ann Marie

One

Anthony "Rags" Ragazza was dressed in his work clothes as he prowled the neighborhood. His jeans, although stylishly tailored, were loose enough to allow him to move rapidly. His leather bomber jacket, dark brown, and meant to be menacing, matched his hawk nose and deep-set crow's eyes. His sallow complexion, in the sparse street light, even at 3:00 A.M., easily marked him as no friend to sunlight. He appeared taller than he actually was because of his gaunt frame. Rags Ragazza was a car thief.

New York City is a smorgasbord of old towns that grew together and now are barely discernible. Albemarle Park is one of those towns in the otherwise congealed neighborhoods of Brooklyn. Its streets are divided by malls with carefully cultivated bushes. The houses, all spacious three-story Victorian homes, meticulously maintained, line the streets like sentinels, guarding the wealth. Parked in the driveway at 30 Buckingham Road was a 2005 Mercedes. Its license plate read: SUPREME COURT 150.

Ragazza looked furtively up and down the street lined with sycamore trees. Although he took advantage of the shadows, he strolled up the driveway, reached into his pocket, and took out a car key. Casually, as if it were his own car, he opened the door and started the engine. Ragazza, carefully and without haste, backed down the driveway. He made a left turn at Church Avenue and another left onto Ocean Parkway. It was at this point that Rags violated the cardinal rule of all car thieves—he ran a red light.

The police cruiser's turret flashed on its blinding red lights, the car burning rubber as it took after the Mercedes.

"Looks like we got a live one." Tom, the recording officer, hit the siren.

"He's going like a bat out of hell," the driver said.

"Maybe we ought to call for backup."

"Nah, we got him now, Bobby."

The three other cars that were stopped for a traffic light were barely a deterrent for Rags; he maneuvered around them. The police cruiser careened around in pursuit.

"Christ, this guy is going to get us killed," Bobby said.

"What're you worried about? Then you won't have to pay alimony."

The Mercedes hit a pothole, causing it to sideswipe a van. Amid a shower of sparks, the car mounted the curb and skidded several hundred feet before it slammed into a large maple tree.

The police officers circled the demolished Mercedes. Their pistols were drawn and their hands trembled. They found Ragazza pounding on the collapsed air bag with his fists.

"What luck!" Ragazza said. "What goddamned luck!"

The tension of the chase was too much for Bobby. He smashed the driver's-side window with his pistol. Shards of glass cascaded upon Ragazza as he moved away from the pistol pointed at his head.

"Hey, oh shit. I'm surrendering!" Ragazza raised his hands. "See?"

"Take it easy," Tom said.

"Take it easy? I'd like to put a bullet right in his frigging brain!" Holstering his pistol, Bobby reached into the broken window and seized Ragazza. Bobby was bulky, like an old-time cop, and he easily yanked Ragazza through the broken window and onto the pavement.

He placed his knee into the small of Rags's back and handcuffed him. He then patted his prisoner down.

"He ain't got any identification."

"They never do," Tom said, "What's your name?"

"Would you believe me if I said Sylvester Stallone?"

"A comedian," Bobby said. He gave Rags a sharp kick to the ribs.

"You fat bastard! You wouldn't do that if there were witnesses."

Tom, too, kicked Rags.

"You want witnesses? Steal a car in rush hour," Tom said.

Two

The interrogation room at the 66th Precinct was meagerly furnished. The barrenness of its green walls was a reminder that no care was necessary for those unlucky enough to be questioned there. Morning light was just now coming through the window.

They sat Ragazza at a table. To his front was a camcorder set on a tripod. Slightly off to the rear but within his field of vision was a big clock placed in a large patch of unpainted plaster. The tiny red light on the camcorder signaled that it was recording.

Martin Tracy, obviously the younger of the two detectives, had reversed his chair and sat, leaning on its spine. Jack Zangara drew the shades and then circled Rags, but he was careful not to get in the picture. Ragazza smiled, but not enough to show his bad teeth.

"Where's the sign?" Ragazza said. He pointed to a spot over the door.

"What are you talking about?" Tracy said.

"The sign—the sign that says: Abandon hope, all ye who enter here."

"They said you were a comedian." Tracy rocked in his chair as if he were going to leap at Rag's throat.

"Come on, you guys. Give me a break."

"That wasn't too bright, Rags," Zangara said. "Stealing a judge's car—not too bright." Zangara picked up the arrest report and thumbed through it. He knitted his brow, as if the truth always puzzled him.

"Something smells here, Marty."

"You getting one of your harebrained ideas again?"

Zangara shook his head. Twelve years, seven as a detective, and still Tracy had not developed that instinct that made a cop a detective. It was just his luck that he was stuck with an unimaginative partner. But, then, he had enough instinct for both of them. Martin Tracy, always neatly dressed, tall and still slender—and, unlike Zangara, not given to baldness—was at least dependable as his backup. Did he really have a complaint? After all, they were both still alive and healthy in a very dangerous business.

"Today's Saturday," Zangara said.

"Yeah, Jack, so what? And tomorrow will be Sunday."

Zangara's thick arms filled his shirtsleeves and matched his bull neck. He moved toward Ragazza, but he was not threatening. His dark eyes bulged slightly as he stared at the perpetrator. "Rags, since when you working a seven-day week?"

"What you mean?"

"Yeah, Ragazza, don't you thieves party on weekends?"

"I was short of cash."

Zangara checked the report again.

"According to this, the key was in the ignition."

"Tell the truth, you found it on the ground," Tracy said.

"Hey, how did you know?" Ragazza said.

"You got a contact at the dealership, Rags?" Zangara asked. His voice was now low and conspiratorial.

"Nah, people make that mistake all the time—leaving the key in the ignition."

"Is that what happened, Rags?" As Zangara spoke, he moved still closer to Rags and dropped his voice to a whisper.

"You're in deep shit, Rags," Tracy said. "I called the judge and woke him up. He didn't leave no key in the ignition. All we want to know is: Where's the chop shop?"

"I want to see my lawyer."

"Now the little shit wants to see his lawyer!" Tracy said.

"Yeah, and it's on tape! You can't question me after I ask for my lawyer."

Ragazza took a Camel from the pack in his jacket and leaned back in his chair.

"Anybody got a match?"

Zangara went to the camcorder and flicked the "off" switch. Then he turned to Tracy.

"When he's right, he's right. Now there's no videotape," Zangara said.

The cigarette only momentarily dangled from Ragazza's lips, because Tracy swiped it from him in one quick, sweeping motion. He kicked the chair and knocked Ragazza to the floor, then picked him up. "You sack of shit!" Tracy said and slammed Ragazza into the wall. The clock shook from the impact.

"We know you know your rights, Rags." Zangara's voice was now as harsh as Tracy's. Zangara was so close that his spittle sprayed Ragazza. Tracy kept Ragazza pressed against the wall and pushed his leather jacket into his throat.

"I'm gonna ask you only once more: Where's the chop shop?" Tracy said.

"Come on, Rags. You know you're facing life imprisonment as a persistent felony offender. We can't help you unless you help us." Zangara's voice was smooth and soothing again.

After a long moment, Ragazza turned and nodded to Zangara.

Tracy released him.

"Just take it easy. You got some name for a detective," Ragazza said. He pulled his jacket back into place. "Yeah, Tracy the Dick—Dick Tracy."

"How did I know this little piece of shit was going to say that?" Tracy swung his forearm and struck hard at Ragazza's vocal cords.

"That's wonderful," Zangara said. "Now he can write out his confession."

"I'm sick and tired of this wiseass."

Ragazza rubbed his throat and tried to clear it. When he was able to speak, his voice was uncertain and hoarse. "What if I give you a name better than a chop shop?"

Three

The Supreme Court of the State of New York is a court of original jurisdiction. In other words, it is not the highest court in New York but rather, the highest *trial* court.

The Brooklyn Courthouse is in the downtown business complex, surrounded by tall office buildings. The courthouse itself, however, a modern eleven-story building, is set in a parklike complex with trees, paths, and benches.

On Monday morning, the area, desolate on weekends, was quickly coming to life as the subway disgorged people hurrying to work. It was obvious that this was no ordinary morning because in addition to civilians entering the courthouse, a number of uniformed police officers were setting up wooden horses.

To one side, a group of African-Americans gathered, while on the other, Hasidim dressed in wide-brimmed hats, black suits, and white stockings, also gathered.

A taxicab pulled up by the office buildings that

framed the other side of the plaza, and Justice Simmons alighted. The permanent on-duty police officer greeted him with a salute.

"What's up, Judge? I didn't expect you to be traveling by public transportation."

"How are you, Mac? They stole my car the other day."

Officer Macarella was a stocky Sicilian-American with a dark complexion and a bright, jovial smile.

Gregory Simmons was the opposite of Mac. He was a little over six feet tall and still lean although, at forty-five, he was beginning to thicken around the middle. His shock of gray hair tumbled boyishly on his forehead as he walked. He was fair-skinned with blue-gray eyes that seemed to shine even when he was serious. As usual, he wore a Brooks Brothers suit with narrow lapels. His shoes were spit-shined, but his brown suit did not quite match his black shoes.

"These things can really upset somebody." Mac looked down at the mismatch.

"You notice everything, don't you, Mac?"

"I better escort you into the courthouse today."

"*Somebody* better help me," Simmons said. "It looks like I dressed in the dark."

"Anything you need, Your Honor, just let me know!"

"I need an Advil. I'm the trial judge in the *McCauley* case."

"Things sure are changing. They don't even wait for a verdict before they picket. They respect *you*, though, Judge."

"It's too bad that the *crooks* have no respect."

Mac took Simmons's briefcase and carried it for him.

"What bothers me is that I just paid eight hundred dollars to service the damned car and a thief raps it up."

"We caught him?"

"Yes. After he totaled my car."

As they reached the side entrance, angry voices came from the Hasidic group.

"Look at her, so fancy. Defending a murderer," said one.

"She doesn't care who she represents," said another.

"You should choke on the money you make on this case!" called out a third.

"That's Barbara Danzig, isn't it?" Mac said.

"Yes."

Barbara Danzig was smartly dressed in a two-piece blue business suit that accentuated her well-proportioned body. She walked briskly up the Supreme Court steps. She took no note of the harassing remarks and ignored the stares of several of the spectators.

"She's some dish," Mac said.

"Yes, she is very attractive," Simmons said.

"Attractive? Did you get a look at those legs?"

"Mac! I'm surprised at you—a married man." Simmons smiled, and his dimples deepened.

"Hey, Judge, the way I look at it, we go to the museums and admire stuff stuck on walls. The way she walks is living art."

Four

When the elevator doors opened at the seventh floor, Barbara allowed herself a cordial smile as several men stepped aside to permit—and watch her, weave her way along the narrow corridor.

"Thank you. . . . Yes. . . . Good morning."

Barbara was in her "congenial to the public" mode, but her thoughts were concentrated on the McCauley case. Rather, she was forcing herself *not* to think about that damned recurring dream.

It had not been a good night for sleeping. Alone and awake. Three years of therapy and nothing to show for it! Doctor Reich? No, Doctor Schmuck! Barbara's smile, this time was directed inwardly—*Schmuck*? What was the feminine equivalent of that Yiddish word? She'd have to ask Uncle Norman.

As at the street entrance, a buzz of conversation trailed after her. Barbara was five feet eight inches tall and wore stiletto heels when she went to court. On those days, dominance prevailed over comfort.

"That's a lawyer?" a spectator said to his friend.

Barbara's hair tended toward kinkiness. It was dark auburn and in pleasing contrast to her creamy complexion. She kept her hair short for easy washing. Barbara's nose was thin and aristocratic despite a small bump that testified to a competitiveness spawned in childhood.

"Come on, throw it harder," she had said to her uncle Norman. "You throw the ball like a girl!"

Disdain breeds carelessness—because as she turned away, her uncle threw the ball. It caught her, and her nose, off guard.

The nose was a minor distraction; it was her eyes that set her apart. They were sky blue and riveted you with their glance. And, then, to make the gods more jealous, she had been endowed with a first-rate mind.

"She's as tough as steel," another spectator said. "She'll get McCauley off. I don't know how, but she'll find a way."

The spectator shook his head. "Not with all those eyewitnesses."

The Part 8 courtroom was blocked by a court officer, who opened the door for her.

"Good morning, Ms. Danzig."

"Hi, Basil. House full again, eh?"

"You bet." Basil was six foot four and weighed three hundred pounds. It was apparent why he had been given the task to guard the courtroom entryway.

The courtroom was an interior one. Floor-to-ceiling wood paneling and bright fluorescent lights compensated for the windowless walls. Every seat was occupied by spectators, who spoke in church whispers as they waited for the trial to begin.

Barbara took her seat at the defendant's counsel table—the table farthest from the jury box. This was a sizable disadvantage that Barbara had attempted to turn around in her opening statement to the jury, the day before.

"Tradition. I believe in tradition," she had said. "It holds our society together. Sometimes it's not fair, but we learn to live with it. For example, why is it that the prosecutor always sits at the table that's closest to the jury? Why? Tradition. The district attorney said to me, 'What's the big deal?' I said to him, 'Well, if it doesn't matter, let's switch.' Would you believe that he said he couldn't switch—because it was tradition? To tell you the truth, it isn't a big deal, because this courtroom isn't a restaurant. The D.A. may have the better table, but I have the better case."

The assistant district attorney had objected, and Justice Simmons had sustained the objection. Barbara figured that the next time she would go a little farther. Justice Simmons, in ruling against her, had not even bothered to bang his gavel. Trials, like wars, were often won by small victories.

As for now, she glanced at the assistant D.A. and nodded. Wallace Macklin was a deep-voiced West Indian who spoke in a clipped, slightly British accent. Young. Can't be more than thirty years old. Where was all the time going? Macklin was at least five years younger than she. He was wearing the same wrinkled gray suit he had worn for the last few days.

The volume in the audience increased as a door to the

right of the bench opened. Reginald McCauley was led into the courtroom. The youth was in handcuffs and flanked by two court officers. McCauley stood sullen as the handcuffs were removed. He was neatly dressed in a sport jacket with a blue shirt and tie. His white running shoes were more dissonant than old-time spats.

"How we doing today?" Barbara asked him.

"You tell me." McCauley's voice was hostile and loud enough to be heard by the audience.

Barbara smiled as if she were perfectly at ease with his anger. She then leaned over and patted him on the shoulder.

"Be nice, you little prick," she whispered.

Five

"We're running late today," Justice Simmons said.

He waited for his law clerk, David Leibowitz, to help him on with his robe. David was tall and gangling. Despite his relative youth, he was the father of five children.

"Making up for the Holocaust?" Simmons had often teased him. "Or are you trying to make Malthus look good?"

Today, however, was not a day for lightness. Justice Simmons went to his desk and picked up the intercom. His voice was unusually brusque.

"Elaine, come in. Bring your steno pad."

The chamber was eclectically furnished. His large mahogany desk dominated the room. Behind him, on either side, were an American flag and a New York State flag. The walls were cluttered with plaques, diplomas, and photographs, with the governor, the mayor, and the former governor. It afforded a history of Gregory Simmons's illustrious career. It told a tale—for those who could read it—of his rise to power and position of prominence.

Elaine Trezza slipped into the chair opposite the desk, and with the easy familiarity of a chore often repeated, flipped open her pad. She held her pen and looked up. She was an elderly, motherly type and had worked as the judge's secretary for many years prior to his ascending to the bench. Many lawyers had discovered her fierce protectiveness only after they had felt the lash of her tongue.

"They're thieves and should be castrated," she said.

"Elaine, I don't have time for this. I need this letter out today. The insurance company requires written notice before they'll consider the loss."

"Balls and all," she said softly.

"Will you please take this down! 'Pursuant to my insurance policy, you have the policy number, please be advised that on October 9th, my Mercedes was stolen from my home. It has been recovered by the police in a severely damaged condition.' Etcetera . . . you know the rest."

He turned next to David, who had been hovering by the bookcase. "David, my golf clubs are in the trunk of my car, and I'm scheduled to play at the Brooklyn and Manhattan Trial Lawyers golf outing. Do you think you could get them for me?"

"Where's the car?" David glanced at his watch.

"They towed it to the sixty-sixth precinct."

"Should I prepare your jury charge, first?"

"Don't worry about that. We still have a few days before summations."

The judge took the key from his pocket and gave it to David. He accepted the key reluctantly because—though already 28, with a brilliant legal career before him—David was just now learning how to drive. "First things first," he had told his wife. She had finally shamed him into going to driving school. "You finished second in your class at Harvard? What a nebbish," she had said.

He had obtained his driving license, but the confidence he had in navigating the law was not transferred to the road.

"I'll have my wife pick them up, Your Honor."

"David, you do it! There might be some legal technicality—some papers to sign."

"Yes, sir."

"Now, let's get to work."

Rose Somma, a diminutive court officer, was in the anteroom to Judge Simmons's chambers. She waited to escort him to the courtroom. In long strides, he breezed past her. She hurried and caught up with him at the judges' elevator.

"So what's new, Rosie?"

"They're waiting for you."

"To be more accurate, they're lying in wait for me."

Rose smiled. No sense in trying to match wits with him.

"They sure are. You should see what's going on in the front of the courthouse."

"I did," Simmons said.

"It's not funny. This whole city is about to explode. What a sight—blacks and Jews picketing each other—and you're in the middle of it."

"No, it's not funny, Rose. What are they saying? I arrived while the police were still setting up."

"The cops have them all marching around but separate from each other. The blacks have signs like NO MORE LYNCHING and FREE REGINALD. The Jews are carrying signs that say: NEVER AGAIN—WHITE OR BLACK and

JUSTICE FOR MENACHEM. There's going to be a riot no matter who wins the case."

"Unless we have a hung jury," Simmons said.

"Then there'll be two unhappy sides instead of one."

"Ah, but when everyone is unhappy, it sometimes takes the sting out of victory or defeat."

"That's too deep for me, Your Honor."

When they reached the rear corridor of the courtroom, the members of the jury were already lined against the wall according to seat number. Simmons moved easily among them. He greeted each one as they waited to be led into the courtroom. The jury was a mix of Caucasians, Asians, and African-Americans. Given the climate, it was practically an invitation for a hung jury. What the hell was on that kid Macklin's mind? Perhaps that was what the district attorney wanted—a hung jury. It meant that the case would have to be retried. Weren't there enough new cases to keep the court busy?

After the jury was seated, Justice Simmons entered the courtroom. He briskly stepped to the bench, and the clerk called out, "All rise."

Simmons remained standing as the clerk delivered the proclamation. "The Supreme Court of the State of New York is now in session. Draw near and give your attention, and ye shall be heard—the Honorable Gregory A. Simmons presiding."

"Have the witness return to the stand," Simmons said.

Abraham Steinhardt, a small man of about 50, walked to the witness stand. He moved slowly, looking as if he had been bent by the endless hours spent hunched over his desk. One could almost see the mark made by the shade on this little accountant's forehead. He was dressed in traditional Hasidic clothes—black suit, white stockings. He wore a yarmulke that rested uneasily on his bald head.

"The witness is reminded that he is still under oath," the clerk said.

"Would you proceed, please, Ms. Danzig?"

Barbara rose and walked to the far end of the jury. She placed her notes on the small ledge by the jury box. She always had papers, either in her hand or on the ledge, but never looked at them. She used the legal pads more as props than for information.

"Now, Mr. Steinhardt, I'm going to ask you some questions. If you cannot answer them with a 'yes' or 'no,' please tell me and I will rephrase them. Will you do that?"

Macklin slowly rose and made a mild objection.

"Can't we just get on with this cross-examination without Ms. Danzig instructing the witness on how to answer questions?"

"Yes, Ms. Danzig, don't try to do my job."

"Yes, Your Honor." Barbara smiled sweetly.

"Mr. Steinhardt, would you tell the jury how many people were surrounding Reginald McCauley."

This time it was a real objection. Macklin had turned from placid to livid in a second. His freckles reddened and made his honey brown complexion seem lighter.

"Surrounding? I object, Your Honor. I most strenuously object."

"An objection is sufficient. It doesn't become more valid by being strenuous."

Simmons smiled. *Youth!* Passion was good; losing control was bad. This young man might get better with time, but this was the here and now!

"The objection is sustained. Counselor, you know better than to ask a question like that." A small rebuke. Had to keep her in her place, too.

"Your Honor, he's the third witness who wants this jury to think that they were all innocent bystanders!" It was a nice try. How far could she push this judge? How hard *should* she push?

Barbara had researched Justice Simmons's background. She knew that he had graduated from Brooklyn College phi beta kappa. An odd fact had jumped out. He had been elected class poet. He had then graduated from St. John's Law School—a poet lawyer? But she could deduce more than that.

Brooklyn College was a public college—not Ivy League. Therefore, he was not from money. He must have worked his way through school. He was not law review. That, too, was curious—top students were selected for law review. How was it that Simmons could be phi beta kappa and not be on law review? No aptitude for law? Not likely. And a poet, too. What baggage was he carrying? It is said, "Know the child and you'll know the man." Unfortunately, Westlaw and Lexis could reveal many facts, but reasons often remained a mystery. Still, private life could be revealed by a résumé or casual inquiries to friends.

For example, she had learned that Simmons was an only child. Catholic and no siblings? Had there been an "Irish divorce"? That is, had his father just disappeared? If so, he seemed to have weathered that storm pretty well, because Simmons was highly regarded. The opinions of lawyers who had tried cases before him was that he was street-smart. Knowledgeable and fair—what more could she want from a judge?

"You will disregard the comments of counsel," Simmons said to the jury. "The objection is sustained."

Then, turning to Barbara, he said, "Please rephrase the question—'surrounding' is a conclusion."

Barbara concealed her satisfaction with the small triumph. Fat chance that they would disregard *that*!

"All right, Mr. Steinhardt. Were there more than six persons present at the time of this incident?"

"Including the victim, yes."

Barbara shook her head in mock despair.

"Seems like we have a lawyer for a witness," Barbara said.

"No, I'm an accountant." Steinhardt smiled for the audience.

"Objection," said Macklin.

"Oh, no, Judge. This time it's my objection, and I move to strike the answer as unresponsive." Barbara pretended annoyance.

"Strike it, as well as the comment about the witness being a lawyer."

"Mr. Steinhardt, this jury will decide who the victim is. Let me ask you again. Were there more than six?" Barbara said.

"There were a number of people. I don't know the exact count."

"All of these people—they were all Hasidim?"

"All except for Mr. McCauley." Mr. Steinhardt's voice was subdued. He stared at Barbara, but his mind was searching for the trap he was certain was being laid for him.

"Let's talk about Reginald McCauley. You've identified him as the person who stabbed Menachem Sackheim?"

"Yes."

Barbara noticed that several of the jurors leaned forward. It couldn't have been in surprise. In jury selection, everyone had acknowledged that they had read about the case in the newspapers or heard about it on television. They, too, it seemed, looked for the trap—if there was one.

"Was there anything distinctive about Reginald that makes you so certain?"

"Yes."

"Was it his clothes—or was it his high-top sneakers?" Barbara said.

"It was his face."

"Not his hairstyle?"

"It was his face," Steinhardt said.

"And he was the only black face there—wasn't he?"

"Should I answer that?" Steinhardt said to Macklin.

"*Should you answer? I demand* an answer!" Barbara shouted.

"A face is a face," Steinhardt said.

"Reginald McCauley was the only African-American there—wasn't he?"

"Yes."

"So, you don't have to worry that they all look alike."

Macklin jumped to his feet. His chair scraped noisily along the floor until it hit the bar rail and bounced back. His objection was ignored by Barbara as she watched the surprised Macklin retrieve the wayward chair.

She was cool now as she mustered up her best sarcasm.

"Do all blacks look alike to you, Mr. Steinhardt?"

"I object, Your Honor. I object! She's playing the race card."

"I am not! I'm questioning the witness's objectivity. I'm attacking his credibility! I'm questioning his motives. . . ." Her voice trailed off.

Simmons banged his gavel.

Barbara picked up all of her papers and returned to her seat. "I have no further questions."

"The jury will disregard the last question," Simmons said.

The question was worth the rebuke that Barbara knew would follow. She heard Simmons adopt an "I'm running out of patience" tone, but she accepted the trade-off. Scalpel or sledgehammer. Did it matter? She had made her point.

"As I have explained to you in my preliminary instructions, a question without an answer is not evidence . . . ." Simmons took off his reading glasses and glared at Barbara. He continued: "Nor, are the statements, remarks, or other comments of counsel—on either side—evidence."

Well, at least he had tarred Macklin with the same brush. On the whole, Barbara was satisfied that she had accomplished as much as she could with Steinhardt. She had laid the foundation for the cross-examination of the other witnesses, who would be paraded before the jury and tell much the same story.

They were all eyewitnesses. So what that they were all Jewish. Would the jury believe, even given the similarities of their backgrounds, that these people were all mistaken—or worse, liars? Would O. J. Simpson have been acquitted if there had been eyewitnesses? No, there were limits to a defense based upon race, regardless of the pickets.

At least Reginald was behaving. He had listened to her advice without protest. Not many clients could do that. He had gotten a modified afro. "I want it close enough to show that you're middle-class. If it's too big, the jury will think you're a bomb thrower," she had told Reginald. "And don't get smart. The jury will look at you whenever a witness is graphic, so don't try to display the right emotion. Leave the grandstanding to me. No laughter, no indignation, nothing."

At another point, Barbara tried to ameliorate the cumulative effect of the eyewitnesses.

"Your Honor, just to save time, the defense is willing to stipulate that those people listed as eyewitnesses will all testify in substantially the same manner."

"The prosecution appreciates the generous offer and thanks the defense for its concern, but we must decline," Macklin said.

"Just trying to speed things along," Barbara offered. To show that she meant it, she limited her cross-examination of several witnesses, especially when one was caught in a stupid lie.

"Mrs. Schwartz, we heard your testimony. Have you spoken with the district attorney, or anyone, about this case?"

"Absolutely not."

"Not even the police?"

"On my word."

"Thank you, Mrs. Schwartz."

As she was about to step down, Barbara asked, "Mrs. Schwartz, do you know what your name means in German?"

"It means 'black.'"

Barbara turned to the jury and smiled. It was harmless, but she could not resist saying, "So, Mr. Steinhardt was mistaken. There was another black present at the incident."

"Your Honor, do we have to listen to all this?"

"Why, Mr. Macklin . . . I did give you a chance to stipulate," Barbara said.

Simmons closed his minute book and shook his head.

"That's enough for today. I'm already late for a Board

of Justices meeting. We'll adjourn now until 9:30 tomorrow morning." He then turned to the jury. "I am obliged to remind you not to discuss this case with anyone."

The jury was dismissed for the day. Before they handcuffed and took Reginald back to the pen, Barbara said to her client, "And don't come back tomorrow with those goddamn sneakers!"

Barbara was stuffing her papers into her briefcase when Sharon, the third court officer, approached her. She was voluptuous even in her court officer's uniform. Her platinum blonde hair was tightly braided, and her beauty, like Barbara's, generated much attention.

"You were wonderful today." Sharon lightly touched Barbara's hand.

"Thank you, Sharon."

"It would be lovely to spend some time together—even if it's only to chat."

"As you can see," Barbara said, "I'm pretty busy these days."

Six

The boardroom contained a huge round table set in the center. Theoretically, all of them were equal, and since Supreme Court Justices tended to be prima donnas, it was quite appropriate that they should be seated in a circle. The room's faux medieval fireplace dominated one side, while shelves of law books occupied the other. The books were rarely used, since duplicates were housed in the spacious library down the hall. What with Westlaw and other computer services, the law books had become truly decorative.

Ronald Franco, the administrative judge, presided at the meeting as thirty other judges, some still in their robes, listened politely. Since none of their prerogatives had yet been infringed upon, the meeting had a convivial air.

Justice Franco was a man who looked like a judge. His hair was gray at the temples, but it was his firm manner and steady gaze, with eyes set behind rimless glasses, that gave him an air of authority. More importantly,

Simmons—and many other judges—counted him as a friend. It was good to have an administrative judge that one could trust. Franco's job was complicated and required finesse. Supreme Court Justices were elected to fourteen-year terms. Assignment to trial parts could be very sensitive in an environment where, as another administrative judge had put it, "we don't hire and we don't fire."

When Justice Simmons entered, Franco was giving his progress report.

"And here comes Simmons—again, just in time to close the meeting," Justice Coughlin said. He was the acknowledged crank in the group. He liked to call himself the "last curmudgeon." Franco ignored him.

"I don't have the latest figures on civil cases, but on the criminal side, we're doing very well. In the last year we have disposed of 12,000 indictments, by plea or otherwise. We've found that, except for protracted trials, the average case takes four days to try."

"I'm still having problems with defense lawyers. They're always stalling," Justice Judith Eissner said. She was relatively new to the bench, and had not yet acquired a commanding presence. It was well known that she was unsure of herself and, as a consequence, had a tendency to scream at lawyers. Naturally, the lawyers then provoked her. The problem was further compounded with her defensive feminism and lack of any humor. The male judges had perceived, of course, that historic gender bias existed and most worked diligently to correct it. What galled the men was the strident presumption of guilt that was being laid on them by the female jurists. It was pure and simple arrogance on the part of their "sister" judges. Consequently, the more provocative judges taunted the thin-skinned female judges.

"Hey, Judy," said Justice Greenberg. "Put 'em in handcuffs. That'll stop their stalling."

Eissner was stone-faced and glared at Greenberg.

Justice Starkey, a courtly man, waited for the laughter to subside before he spoke. "Isn't that the name of the game? The defendant is always ready, unless the district attorney is ready. Then the defense wants an adjournment."

"Well, we're all conscious of the speedy-trial rule," Franco said.

Greenberg was unwilling to quit. "Put 'em all in handcuffs, I say. Even if they're *not* stalling."

"This meeting is adjourned," said Franco.

Above the din of general banter that usually attended the end of a meeting, Judge Alice Rankell called out, "Those men are unruly and disrespectful. I think you should make our judges aware of their responsibilities, Judge Franco."

Franco shrugged.

Judy Eissner shouted out, "I hope their demeanor on the bench is more sober."

"Don't worry, sweetheart," Justice Pappas said, joining in the teasing. "I haven't called any lawyer 'little girl' for days now."

"*Sweetheart?* Sweet . . ." Eissner sputtered.

As the judges filed from the boardroom, Franco motioned to Simmons and walked to the corner. He leaned on the fireplace's mantel and turned his body just enough to show that he wanted to speak privately with Simmons.

"What's going on with your trial?"

"Tomorrow the mother testifies. Afterwards, the People will probably rest," Simmons said.

Franco glanced around, so as to ward off several

judges who waited to speak with him. "I received a very strange phone call this afternoon from Ray Manning."

"The district attorney, himself, eh? I can understand his concern. He's caught between a rock and a hard place. He's up for reelection, and if he loses the case, then he loses the Jewish vote. If he wins, he loses the black vote. He was pretty smart to have a black assistant try the case."

"That's the point, Greg, he didn't ask about the case at all. He called and acted like I was his long-lost friend. Then he began to ask questions about you—your personal life."

"Did you tell him I was separated from Caroline?" Simmons asked.

"I didn't tell him anything. I pussyfooted around it."

"Is anything happening in the trial that's strange or unusual?" Franco said.

Simmons chuckled. "No, nothing—except there are a hundred cops in front of the courthouse, and five television trucks with a gang of reporters. Then, of course, there are about a thousand spectators ready to maim each other."

"Well, you watch your ass. Be careful, Greg, especially of Danzig. She'll do anything to win."

"Don't I know it."

Seven

The private office of the District Attorney of Kings County was a cavernous room. The heavy drapes only partly obscured the Gothic-style windows. Ray Manning's desk was off to the side and rested on a bright Navajo Indian rug. A sofa and several stuffed chairs surrounded a coffee table in a lame attempt to make the room homey, but there was no mistaking the message: You are in the boss's office.

When Wallace Macklin entered, Manning, who was in his shirtsleeves, rose from his desk and smiled. Time had not been kind to Manning. His nose, the product of one too many drinks, was pockmarked and bulbous. His sloping shoulders were supported by ample buttocks that caused his body to be pear-shaped.

"Well, Wallace, it's good to see you."

Manning extended his hand, which Macklin took tentatively—his eyes transfixed upon his boss's green suspenders.

"You know Sidney, don't you?" Manning said, and pointed to his deputy, Sidney Grossman, who sat on the stuffed chair.

Macklin nodded, and Grossman returned the nod, without bothering to rise.

Manning took Macklin by the arm and led him to the sofa.

"Sit. Sit. Make yourself comfortable."

Macklin sank into the sofa and tried to look relaxed.

"How's the trial going?" Grossman asked. His voice croaked through his bushy beard.

"Great, Chief," Macklin said to Manning.

"We have great confidence in you, Wallace."

"I really appreciate this opportunity," Macklin said, blatantly concealing his real feelings. *Some opportunity. Black on black. How could he ever go out into private practice? Win or lose, Jews would never retain him now. And what if he won this damned McCauley case? He could kiss the black clients goodbye, too!*

He gave his best smile to Grossman and tried not to stare at the man's yarmulke.

"Wallace, we need some time on the McCauley case," Manning said. He sat down next to Macklin and leaned close to him. His voice was soft and confidential, but the tone was unmistakable. Manning was giving him a command.

"But, Chief, we're in the middle of the trial."

"So?"

"But we have an open-and-shut case."

"There are other considerations, here, Wallace—considerations that do not concern you."

"Judge Simmons will never grant it."

"Get the damned adjournment," Grossman said.

"On what grounds?"

"Are you a lawyer? Find one." Grossman's voice carried the threat of a salary raise going out the window.

"It's only for a day or two," Manning said.

"I'll try."

"Just do it!" This time it was Manning, with his steel gray eyes and white shark teeth, who gave the order. The intensity of his tone obliterated his slight Irish brogue.

Eight

Barbara sat in the green leather settee in Simmons's anteroom while Macklin paced back and forth.

"I'm not consenting to any adjournment, Wallace," Barbara said.

"Maybe you will."

"You want to tell me what this is all about?"

"Let's wait." Macklin smiled and sat down. He crammed himself next to Barbara.

The inner door to Justice Simmons's chamber opened, and David ushered them into the room.

"You know my clerk, David Leibowitz," Simmons said, motioning for the lawyers to sit.

Barbara noticed that Simmons looked at her a moment too long, so when she sat down, she adjusted her skirt and demurely crossed her legs. All's fair in love and war.

"Now, counselors, what's the problem?"

"I think we ought to settle this case, Judge," Macklin said.

"What do you have in mind?" Barbara said.

"Manslaughter in the second degree."

"You have got to be kidding."

"This does seem like a case where there should be a plea bargain," Simmons said.

"That's why I'm authorized to make that offer. With two communities at each other's throats, it's in the best interests of everybody for us to offer a lesser plea."

"Not for my client. He's innocent."

"What's the offer?" Justice Simmons said.

"Five to fifteen."

"Judge, this is all nonsense. We'll plea if we have a promise of Youth Offender treatment with five years' probation," Barbara said.

"On a murder charge—in a case you can't win?" Macklin asked.

"Says you," Barbara said.

"What if I agree to the Y.O. with a sentence of one to three years?" Simmons said. "With the Y.O. treatment, there is no conviction and your client won't have a record."

"Is that the offer?" Barbara asked Macklin.

"If the judge says he'll accept that plea, I'll go along with it—but I have to get permission. What about you, Barbara? I'm not going to talk to Mr. Manning unless I know it's a deal." Macklin smiled. He was going to get an adjournment without even fighting for it. He had boxed her in with an obligation.

"I smell a rat, Judge. Why is the prosecution suddenly coming up with an offer to plea bargain? Have they lost their main witness?"

"The mother is ready to testify. If we can spare her the agony, we will." That was a nice touch. "Are we in the ballpark or not?"

"I have to consult with my client," Barbara said.

"Of course," Simmons said.

"Why don't we just adjourn for a day or two so we can straighten this out?" Macklin asked.

"I don't need an adjournment, Judge. You know they get the prisoners up at four o'clock in the morning at Rikers, so that they can be in court on time."

"But I'm not talking to my boss until you tell me a plea is possible. I'll need at least a day," said Macklin.

"That's not unreasonable," Simmons said.

Barbara found herself looking instead of listening. Was Simmons too old for her? Ten years, maybe. Heard he was separated. That's *almost* not married. He was sexy, too. Square jaw and dimples. Wasn't she a sucker for dimples every time?

"Well—Ms. Danzig?"

"They're stalling," Barbara said. Her voice had little conviction.

"Let's adjourn this for a day just in case you're wrong," Justice Simmons said.

Nine

Barbara used the unexpected time to clean up paperwork in the office, but not before a hectic morning with McCauley.

"I ain't taking a plea. You selling me out, Barbara?"

"It's the judge's suggestion, Reggie."

"Fuck him, too."

"You're not going to provoke me, Reginald. You're damned lucky to have Simmons as the judge; he has a heart, but if you're convicted, his hands are tied. You're facing mandatory life imprisonment if you're found guilty."

"Even if I'm *not* guilty?"

"What's that got to do with it? You looking to be a martyr?"

"You said we could win."

"No, I said we *should* win. We have a hell of a defense, but suppose it backfires? I never gave you any guarantees, Reggie."

"You're telling me that I have no choice."

"I'm not even sure the D.A. will go along with it. I have to call him and let him know that you agree."

McCauley paced about the holding pen, murmuring, "Got no choice, got no choice."

Ten

As Barbara was to learn, there *was* no choice, because Macklin called her. Manning would not agree to anything less than five to fifteen years in jail.

After the telephone call with Macklin, the thought nagged Barbara that she had been deceived. But why? And for what purpose? Was there anything she had forgotten?

Barbara fidgeted through several calls and tried to involve herself in an omnibus motion on another case, but the adrenaline rush of the trial refused to turn off. She paced back and forth while her secretary, Lucy Sparrow, waited to take dictation.

"How much time do we have on the omnibus motion?"

"The usual forty-five days," Lucy said. She was petite and, like many short people, tended to be sassy.

"I know that! I mean how many days do we have left?"

"The usual three days." Lucy served as office manager, secretary, and paralegal. She had a prodigious memory and was familiar with every case in the office. More importantly, she sent out the bills and was relentless in pursuing deadbeat clients.

"Lucy, I'm in no mood for your sarcasm."

"Well, you're always waiting till the last minute to file these motions."

"Let's start over." Barbara picked up a client's file and examined it. "All right, Lucy. We need a motion to sever, a motion for permission to get the grand jury minutes, and applications to suppress the confession and gun."

"What about the Wade hearing for the improper lineup?" Lucy asked.

"There's no identification issue here," Barbara said.

"Yes, there is," Lucy said. "You're looking at the wrong file."

Barbara thumbed through the pages and tossed the file back onto the desk. Without another word, she walked out of the room and down the corridor to the next office.

"I'm no good here, Uncle Norman," Barbara said.

Norman Horowitz, who doubled as her uncle and her investigator, was almost sixty years old but still rail thin. His drooping mustache and missing right bicuspid gave him a slightly comical expression.

"So go, already. Go to the gym or something. Better yet, go get laid." Norman, a retired cop, enjoyed making shocking statements.

"Uncle Norman!"

"And leave the jelly donuts," he said. "It's good for hair growth." He patted his bald head.

Barbara looked at her watch. It was not yet two o'clock.

"I do have an appointment with Dr. Reich at five-thirty," Barbara said.

"Why you paying good money for that nutty psychologist when you don't listen to him, anyway?"

Eleven

The gym *did* lessen her anxious state as she settled into a steady jog on the treadmill. The treadmills were lined up five in a row and faced the ground-floor picture window.

Pulchritude was on display as pedestrians gave sidelong glances at the bouncing assets of the various women. Barbara, clad in a black leotard, was not offended as she watched them, watching her. She worked up a good sweat after three miles and then took a massage.

"You'd better start coming here more often," Regina, her sometimes masseuse said. "Those buns are going to start falling."

Regina's perfect figure was augmented by silicone breasts. Barbara liked Regina, but she had to suppress a smile. Regina's breasts would surely fall before Barbara's buns.

Barbara rested her head on the table and allowed Regina's kneading hands to search out the fatigue in her muscles.

"That feels good."

"Barbara, what you need . . ."

"Don't say it." Barbara laughed. "I've already been told."

"Are you seeing Bill Scharf?" Regina said.

"On and off." Barbara sat up. "Oh, Regina, not you, too?"

"He's rich and good-looking, and he's in excellent shape."

"He's a satyr," Barbara said.

"What's that?"

"Somebody who can't get enough."

"You can say that again." Regina giggled, but her hands were nervously working on Barbara's torso. "I mean, I don't want to interfere . . . you know."

"It's a wide-open field," Barbara said. "Is he still coming to the gym?" She did not tell Regina that one of the messages at the office had been a call from Scharf.

More out of pique than desire, she returned Scharf's phone call. She then showered and dressed. Wouldn't Uncle Norman be surprised if he learned that she was availing herself of both his suggestions?

Twelve

Gershon Reich was almost seventy years old. Obese and extremely short, five foot one or something. He always sat on a stool when he treated patients. His mustache was an admitted affectation that he waxed frequently and then tightly twisted both ends. He relished the appearance of an old-style silent movie villain. Dr. Reich, however, was far from silent. His office was in a small apartment on 87th Street just off Park Avenue and decorated, as he often complained, by an interior decorator who was one of his patients.

"I must have been crazy to let him touch this place."

In reality, it was perfectly decorated. The oriental rugs were thick, and the windows were covered with heavy velvet drapes. The floor-to-ceiling bookcases surrounded the room, leaving no space for paintings. It was a perfect place to hide. A perfect place for confiding secrets. An existential womb.

He was an unconventional psychotherapist in that he was often verbose and inclined to yell at or insult his patients. His charm was that he allowed reciprocity. Also, he did not pander to the whims of his profession or his patients. He refused to add a couch to the furniture and required his patients to sit up straight in an armchair—"better we should look each other in the eye."

Barbara began her session with Dr. Reich by asking, "How's my little Nazi today?"

"About to go out of business. Three cures yesterday. At this rate I'm going to run out of patients." He twisted his mustache and smiled in mock satisfaction.

"When do you call it a cure? When they run out of money?" Barbara asked.

"Sarcastic! Always wanting to be in control. You don't listen and you don't learn."

"I'm learning, all right. I'm learning that I'm wasting my money with you."

"If I don't charge for failure, will you pay double if I succeed?" He twisted his mustache again.

"Dammit, I wish you'd stop that!"

"You're that strung out?" This time his voice was soft and solicitous.

Barbara, however, was not to be placated. "And another thing I wish you'd stop trying to imitate some '60s hippie therapist. *Strung out! What the hell does that mean?*"

"It means that you've had another bad night and you don't want to talk about it."

"Gershon, that's precisely why I'm here."

"You could have fooled me. You come in here and waste precious time. You refuse to address any subject except the most superficial. How am I supposed to help you?"

"That's a goddamn lie." Color drained from her face, and Barbara bit her lip.

Dr. Reich elaborately twisted his mustache—this time with both hands. "Is it?"

"Okay what shall we talk about today, you son of a bitch?"

"Anything you want. Maybe your dreams?"

"I've been thinking about my middle name."

"That's new. I didn't know you had one. What is it?"

"Alicia."

"That's a pretty name."

"Don't you see, Gershon? My name is Barbara Alicia Danzig—B.A.D. Those are not good initials for a gold pin or for some luggage."

"Today, it's not so *bad.*"

"Christ, you're hopeless, Gershon. Are you sure you graduated from high school?"

"You sure you're dealing with profound problems? What's the big deal?"

"I just wondered why my mother would give me a name without considering the unfortunate initials."

"Maybe it was your father's idea," Reich said.

"No, my father would have deferred to my mother."

"As he does in everything else?"

"You said it, not me."

"No, Barbara, you said it. You're not going to deny your hostility, are you?"

"Why shouldn't I resent him? He's a goddamn cipher. My father never faced a problem in his life."

"Some people are not confrontational. It could be a life-saving attribute," Reich said.

"Or a life-destroying one."

"In what way, Barbara?"

"I'm a lawyer. I thrive on confrontation."

"Face a problem head-on—don't sweep it under the rug!"

"You're making fun of me, Gershon."

"I'm making fun of your bullshit. You're the best 'sweeper under the rug' patient I have. You can't sleep. You have nightmares. You call me a Nazi, but it's pure projection. *You're* the one who has to be in control all the time. Dominate the courtroom. Dominate. Dominate!" Gershon Reich hopped off the stool and wagged his finger in Barbara's face. "I'm sick and tired of *your* bullshit." He went back to the stool and wiped the perspiration from his brow. "Face it. You became a lawyer so that you could get even with your family."

Barbara returned his steady gaze.

"Is this the latest mode of treatment in psychotherapy?" she asked.

"I'm serious, Barbara. I don't want to hear about your nightmares until you face facts. So you don't respect your father. So what?"

"So what? I was twelve years old and his brother Isaac took me up to the bathroom and started touching me. Touching me. All over, goddammit. I told my father, and you know what he did? Nothing! 'I imagined it,' he said. Uncle Izzy did it again, and my father again did nothing. But when I told my mother, she kicked his ass out of the house. She bashed his head in with a broomstick. Yes, Dr. Reich. I love my father, but you'll have to tell me why."

"The horror came at an age when you were most vulnerable, Barbara. I think you understand that."

"I just feel so stupid about it. I look at the incidents and don't repress them, but I'm still affected by them."

"Barbara, you're so unique. You recognize it and you don't recognize it. You just said it! Tell me, did these childhood incidents screw you up sexually?"

"I enjoy sex, but I'm afraid that I'm not very discriminating."

"Do you mean you're promiscuous? Could it be something else?"

"Come on, Gershon, the next thing you'll be telling me is that I haven't resolved my Electra complex."

"To not say it doesn't make it not true." Reich twisted his mustache.

"Why are we affected so by our past?" Her voice seemed to come from another woman as her eyes fixed on the drapes. It was as if they, too, were veils that concealed secrets. "I mean, I know it's stupid to dwell on the past, but it still seems to control me."

She had said the word and it brought her back to Dr. Reich. *Control.* Always in control. Never lose control. That bastard, Uncle Izzy. Were the two really connected, or was she just using him as an excuse? The pervert! She never should have let him "kiss the boo-boo."

"Puberty and beauty can be an ugly combination."

"Christ, Gershon. You're not saying it was my fault?"

"Not at all. I just meant that a homely child is less likely to be a victim."

"What the hell kind of an analyst are you?"

"Psychotherapist. Not analyst."

"You're not a Freudian or a Jungian?" Sarcasm. She was good at that.

"Jung at heart." Reich gave his mustache a solid twist and it matched his smile. It was not often that he revealed his crooked teeth.

"You're not much help, but you're always good for a laugh!" Barbara headed for the door. It seemed these sessions always ended with her walking out angry. So much for the gym workout and the massage. But, then, there was still Billy Scharf. He could still, like Clint Eastwood said, "make her day."

"Where are you going? Your hour's not up yet."

"You should change those dirty drapes," Barbara said. "Make them red next time. Put some life into this hole you call an office."

"See you next week," Dr. Reich said.

"Yeah, sweet dreams," said Barbara.

Thirteen

"And here is my cheap date," Bill Scharf said. His body filled the doorway to his apartment. "I don't even have to spring for dinner."

"I sweated all afternoon. It would be a shame to put all those calories back on," Barbara replied.

She brushed him aside as he attempted to embrace her. "Later," she said, and made a feint for his crotch. Scharf's considerable pectorals danced beneath his shirt as he stepped back from the unexpected move.

"Christ, Barbara!"

Scharf was wearing slacks. His red silk shirt was open half-way down his chest. His bare feet, despite all protestations, showed that he was ready for action.

"I'm surprised you're not in your pajamas."

"Cut the crap, Barbara. You know that if you want-commitment, you just have to say the word."

"You mean you'd give up all your girlfriends for little old me?"

"You're a sarcastic bitch."

Barbara cocked her head, and her blue eyes never left his face. She slowly unbuttoned her blouse. She was not wearing a bra.

She took his hand and led him to the large ski bed. She kissed him hard on the mouth before pushing him down. She fell on top of him and clutched him. Barbara did not allow him to move, except in the precise way that she wanted.

The joy in sex was not unlike the joy in court. Court and sex. *Courting.* That was an interesting connection. That little Nazi was right. But, then, he was always right. The problem was that you had to guess where he was going. It was obvious that control was good sometimes. Necessary? Often. Harmful? Maybe. Out of control? Never. At times like this? She'd have to draw more lines. Not in control did not have to mean submission or even abandonment. She'd have to discuss that with Gershon.

As they lay back in bed, Scharf kept talking. She pretended to hear him, but as far as she was concerned, he had fulfilled his function.

"You know, I'm a pretty popular guy. In demand."

"What do you want from me, Billy?"

"How about a little love?"

"Isn't that what you just got?" Barbara said.

"Perfunctory. That's what *you* like!"

"I'm a Timex? I take a licking and keep on ticking?"

"You like to play with words? Play with . . ." He grabbed for her.

Barbara, however, was too quick for Scharf. She cupped his face in her hands and crooned softly, "Fairy tales may come true, they can happen to you, when you're young at heart."

"You really know how to concentrate, don't you, Barbara?"

"... when you're *Jung* at heart." She giggled at her private joke.

"You never give me a chance, do you?"

"Stop whining, Billy. You came, didn't you? If passion was determined by swiftness, you'd win first place." She knew that that was not fair. She was accusing him of her own faults. But, then, fight fire with fire. It was not she who was inadequate, it was Scharf who didn't measure up. Arguments, arguments. Everything's an argument.

"It's your choice, Barbara. It's always your choice. You even dictate how and when we make love. I'm not used to this sort of treatment. I have a seat on the stock exchange, I'm reasonably good-looking, and you treat me like shit."

"It's funny, Billy, but you never complain beforehand."

"Funny? I can have just about any girl in town and I'm stuck with you."

"You're not stuck *with* me or *on* me, Bill. You're just a spoiled brat. Your emotional development stopped in your teens." She leaned back and caressed his blond hair. "I do like you and I do enjoy you, but *love*? I think I could fall in love with an *octopus* before you, Billy Scharf."

He stroked her thigh, ever so lightly.

"You have great legs."

"You know, in this light your eyes are green. You're a hunk of man, Billy—but not my type." She tapped the cleft in his chin.

"And what type is that?"

She leaned over and kissed his chest. "I don't know. Rich is nice."

"I'm rich."

"Faithful is good. Intellectual is better."

He reached and touched her breast. "I'm your man. You just don't know it."

"Is that right? Billy, what do you think of Brancusi?"

"Who?"

"How about Giacometti?"

"You on an Italian kick?"

"Neither of them were Italian," Barbara said.

"Give me a hint . . . the double-play combination for the San Diego Padres?"

"Go ahead. Joke away your ignorance."

"I'll bet they never made two million a year."

Barbara shook her head. "You have to be putting me on. Nobody can be that crass." She left the bed and began to dress, blouse first.

Scharf reached over to draw her back to the bed, but she pulled her arm away.

"I have a big day tomorrow. I shouldn't have come at all." On her way to the living room, she tripped on an end table. She caught the tall lamp before it hit the floor.

"Go ahead, break up the place," Scharf said.

"Keep it lighted next time. Regina, with her big tits, might trip over it, too." She paused and stuck out her tongue at him. "Good night, Hercules."

"You know, Barbara, with all your bullshit, you use people, too!"

Fourteen

Barbara was daydreaming when Macklin rose from his counsel table and said, "The People of the State of New York call Chanah Sackheim to the witness stand."

It was odd how engrossed one could become in a case, so that time, if not standing still, seemed to proceed in slow motion. She had awakened, picked out the day's clothes, and brushed her teeth, just like every morning. She had taken the train to court and had entered the building just as she had done hundreds of times before. But now she was amazed that she did not remember a single detail that had brought her to the counsel table. She forced herself to concentrate even more, so that she could appear unconcerned, as she watched Mrs. Sackheim laboriously walk to the stand.

Chanah Sackheim was a ruddy-faced, small woman of about fifty. Matronly. That was it. Barbara gazed at the jury. How could she have been so stupid? Five African-American women. Yes, they were black and would identify with McCauley, but they were matronly and middle-class. Each day they had come to court dressed like they were going to church. And they were all mothers!

Barbara fought a panic attack. In the heat of battle, hadn't she always worried that she had made a fatal mistake? She had succeeded in keeping Jews off the jury. They would doubtless be inclined to find Reginald guilty. But what about those mothers? Love knew no color. She looked at Macklin—so confident, that son of a bitch.

Barbara knew approximately what Mrs. Sackheim's testimony would be. The details, however, would be important, and Barbara knew that she had to listen closely and wait for an opening. Why had Macklin sought to plea-bargain in the middle of a trial, especially this one, when there had been no offer before? Was it because her testimony would be different from the other witnesses?

Mrs. Sackheim did not look like a woman thirsty for blood, but she *had* lost a son. It was not *what* she would say but *how* she would say it that would determine the impact on the jury. Most important was how she looked at the jury. Chanah Sackheim wore a long-sleeved dress, and her hair was covered by a babushka.

Barbara wrote on her legal pad, "Be careful. This little lady is ten feet tall."

The clerk took the witness through the formalities.

"We don't swear, we affirm," she said. Her voice was listless and hollow.

"Relax, Mrs. Sackheim, don't be nervous," Macklin said.

When Macklin asked her to point to the person who had plunged a knife into her son, she lifted her arm and pointed to McCauley.

"That's the one. He murdered my Menachem." Her voice was without inflection—as if life had also been drained from her.

Fifteen

Chanah Sackheim had been walking with her son, Menachem, on Eastern Parkway, a broad avenue with malls on each side.

It was Sabbath, and the benches that lined the mall were filled with people. Whites and blacks, talking, some even playing together.

Menachem, tall and straight, his blond beard just blooming into maturity, walked by her side. She had clutched his arm—like a groom. So proud. Hadn't she just been bragging about his becoming a rabbi? Was all of this the Almighty punishing her for her pride?

She had told the police that this man—or was he a boy, too—caught up in the madness of race and hatred who killed her son. Did it really matter whether it was murder or an accident? Worst of all, what part had her own prejudices played in the death of her son? Her people, the blacks, the authorities—all believed it mattered. But the reality of it, at least for her, was that her son was dead.

It had all started with a ball. A bouncing ball and misunderstanding of people too quick to accuse—too quick to take offense.

As they walked, McCauley, who had been backing up to catch the ball, brushed against Chanah. Her *shaytel* fell from her head as she staggered from the contact. Instinctively, one hand tried to catch the wig while the other protected her purse.

Chanah recalled saying something like "Oh, my goodness" as the boy stopped and turned. It was evident from his surprised and contrite expression that this boy, McCauley, was about to apologize, but then, suddenly, his face contorted in anger.

"Hey, I'm not robbing you!"

Menachem, always protective had replied, "Who said you were?"

"She grabbed her purse like I was a thief."

"You should watch where you're going," Menachem had said.

And so it started.

"You fucking Jews—think you own the sidewalk!"

"Don't talk like that in front of my mother!"

"Leave him be, Menachem. I have my purse."

It was then that she noticed that anger gave way to nervousness and a group of Hasidim gathered around them. Was it Steinhardt who said, "He tried to steal your purse?"

"He knocked off her *shaytel*—I saw it," a bystander said.

"These *schvartzes* should be taught a lesson," another bystander said and raised his fist.

McCauley, now fearful, had tried to back away but

was surrounded. He took a knife from his pocket and waved it in warning.

"You're not beating up this nigger!"

Sixteen

It was at this point that the testimony diverged. There was no doubt that McCauley had stabbed Menachem and then, in the confusion, had run away. Mrs. Sackheim had testified in a manner similar to that of the other eyewitnesses, but her scrupulousness gave an opening that Barbara could exploit. Could it be that when Menachem had interposed himself between Reginald and Chanah, he had been pushed by the crowd? That the stabbing had been at least self-defense—if not an accident?

When Macklin said, "I have no further questions," Barbara rose. She waited until Macklin sat down. Then with her pen she tapped on the well rail, as if she were sending a message in Morse code. She was acutely aware of the overwhelming silence in the courtroom. Everyone looked at Barbara.

It was decision time. This was one of those times when preparation was subordinated to instinct. To what extent should she cross-examine this nice, little old lady whose most terrible fears had been realized? With the slightest of effort, Barbara felt that she could dispose of the murder count. It was a street encounter—where was the intent to kill? No, it was time for her trump card.

"I have no cross-examination—if the prosecution rests," Barbara said.

A murmur sounded throughout the courtroom. Macklin was not sure what to make of this maneuver, but he was clearly surprised.

"No cross? Then the People rest."

Mrs. Sackheim started to rise from the witness stand, but Barbara motioned her to sit back.

"Your Honor, may I request that Mrs. Sackheim remain on the stand?"

"I object," Macklin said. "Judge, she said she had no cross-examination."

"May we have a sidebar, Your Honor?"

Justice Simmons waved his hand impatiently, and both lawyers went to the bench. Off to the side, they all spoke in hushed voices, well out of earshot of the jury.

"What are you trying to pull?" Macklin asked.

"I wanted to make sure that you had no other witnesses."

"I don't understand, Ms. Danzig. You intend to call the deceased's mother as a *witness* instead of cross-examining her?" Simmons's voice rose slightly in disbelief.

"It doesn't matter, Your Honor. This may seem unorthodox, but I would appreciate a little leeway."

"Like what?"

"Like allowing me to have another person sit at the counsel table with the defendant."

"To assist you?" Simmons asked.

"Not exactly."

"Is this part of an alibi defense?" Simmons said.

"Oh no, Judge. She can't do that. We never received notice of any alibi witnesses," said Macklin.

"You know, Ms. Danzig, that you're required to give the district attorney prior notice of any person who you intend to call to establish an alibi."

"Trust me. There is no alibi defense." Barbara knew that if a person intended to rely on an alibi defense, that is, claim that a defendant could not have committed the crime because he was elsewhere at the time the crime was committed, then the prosecutor was entitled to be notified of the names of the witnesses. The district attorney would then be allowed to question these "alibi witnesses."

Simmons smiled. "I'm going to permit you to question Mrs. Sackheim, but not on the basis of trust."

"Mrs. Sackheim, I want you to close your eyes for a moment." Barbara's voice was low and soft.

Mrs. Sackheim glanced toward Simmons. He nodded and she closed her eyes. Barbara turned to her uncle Norman, who was waiting in the rear of the courtroom. The door opened, and a man wearing clothing identical to McCauley's walked down the aisle. Richard McCauley sat next to his twin brother. The sound from the audience gradually increased as they realized what was occurring. Justice Simmons banged his gavel, and the clerk cried out, "Order in the court—order!"

Barbara moved closer to the jury, as if she were becoming part of it. She walked along its length, treading dangerously near the witness. She did not want an objection now. The audience was pin silent.

Everyone was so mesmerized by the silence that several in the audience involuntarily flinched at the sound of the two brothers rising and shuffling their chairs—as if they were trading places. Reginald and Richard McCauley, however, did not change seats.

Barbara waited until the courtroom seemed no longer to be able to hold its collective breath. "Mrs. Sackheim, I want you to open your eyes," she said. Her voice was still soft—neither commanding nor triumphant. "Open your eyes and point to the boy who stabbed your son."

Seventeen

The glory of our legal system is that society has fashioned a method to resolve disputes in a civilized manner. That is, without violence. Sometimes. The dismissal of the indictment against Reginald McCauley did nothing to diminish conflict. Jews and African-Americans were still at odds with each other.

On the spacious approach to the courthouse, television trucks from the major networks had mounted the roadway and parked. Their telescopic antennae were extended skyward, announcing their operation. The reporters blocked the entrance as they fought for interviews.

The Jews were irate and seemed to increase in numbers as they marched along the oval path. The police had formed an outer ring of blue about the picketers and interposed themselves between the African-Americans and the courthouse. There would be no invasion of this building.

The Jews no longer carried signs—some tore them up and stomped on them, contenting themselves with shouting.

"Justice? Only blacks get justice!"

"Trickery—is that the law?"

"Menachem must be avenged," they chanted. "Menachem must be avenged."

The African-Americans, though no longer picketing, crowded around the several reporters. The television journalists quickly found a spokesman.

Reverend Dalgren, portly and light-skinned, was dressed in clerical garb. The folds of his double chin almost concealed his collar.

"Reverend, why aren't you pleased with the dismissal of the charges against Reginald McCauley?"

The reporters pushed their microphones into his face to insure adequate audio, while the cameramen, their instruments heavy on their shoulders, fought each other for space. Dalgren was now backed against his followers, who pushed to get into the picture.

"Reverend, weren't you just picketing—demanding that Reginald be freed?"

"He should have been acquitted on the ground of self-defense."

"That's a technicality. Does Reginald care?"

Dalgren raised his arms and intoned, "*He* may not care, but the *community* does! These Hasidic Jews have to learn that they cannot take the law into their own hands."

His followers nodded forcefully and in unison, preserving the moment for posterity.

"Are you saying that the Jews of Crown Heights are vigilantes?"

"I'm saying that whenever they think an African-American youth has committed a crime, they beat him up. That boy, Reginald, was in fear for his life."

Like a chorus congregation listening to a sermon, Dalgren's adherents replied, "Amen."

"That boy had a right to defend himself," one said.

"With a knife?" A reporter pushed the microphone too close, and Dalgren waved him off.

"When a white attacks a black, you make him a hero."

"Amen. You heard of Bernhard Goetz, the subway gunman?" another follower said.

"Thank you very much, Reverend." The reporter signaled to the cameraman to stop filming. Then, as if the news media had one mind, they turned, pushed aside the other spectators, and walked, parade fashion, to the Hasidic picketers.

Unable to pick out their leader, since the Jews were dressed alike, the reporters waited until a gray-bearded man pushed himself forward.

"Rabbi, Reverend Dalgren claims that the Jews of Crown Heights are vigilantes," a newscaster said.

"Vigilantes? It's strange that he should call the victims 'vigilantes.' Someone killed Menachem Sackheim, and that person has just gotten away with murder."

"Rabbi, do you feel that the court system is too lenient?"

"Justice should not be cheated by cheap theatrical tricks. Furthermore . . ."

At that moment, a news staffer pushed her way through the group and whispered to the reporter.

"*What?*" the reporter said. He abruptly withdrew his microphone from the rabbi's face and grabbed the surprised cameraman by the arm.

"Let's go!" The reporter dragged the cameraman away, pushing aside everyone in his path.

"Take it easy, Morty—you try lugging this camera around."

"Stop complaining . . . this is really breaking news!"

Eighteen

"I didn't get into an accident, but I didn't get the golf clubs, either," David Leibowitz said. He straightened his tie, which he had loosened during his trip to the police station. He omitted the fact that he had called his wife, and she had done most of the driving.

The law clerk looked morose, as if the failure of his mission was as damaging as a misquoted legal citation.

"Why wouldn't they give you the golf clubs?" Simmons leaned back in his desk chair. His voice was more angry than puzzled.

"They said everything was impounded," David said.

"Did you talk to the captain?"

"The detectives and the lieutenant. The captain wasn't in."

"I can understand waiting to hold the car as evidence—but my clubs?" Simmons said.

"Something's going on, Judge. I think you'd better call the district attorney's office."

"Why?"

"They even tried to take your key away from me."
David handed the key to Simmons.

It was then that Detectives Zangara and Tracy brushed aside Elaine Trezza and entered the inner chamber. They intruded so quickly that Elaine had no time to protest. She hurried in behind them but stopped when Tracy turned and showed her his badge.

"Your Honor, we are here to place you under arrest." Zangara was clearly uneasy, and his voice betrayed his nervousness. He shifted his weight and looked down at his shoes.

"You've got to be kidding." Simmons rose from his desk. "All right, fellows, what's the joke?"

"No joke, sir," Zangara said, and nodded to Tracy.

Tracy moved his hand from inside his jacket and then to his pocket. He took out a card and commenced to read aloud, "You have the right to remain silent . . ."

"This has gone far enough!"

"Anything you say can be used against you in a court of law."

"I'm sorry, Judge," Zangara said. He took a pair of handcuffs from under his jacket. The cuffs hit a lamp and made a curious metallic sound, like a cheap clock chiming the hour.

"What are the charges?"

"Insurance fraud and filing a false report," Zangara said.

"What are you talking about?"

"The vehicle you reported stolen was taken by an accomplice. When you reported it stolen, you made a false report, perpetrating a fraud on your insurance company."

"That's absurd!"

"I'm sorry, Judge, but you asked me."

Zangara glanced toward Tracy, who was impatiently waiting to continue the *Miranda* warnings.

"You have the right to an attorney, and if you cannot afford one . . ."

"Will you stop that! I sure as hell know my rights."

"It's routine, sir," Zangara said. He turned the judge around and handcuffed him.

"Is that necessary?" David said.

"You want to get locked up, too?" Tracy threatened.

"I'm just asking—why are you doing this?"

"It's police procedure. Every arrested person must be handcuffed." Zangara's voice was conciliatory as if he were apologizing for Tracy.

"If there's a charge against the judge, wouldn't it be common courtesy to have him surrender at the precinct?"

"I'm sorry, sir, but my orders are to treat the judge like everybody else."

"Who gave those orders?" Elaine said, and interposed herself between them.

"Don't be a hero, lady," Tracy said.

Nineteen

Word spread more quickly than if a fire alarm had sounded. Court officers, clerks, and office personnel left their rooms to gawk at the procession as Justice Simmons was led away. David walked in front, running interference. He noted the sad faces in the crowd—as if sadness was a way of objecting to the arrest. But, then, were they really so distressed? Didn't the hoi polloi take pleasure in witnessing the fall of the mighty? There would be no presumption of innocence for Justice Simmons!

By the time the judge had reached the lobby foyer, the crowd had coalesced outside and was waiting for the television cameras to memorialize the event. An unintended effect was that Jews and African-Americans mingled together in apparent harmony, their differences now deflected by their common curiosity.

Morton Fraser, one of the more aggressive reporters, stalled for time as he awaited the appearance of Simmons.

"From what we have learned, Justice Gregory A.

Simmons, the presiding judge at the Reginald McCauley trial, has been arrested. We are not sure of the charge—only this afternoon, Justice Simmons dismissed the charges against McCauley when the victim's mother was unable to distinguish between the defendant and his twin brother."

Zangara had wanted to exit from the rear of the building and was annoyed that he had been ordered to use the front entrance. Maybe the judge was guilty, but why the humiliation? It just wasn't right.

Justice Simmons was in an obvious state of disbelief and continually shook his head. His normally ruddy face was ashen.

The detectives enlisted the aid of several court officers to serve as a phalanx for its prisoner. They moved into the crowd clearing a path, but the onlookers, like the pseudopod of a giant amoeba, flowed with them down the steps of the building.

Fraser lost his microphone when his outstretched arm was knocked away by the stumbling crowd. He was out of the frame, but his cameraman still had an angle. Fraser called out: "Does this have anything to do with the McCauley trial?"

Twenty

The speedy-trial rule required that every indictment be disposed of within one hundred and eighty days. With approximately forty judges to handle the workload, and given the number of indictments, it was obvious that all defendants who demanded trials could not be accommodated. One of the makeshift solutions was that generous plea bargains were often offered to encourage dispositions.

Accordingly, the punishment seldom fit the crime and the judiciary left itself open to the charge that it was "giving away the courthouse." The district attorney, Ray Manning, having to run for office every four years, was particularly sensitive to political and media pressure and never missed an opportunity to blame the court for any perceived failure.

Nevertheless, a close working relationship, however wary, was necessary between the administrative judge and the district attorney to keep the system from collapsing. Justice Franco and Manning frequently telephoned each other as they resolved day-to-day problems, but they rarely met in person. Today was different.

Ron Franco was incensed by the arrest of Simmons. He stormed into the district attorney's office without an appointment.

It was late afternoon when he entered the marble-walled lobby. The guard's smile of recognition faded when he saw the stern look on the judge's face.

The guard picked up the phone and called Manning.

"You tell the judge that I'd be delighted to see him. Send him right up," Manning said.

"It didn't take him long," Sidney Grossman said.

"I expected him an hour ago." Manning donned his jacket. Today he was wearing red suspenders. "Put on your jacket, too, Sidney. I think this is going to be a very formal meeting."

"He's probably mad as hell, Chief."

"Screw him. We've got nothing to lose."

"We do have forty potentially hostile judges, now."

"No, Sidney, we have forty judges who'll be scared shitless that it could happen to them."

"Maybe you're right. Arresting Simmons might have some advantages."

"You're damned right. It'll take the heat off us. Just remember, the jury didn't acquit McCauley—Simmons threw the case out. He's the one that's soft on crime."

"The Orthodox and the Hasidim are too smart to fall for that." Sidney took out his pipe and sucked on it. He had stopped smoking years ago, but he used the pipe to show reflection.

The intercom sounded, but Manning ignored it.

"It's your job to convince them."

"Yes, I know, if you lose the election, then we're both out of jobs," Sidney said, as if he had said it a thousand times.

"I'm going to try this case myself. What do you think of that?"

"The best trial lawyer in Brooklyn," Grossman said.

"You know, sometimes you piss me off. You don't have to suck up to me."

Sidney, who had been sitting on the sofa, stood up and slowly put on his jacket. He definitely knew that he always had to suck up to Manning. Embarrassed, he fingered his pipe.

Despite his direction to "send him right up," Manning had Grace, his secretary, make Justice Franco wait in his outer office. Franco paced there as he waited to be announced.

"Dammit, Grace, I'm going in!"

"He'll be with you in a minute, Judge."

"He's playing games, and I'm not going to tolerate it."

"Let me buzz him again," Grace said. She picked up the phone and pressed the intercom, but Franco did not wait. Grace bolted from her desk and chased after him as he opened the inner door and stormed in.

Manning was momentarily surprised by the entrance and cast a dour look at his flustered secretary. He quickly recovered, however, and rushed to shake Franco's hand.

"Ronnie—it's so good to see you."

"Cut the crap. What the hell is going on? . . . I'm really angry with you, Ray. The other day you call me and start asking me personal questions about Greg Simmons, and today you arrest him. That's pretty sneaky."

"Just a minute, Ronnie. What was I supposed to tell you—that a grand jury was meeting to return an indictment?"

"Come on, Judge, we had a complaint and we had to act on it."

"Is this your work, Sidney?"

"See, I told you I'd get the blame, Ray."

"There's no blame here. Only a crime," Manning said.

"I never heard of such bullshit charges."

Now it was Manning's turn to be irate. His face flushed and his pock-marked nose seemed to get even redder.

"Insurance fraud is a class D felony—seven years in jail. Does that sound like bullshit, Ronnie? Besides, we have the accomplice."

"A car thief? A three-time felon?"

Manning looked sharply at Sidney. Sidney sighed as he contemplated Manning ordering another internal investigation.

"That's confidential information. Where did you hear that?" Manning said.

"Never mind. I have my sources, too."

"We had no choice. We can't just decide who's lying and who isn't," Grossman said. He puffed on his pipe. "That's for the jury to decide."

"Cut the shit, Sidney. You're talking to *me*. Remember, I used to be a district attorney."

"A crime is a crime," Manning said.

"No, you're looking to crucify him, and I can't figure out why."

"He's no different from any other perpetrator."

"Is that why you had him taken out of the court in handcuffs?"

"There's precedent for it. The feds did it on Wall Street, so why not in the courthouse."

"Then this *is* political. You're destroying one of my best judges just for publicity?"

"You have no idea of the pressure on me from insurance companies. It's not for publicity," Manning said. "Simmons is guilty."

This was killing two birds, or was it three?—with one stone, wasn't it? There was the publicity. This case would get his name before the public for months. No more local press. He'd be known statewide. Governor? Perhaps even nationally. People would forget the McCauley debacle. And finally, there was revenge for his sister, Agnes. Had she heard about Simmons's arrest? Manning would have to call her. It might take years! Years. But a Manning could wait to avenge an insult. Lace-curtain Irish and too good for his family?

"I have nothing against Simmons," Manning said. "After all, we're both Irish."

"Greg is a class act. You're *Shanty* Irish."

"A wop shouldn't make that kind of judgment."

"This is one wop who doesn't get ahead by walking on other people's graves."

"Come on, fellows," Sidney said. "No more name calling. We still have to work together."

Manning sat down at his desk. He took up a pen but, instead of writing, leaned back. He rocked slightly in his high-back swivel chair.

"Tomorrow morning, you will have my written request for an impartial judge to try the Simmons case."

"All my judges are impartial!"

"He means a judge from outside of Brooklyn," Grossman said.

"You make me want to vomit!"

Franco leaned over the desk and glared at Manning. For just a moment it appeared that he was actually going to throw up. Then Ronald Franco turned and left. He slammed the door behind him.

Manning swivelled from side to side in his chair and gently rocked, nodding to its rhythm. "Sometimes I feel like the reincarnation of J. Edgar Hoover."

Twenty-one

It might have been intentional, but by the time they had booked, fingerprinted, and photographed Justice Simmons, it was too late for night court. "No exceptions," they had said, so he had to spend the night in Central Booking, where they had transferred him.

Simmons, with his Brooks Brothers suit, white shirt, and striped tie, clearly stood out in the common jail cell. He sat despondently, his head in his hands, as two transvestite prostitutes traded comments with each other. He kept his head down, trying to ignore them. It was curious how the shadow of the bars to the cell seemed to bend in the light.

"It's about time they started arresting johns," said one hooker.

"We can have a party right here, honey," said the other.

A man who had been arrested for driving while intoxicated had passed out on the floor.

When Simmons tried to help him to a bench, the man awoke from his stupor and began to flail his arms.

"Leave me alone, son of a bitch," the drunk said.

"Yeah, leave him alone," the hooker said. She went over to him as the man lay prostrate and began going through his pockets.

"They took his money when they threw him in here," the other prostitute said.

"I know that! I'm looking for a damned match."

"You're sticking out like a sore thumb," said a clear male voice.

Simmons glanced up. It was Officer Macarella. Simmons went to the bars and grasped them tightly.

"Mac. Mac. You're . . . the only one." His voice cracked.

"I thought you might need some help."

"Help? I feel like the gods are dumping on me."

"Hey, Flanagan. Open this damned cell door! I can't talk to the judge through the bars."

Flanagan, a florid-faced cop, shook his head.

"No way, Mac. I let you see him, but I ain't letting him out."

"Don't be an asshole. You think he's gonna escape?"

"It's against regulations."

"Open the fucking door, you dumb mick."

Flanagan relented and opened the door, allowing Simmons to sit outside the pen. It wasn't that comfortable, but it was better than the slab bench in the cell.

"When you leave, he goes back in," Flanagan said. "I ain't putting my neck in a noose for nobody."

"I'm sorry for the cursing, Your Honor, but that's the only language he understands."

"Dumb mick?" Simmons said.

"You're getting some education in here, Your Honor."

"It's more like an out-of-body experience."

"You believe in guardian angels?" Mac asked.

"Mine must be on vacation," said Simmons.

"That's a good one, Your Honor—at least you ain't lost your sense of humor."

Macarella stayed with Simmons for hours. Talking. Small talk. Easing the embarrassment. Passing the time that now seemed to enter into slow-motion mode.

"I'll never forget this, Mac."

Twenty-two

Utica Avenue was a street no longer occupied by mom-and-pop stores. It now ran through a dingy, commercial section of town. It was dark because the thieves wanted it that way—breaking the streetlamps as soon as they were replaced. It was ideal for body and fender businesses. The rent was cheap and the garages spacious. A nearby junkyard supplied the hard-to-get parts for early-model cars.

Zangara and Tracy sat in their old Ford and watched as a Lincoln Continental pulled up to Tony's Body Shop and honked its horn. The garage door opened exposing a brightly lighted interior. The Lincoln quickly drove in and the door closed behind it.

"That's the third car in less than an hour," Tracy said.

"Yep. It's a nighttime business."

Zangara had parked down the block between two stripped cars. In the gloom he waited—patiently.

"You know what pisses me off the most?" Tracy said.

"What?"

"Here we are in this dinky car and they're driving BMWs and Lincolns."

"It's the tools of the trade," Zangara said.

"Some hunt with guns. We use beat-up cars."

"It don't seem fair."

"Sure it's fair," replied Zangara. "It's like we're in the jungle stalking prey."

"Yeah, the city's a jungle."

"You're an idiot, Marty. I'm talking about being a predator. A cop's no good if he's not a hunter."

"I'm not a hunter, Jack."

Zangara punched Tracy's shoulder.

"You're a hunter. You're just not a good hunter."

"You know what, Jack? You're full of shit. I tell my friends the things you say, and you know what they say?"

"What do your brilliant friends say?"

"They say, 'Is this guy a cop? Cops don't talk like that.'"

"And what do you say?" Zangara said.

"Me, I make excuses for you. I tell them you were kicked in the head by a horse when you were on the mounted patrol." Tracy smiled and then paused as another car arrived.

This time it was a Cadillac.

Zangara's eyes took in the scene but his mind was elsewhere. "Can you imagine what a jaguar is thinking when he takes off after an antelope. What excitement!"

"I get enough excitement giving out tickets."

"Yes, we're like jaguars."

"We're driving a Ford." Tracy grinned.

"You *are* dumb!"

"Come on, Jack. Let's cut out all this bullshit. Let's call for the swat team and bust their asses."

"Not yet. They must have fifteen guys working there—probably tear a car apart in fifteen minutes."

"That's a man a minute," Tracy said. "So while you're playing Hamlet, another car gets chopped up."

"What's the hurry? They'll be here tomorrow—and the day after tomorrow. We bust them today, they'll be someplace else tomorrow."

"Then what the hell are we doing here?"

"Counting. Just counting. We'll take them down when I know we can hurt them," Zangara said.

Twenty-three

The *Daily News* headline, in twenty-point type, proclaimed: SIMMONS INDICTED. The *New York Times* dealt with the event on page seven. The effect was the same.

The courtroom was filled this time with reporters, family members of other defendants who were to be arraigned, and a few lucky court buffs. The jury box was occupied not with jurors, but with lawyers who were awaiting the arraignment of their clients.

The arraignment to the indictment was the first step, and sometimes the final one, in the trial process.

Simmons and other indicted defendants were brought before the court and informed of the charges against them, their bails set, and attorneys furnished, and then they were remanded for trial dates.

Justice Franco, exercising his right to select the arraignment judge, presided. He sat on the bench, patiently reviewing each case as it was called. Occasionally, he called counsel to the bench so that they could discuss the pleas being offered. A plea to a lesser offense, with less jail time, was often the *quid pro quo* for a quick disposition of a case.

The counsel table was stacked high with case folders, as Bob Minowitz, a young assistant district attorney, fumbled through the folders. He checked his notes, spoke with lawyers and accompanied them to the bench. Everyone knew that this was the marketplace of criminal law. It was the venue for a lawyer to make his best deal—if it could be done. Occasionally, Minowitz would pick up a folder and advise the lawyer, "No deal on this one."

"Why not? It's the kid's first offense."

"It was a rape and robbery!"

"It was his girlfriend," the defense lawyer said.

"In an elevator? No, counselor, you're going to have to plead to the indictment," Minowitz said.

And so it went on, case after case, the heinous mixed with the ugly, the usual with the unusual. The robbers, the burglars, the murderers, the arsonists, the kidnappers, the car thieves, the sexual perverts—all were paraded in, cloaked in the only legal garment allowed, the presumption of innocence.

When a defendant was arraigned and no private lawyer answered, Belle Silverman, the equally young Legal Aid lawyer, stood up and was assigned to represent a defendant. A knowledgeable defendant knew that Legal Aid lawyers were tough, dedicated, and often better lawyers than assistant district attorneys.

The calendar—the list of cases to be heard—would take up the entire day.

The clerk constantly shouted, "Quiet! Sit down!" There were too many busy people, however, to keep the volume down to manageable levels. And while the command to silence was obeyed, it was only momentarily.

As with other defendants, Justice Simmons entered

the courtroom from the rear door. As with other defendants, he was handcuffed. He had not been afforded an opportunity to change and was wearing yesterday's suit. Although he was unshaven, he had straightened his tie so that he appeared presentable and only slightly haggard.

"The People of the State of New York against Gregory A. Simmons," the clerk called out.

"Take those handcuffs off," Franco said.

A court officer removed the handcuffs and Simmons visibly straightened. There was no need for the clerk to call for order as the audience strained to catch every word.

"Judge, the defendant has been indicted and I have here . . ." He held the indictment in his hand and waved it as if it were a flag.

". . . Just a minute, Mr. Minowitz. . . ." Franco looked at the crestfallen Simmons bravely trying to muster his dignity.

"Does the defendant have a lawyer?"

"Not yet, Your Honor, but I can represent myself." Simmons attempted a smile.

"Not today, you won't. Legal Aid will represent you at this arraignment—Miss Silverman?"

Minowitz handed her a copy of the indictment and several other forms.

Silverman accepted them and cavalierly tossed them on her table without looking at them.

"The defendant pleads 'not guilty.' "

"You didn't even ask me," Simmons said.

"Never do. Didn't you ever notice?"

Minowitz ignored the interplay between defendant and lawyer.

"The record should reflect that the defendant has

been served with the required notice for any omnibus motion. On the question of bail . . ."

"Don't say a word, Mr. Minowitz," said Franco. "The defendant is released on his own recognizance."

"I was only going to say that the district attorney has no objection to the defendant's release without bail."

Franco banged his gavel.

"This case is adjourned. Justice Theodore N. Taylor from Manhattan will be the trial judge. He will advise the parties when he is available. All pretrial motions are to be made to him."

The spectators erupted in a loud murmur at the mention of Justice Taylor.

"They're bringing in TNT!" a court buff said.

"There'll be no nonsense at this trial," said another.

Twenty-four

It was late in the afternoon when a black stretch limousine crossed the bridge onto Rikers Island. Department of Corrections personnel were allowed to drive there, but visitors were required to park their cars and take a bus to the prison complex. Money, however, like rank, had its privileges.

A liveried chauffeur drove the vehicle. Seated in the rear was Albert Modansky, a heavy-set man of about fifty. He was dressed in a striped gray flannel suit. His tie was garish, as was his large diamond pinky ring. They reinforced his image of being "Big Al," lawyer to the mob.

Two correction officers who guarded the entrance nodded politely to Modansky as he entered the building.

In the conference room he paced the floor, tapping the table each time he walked around it. Modansky waited until Ragazza entered before he sat down.

"Big Al. Great to see you," Rags said.

Modansky ignored the extended hand and motioned

for him to sit down opposite him. He then leaned forward and thrust his face at Ragazza.

"What the fuck have you done?"

"Come on, Mr. Modansky. I had no choice."

"Of course, you had a choice, you little shit! You turned a simple auto theft into headlines. Our people are very upset with you."

"They caught me red-handed; what was I supposed to do?"

"Take the rap and trust me to take care of it."

"It's gonna work out," Ragazza said. "The D.A. promised me that I walk—even if he don't get Simmons."

"They told me that you were stupid," Modansky replied.

Twenty-five

The Woolworth Building was, for the briefest time, the tallest building in the world. Now it was merely another midsized skyscraper on Broadway. Still, with its brown brick facade and white trim around the windows, it maintained a unique beauty when compared with the surrounding structures.

Barbara Danzig, along with scores of other lawyers who specialized in trial practice, maintained offices in the Woolworth Building. The rent was relatively inexpensive, the rooms were spacious, with high ceilings, and—most important—it was close to the courthouses, both in Manhattan and Brooklyn.

Barbara, before renewing the lease, and at the urging of Uncle Norman, had arranged for several features in the design of their offices. Norman's room was small and had no window. It was plainly furnished with a nondescript desk and several chairs. The walls were painted midnight blue, except for one adjacent to Barbara, where a two-way mirror had been installed.

"Keep it dark," Norman had said. "I don't need anything fancy. You're the one who has to look successful."

Care had been taken in the decoration of the waiting room. This would be the first assessment by a new client.

Lucy Sparrow was surrounded by her desk and tables, which contained a computer, fax machine, calculator, telephone system, and other items she used as the major factotum of the office. Original paintings in simple frames hung on the walls—most of them Impressionist.

Gregory Simmons sat on the brown suede sofa. Waiting. He was wearing a business suit. Conservative. Still Brooks Brothers. Battleship gray—that seemed appropriate. His white shirt was starched and the thin stripes of his tie alternated red and blue. His briefcase rested upright between his legs. His only concession to informality was his soft Italian leather loafers.

"I see Miss Danzig is partial to Impressionism."

"As a matter of fact, she's not," Lucy said. "*I* decorated this room."

"It's very tasteful."

"Thank you, Judge. Most of the paintings I pick up when they have the Greenwich Village Outdoor Art Show. I don't like copies."

"They still have artists painting like Monet or Seurat?"

"Sure, you just have to keep your eyes open." Lucy was neatly dressed in a long black skirt, and when she moved, Simmons could see her leather boots. The whiteness of her starched blouse was accentuated by her onyx broach.

Lucy glanced at her watch as if she were apologizing for him having to wait.

"I'm in no hurry," Simmons said.

"Ms. Danzig is running a little late."

"That's all right. I'm enjoying watching you work."

The telephone had been constantly ringing, but Lucy kept typing. At one point, she typed with one hand while answering the phone with the other.

"I'm like a one-man band—playing out of tune."

"You can't fool me, young lady. Obviously, you love working here."

"Like a *luch in cup*."

"A what?"

"A hole in the head! A judge from Brooklyn and you don't know Yiddish?"

"It's only moments like this that I realize my education is incomplete." He gave her a big smile.

When the interior door opened, a slim African-American walked out. Simmons half rose from the sofa.

"I'm sorry for your troubles, man." The young man extended his right hand.

"Reginald McCauley?"

"No, I'm Richard." He enjoyed the startled look on Simmons's face. Richard McCauley shook his hand and then strode out of the office. "See you, Lucy baby."

A moment later the intercom buzzed and Lucy answered.

"Miss Danzig will see you now." She led him down the corridor to Barbara's office and, stepping aside, allowed him to enter.

Barbara was on the phone. She pointed to an armchair opposite her desk. She swivelled in her high-backed chair and turned her back, cupping her hand over the phone and speaking in a whisper that she was sure was inaudible to Simmons.

"Billy is nice. Yes, he's rich. . . . I can train him. . . . But he's a jock. . . . No. . . . Gershon, your insights are shit. . . . What am I supposed to do in the meanwhile, masturbate? . . . I don't need advice. . . . I need some guidance here, Gershon. . . . I do my job. Why don't you do yours, you Nazi?"

She turned and smiled sweetly as Simmons's eyes swept over the room.

Barbara's office was furnished much like a medieval castle. Tapestries hung on darkly stained oak panels. A large mirror on one wall reflected another, where a knight's shield framed a sword and a mace. A thick Persian rug muffled the sounds. In all, the decor left no doubt that she was always ready for combat.

Barbara was dressed in a navy blue suit. She wore a scarlet blouse with a ruffled collar that highlighted her red hair.

After hanging up the phone, she turned and leaned forward on her desk. She played with her pen—and waited.

"Do you treat all of your clients this way?" Simmons said.

"You're not my client. . . ."

Simmons rose as if to leave.

"Not yet, anyway. Sit down."

It was Simmons's turn to ignore her. He wandered about the room. He inspected a mail glove, then a helmet. He picked them up and felt their weight.

"They're authentic?" Simmons said.

"The helmet, I bought in France. The glove comes from Germany."

"Quite a collection—and the escutcheon?"

"The shield is English, as is the sword. The mace is Italian."

"Nothing Irish?" Simmons said.

"The lectern. It was in a monastery outside of Dublin."

"How appropriate." He had his back to her now and peered into the mirror.

"Is this a two-way mirror?"

"Maybe."

"You videotape your interviews?"

"Not necessarily. More often it's for my investigator. I like him to see my clients but not vice versa."

"Any reason?"

"Sure—but it's none of your business," Barbara said.

Simmons returned to the armchair. He did not just sit down. He sat back and crossed his legs. Both were silent for a very long moment, as if the first person to speak would lose the advantage.

"You like to play games," he said.

"That's how I win my cases. And that's why you're here, isn't it?"

"Yes and no. My being acquitted may not be enough. People always believe the worst."

"I just get my clients off. I don't prove them innocent. If you're looking for more than that, you've come to the wrong lawyer."

"You don't understand. I need a principled defense."

"Like no shyster tricks?"

"Exactly."

Barbara rose from her chair and leaned forward—both hands on her desk.

"You're an insulting son of a bitch, aren't you?"

"I don't mean to be," Simmons said.

"Do you realize what you've just said to me? I use shyster tricks? You sanctimonious son of a bitch! You come to me because you think I'm unethical and unscrupulous—but you want a 'principled defense.' "

Simmons was not fazed by her anger. He knew her talents—he had personally witnessed them. In addition, he had researched her credentials.

Comfortable background—not necessarily a strike against her, but it did explain her self-confidence. Private school. Vassar, then Columbia University Law School. Law Review. Why hadn't she taken a job with an old-line WASP firm, like Sullivan & Cromwell or White & Case. She would have been a partner by now and making ten times as much as she did. Perhaps she merely wanted to be her own boss.

Danzig was obviously not the altruistic type—an idealistic lawyer that was going to forego money for public service to the poor and needy.

"Why don't you retain one of the big white collar crime lawyers . . . they might just listen to your bullshit. Just why are you coming to me, Judge Simmons?"

"I'm coming to you because you are the most brilliant criminal lawyer I know."

Barbara stared at him. She searched for any hint of duplicity. She sat down and rocked in her judge's chair.

"If I represent you at all, it will be on my terms. You'd be only a lousy defendant—not a judge. Do you understand?"

"Yes, but . . ."

"No buts. You've been sitting on your throne presiding like Zeus for years, but now you're going to get down and dirty with me."

"I don't want to win on a technicality."

Now she was really angry.

"How did you ever get to be a judge? You're a schmuck! You think I won the McCauley case by trickery? Let me tell you something. Reginald was innocent! His brother really killed Menachem Sackheim. What was Reginald supposed to do? Turn his brother in? Besides, I had a terrific self-defense argument as a backup. What would you do if you were surrounded by ten hostile people who had a history of violence toward your race—at least in that community?"

"But you waited. Couldn't you have eased tensions in the community by revealing the truth?" Simmons said.

"In the community? I'm a lawyer, not a social worker. Get real, Judge. If I disclosed it to the district attorney, his investigators would be all over the place checking on the whereabouts of the other twin. Macklin would change his strategy and I'd lose the case. McCauley was looking at a life sentence. Go ask Reggie what he thinks of winning on a technicality!"

"You have to understand. I'm sure I'll be acquitted . . ."

"You really believe that only guilty people are convicted?" Barbara said.

"Of course not, but . . ."

"You're not used to being interrupted?"

"No, I'm not but I can't get a word in edgewise with you."

"Go ahead. I'm really a good listener." Barbara smiled. This man was difficult to provoke. Perhaps when she probed a little deeper she'd find the switch that would set him off—or turn him on. Either seemed like a pleasant prospect—the Class Poet?

"As I was saying . . . I'm worried that I might be acquitted but be unable to return to the bench—with honor."

"Just worry about how you're going to pay my very large fee."

"That's some worry. I've been suspended without pay."

"I'm sure you'll find the money. Why don't we go over some of the details, for now."

Simmons reached into his briefcase and gave her a copy of the indictment. Barbara read it and then made notes. Simmons waited patiently for her questions.

"The district attorney really has it in for you. What did you do? Sleep with his wife?"

"That's not funny, Miss Danzig. He might harbor some resentment because he thinks I jilted his sister, Agnes."

Twenty-six

Norman Horowitz sat in his darkened office. He could hear and see them as Barbara asked him rapid-fire questions. She was assessing him—in effect, cross-examining him. There was no doubt about that. It was the start of an evaluating process that usually did not terminate until the foreperson of a jury stood up and read the verdict.

"How many car keys do you have?" Norman heard her ask.

"I have two."

"What about your wife?"

"Caroline? She did have a key, but I think that she left it when she left me."

"Are you sure?"

"I'll look for it."

"Was the separation friendly?"

"She hates me."

"Is there any reason for that?"

"I slept with her sister."

"You are a son of a bitch."

"It was before we were married. It was a mistake."

Barbara threw her pen down so hard that it bounced off the desk and onto the floor.

"Some mistake! What did you figure, that you had to sleep with the whole family before you got married?"

He reached to retrieve her pen.

"You're inclined to jump to conclusions, aren't you, Miss Danzig? I was living with Caroline at the time. Caroline and her sister are identical twins."

Barbara looked at Simmons for some time before she began to laugh.

"Is that why you nearly fell off the bench when I brought Reginald's brother into the courtroom?"

"I was disturbed by the parallel. The odd part is that it happened years ago, but she only blew up last week. She came home, packed her bags, and stalked out, screaming about being humiliated. The sisters are having a terrible battle over money. I guess, Christine—that's her sister—told her about us in order to hurt Caroline."

"You're telling me you couldn't tell them apart? Come on, Judge."

"Mrs. Sackheim couldn't tell *your* twins apart."

"Mrs. Sackheim didn't sleep with one of them!"

"Truly, besides Christine's passion for the color yellow, I still have trouble differentiating between them. The one sure way you can tell them apart is the smoking. Caroline doesn't and Christine smokes like a chimney. If you can get the two together, Christine is the one with the nicotine stains on her fingers."

"Aren't we observant," Barbara said.

Norman picked up the phone and buzzed Barbara. Norman saw Barbara glance at the mirror and then ignore him. "Damn it," he said and buzzed longer.

"Yes? Lucy, I told you that I didn't want to be disturbed."

"It's me, Norman."

"Yes, I know."

"Barbara, you can't represent this guy." Norman found himself whispering even though Simmons could not hear him.

"Why not?"

"Christine Palmer—the woman who retained us last month in the will contest between her and her sister. Guess what the other sister's name is?"

A will contest. Those fights could be more vicious than any criminal trial. Family members clawing over an inheritance. Was there duress? Overreaching? Undue influence? Or was there outright forgery? Barbara's adrenaline flowed on those cases, too, and the fees were both more certain and larger. Norman was right, of course. The safe way was to handle the civil case rather than the criminal one. Barbara, however, like a warhorse, preferred to put the bit in her mouth and abandon herself to the battle.

"Yes, Lucy. Then cancel the flight," Barbara said. She was not yet ready to make a decision.

"Barbara, we're talking about ten million dollars!" Norman said.

"The air fare is not refundable? Oh, well."

Norman watched Barbara hang up. "Damned pain in the ass. You never listen," Norman forgot that Barbara could not hear him.

"Who has time for a vacation, anyway?" Barbara said.

"Me," Simmons said.

"No, you don't. I plan to use you to prepare the omnibus motion and any trial memoranda we'll need. Meanwhile, I want you to do all the things you would normally do, that is, what you can do. If you look like you're feeling sorry for yourself, people will interpret that as guilt."

"I think I'm going to be a difficult client."

"No way. Without your black dress, you're a pussycat."

Barbara rose, signaling the end of the conference and escorted Simmons to the door.

When he left, Barbara did not bother to close the door. It would be only seconds before Uncle Norman, her protector and her conscience, would barge into the room.

"Why don't you ever listen to me?"

"Uncle Norman, why do you always tell me what I can't do?"

"I'm trying to keep you from being disbarred, dammit!"

"Where's the conflict? We represent Simmons in one case and his sister-in-law in the other. We're not representing his wife in any divorce action."

"I don't like it." Norman sniffed the air as if food had gone bad.

"This is too juicy to pass up. Christine kisses and tells on Caroline, hmm . . . trying to break up a marriage and a will. That lady plays hardball."

"Don't be dumb, Barbara. We take the civil case, make money and stay out of trouble!"

"An old cop like you can get me out of anything. It'll be a challenge."

"You'd better save your challenges for the jury."

"We're taking the case, Norman. Stop playing with words and start playing detective. The first thing that has to be checked is the car key taken from Ragazza."

"How do you know Ragazza had a key?"

"I have my sources." Barbara smiled her mischievous smile.

"Bullshit. The judge gave you a copy of the arrest report."

"My, aren't you quick, Norman! Do you think that you could be as quick delivering the petition for the court order that Lucy's typing up?"

"I don't need a court order," Norman said.

Twenty-seven

"Absolutely not, Norman. You need a court order," Stanley Mleski said. "And I don't wanna hear any of your lousy jokes."

Mleski was the property clerk, and he was known to look the other way at times to help a friend, provided, of course, there was little danger. This was not one of those times. He was a huge man whose uniform had long ago surrendered to his appetite. The buttons to his shirt were stretched so tight that it seemed that several loose ones were straining to pop. Mleski's red cheeks were in stark contrast to the rest of his pale white skin. He kept his blond hair in a crewcut, the last remnant of this once-trim Marine.

Going by size alone, he was not a man to be trifled with. But he was good-natured and permitted Norman to tease him.

"Did you hear the one about the Polish firing squad?"

"Yeah, they lined up in a circle."

"How about the one . . ."

"Norman, your jokes stink. For chrissake, give me a break."

As they talked, Norman moved along the counter. He tried to spot the area where the key would be kept. Mleski shifted with him to block his view, as if it were possible to pick out what he wanted from the teeming material that overflowed onto the floor.

The property room was in the basement of the 66th Precinct. It was a windowless room with cubicles on each side, all of which were stuffed to varying degrees with physical evidence. Handguns, rifles, bats, tire irons, machetes, chains, and assorted knives in cubbyholes, along with stacks of sealed envelopes and cartons—all the paraphernalia used in the commission of crimes and the other contraband that would be needed at trial. In the rear was a walk-in safe where the drug evidence was kept.

Norman leaned on the counter and playfully clawed with his fingers at the wire mesh that ran from the counter to the ceiling.

"Seriously, Stan. I need a favor."

"You want a favor and you tell Polish jokes? That ain't too smart."

"If I thought it would offend you, would I tell that kind of joke?"

"Yes." The button closest to his navel did pop when Mleski laughed.

"Come on, Mleski. What's the big deal?"

"What's the big deal? Just my job. The evidence is sealed."

"We've broken seals before. I just want to take a quick look."

Mleski grabbed the mesh and shook it for emphasis. The old screen rattled as its aged screws threatened to give way.

"Norman, the key is in an envelope with Zangara's initials across the seal. You want a peek, get a court order or see Zangara. I saw him a few minutes ago."

Norman left, but not before he said, "We'll get even with you yet."

"What are you talking about?"

"You bastards gave up my people to the Nazis." Norman closed the door quickly so that Mleski could not reply.

Norman caught up with Zangara in the corridor outside the detective room.

"Hey, Norman, you old flatfoot, how are you doing?"

"So, so, Jack. Why does it take four Irishmen to change a light bulb?" Norman asked.

"One to hold the bulb and the others to drink until the room revolves?" Zangara replied.

"Son of a bitch! Everyone knows my jokes."

"Everyone knows *you,* Norman. For instance, you want something from me."

Zangara reached out and tugged gently on Norman's mustache.

"What makes you think that?"

"For one thing, you came looking for me. For another, you told an Irish joke instead of an Italian one."

"What a marvelous deduction. No wonder they made you a detective."

"Don't bullshit a bullshitter, Norman. What do you want?"

"I need a small favor."

"I never heard you ask for a big one."

"I want to take a look at the key in the Simmons case."

Zangara stepped away as he pondered the implication of the request.

"Son of a bitch! Simmons retained your niece!"

"Yes."

"Judge Taylor's going to enjoy overruling her."

"What about the key? I just want to take a look."

Zangara shook his head.

"Norman, this one's a hot potato. I can't help you. You should know better. It would be my ass if I broke the chain of custody."

"Come on, Jack. I won't even touch it."

"What the hell is so important about a key? What am I missing?" Zangara said.

"Now you want me to teach you the business?"

"Never too old to learn," Zangara said. In the dim light of the corridor, his eyes seemed to protrude more than usual.

"You ought to see a doctor. You don't look so hot."

"Christ, Norman, I take fifty milligrams of Lopressor for my blood pressure, Coumadin for my irregular heartbeat, and—are you ready for this—Propylthiouracil for my thyroid."

"My God, you're a walking drug store."

"You're not funny, Norman. When you gonna learn? Now what about the key?"

"A steel-trap mind. That's what you got," Norman said.

"So, you're not going to tell me!"

"No, Jack. You have to tell me. Was it a key made in a hardware store?"

"You can't trace it." Zangara smiled. He was satisfied that it was a clue that would lead nowhere. "The key was not made by any locksmith."

"Factory-made?"

"Norman, let your niece be brilliant on this one."

"Can I at least inspect the car?"

"*That* you can do."

The police parking lot adjoined the precinct and was enclosed with a ten-foot cyclone fence. There were about fifteen automobiles there. Some were undamaged, confiscated for allegedly being used in the commission of crimes. Others were banged up and awaiting expert evaluations. *Did the brakes fail, or was the driver operating the vehicle recklessly? Was the location of the damage consistent with the injuries inflicted by a hit-and-run driver?*

The district attorney had already photographed the Mercedes. "Keep it on ice," Manning had said. "We may need it at the trial."

Norman walked slowly around the car. Zangara watched.

"What happened to the license plates?" Norman took out his pad and jotted down, "Plates missing. License frame reads: PARAMOUNT MERCEDES."

"You making a big deal out of this?" Zangara said.

"Well, someone tampered with the evidence."

"Bullshit. The plates are with Mleski. Those Supreme Court plates are too tempting. They're a trophy item—like a moose head on a wall."

Norman bent over the missing windshield and noted in his pad the vehicle identification number.

"Did you save the VIN number that was on the windshield?"

"The windshield was smashed."

"How do I know this is the judge's car?"

"Come on, Norman. The insurance certificate is in the glove compartment."

Norman went to the passenger side, opened the door and popped open the glove compartment. He scribbled another note in his pad. Norman took out a little pen light and dropped to the ground. He slid under the Mercedes and shined his light on the oil pan. When he finished, he dusted himself off and made another note in his pad.

"What the hell are you doing? This is Simmons's car—not a tag job," Zangara said.

A tag job? Auto thieves sometimes altered the vehicle identification numbers so skillfully that detection was almost impossible. To counter that, car manufacturers hid the VIN in several less obvious places. If someone wanted to check all the numbers—well, good luck to them.

"Don't be annoyed, Jack. It's habit, just habit," Norman said.

Twenty-eight

The apartment building on Riverside Drive off West 120th Street was a prewar building with a sweeping view of the Hudson River. The rooms were immense, with high ceilings, ornate moldings, and huge windows.

Christine's apartment—or, more accurately, the home of her deceased parents—was a six-room duplex. It was furnished in the old style, but it was obviously expensive. Alone, the three Tiffany lamps with their stained glass shades were worth a small fortune, though the heavy velvet drapes did give the apartment a musty feel. The overstuffed paisley sofa matched the chairs and rested on a threadbare, genuine Aubusson.

Carmine Miano turned the rug over to verify that it was handwoven and not machine made. He made a sour face to show that he did not think much of the decor.

Carmine sat back in the deep sofa and watched as Christine Palmer nervously walked around the room. Her yellow jumpsuit seemed engulfed in a fog as she chain-smoked. Christine's long blonde hair flowed about her face as she paced about. She puffed on a cigarette, put it out, and then lit another.

"Goddammit! You're going to give me goddamn cancer," Carmine said.

Carmine Miano was of average height and wore lifts in his shoes in order to appear taller. His dark complexion was in contrast to Christine's fairness. In fact, in appearances at least, they were opposites. Where his eyes were brown, hers were gray. Where his nose was large and curved, hers was small. Where he was heavy-set, she was slim.

"This is getting out of hand ... out of hand, Carmine."

"Relax, Christine."

"Everything is getting screwed up!"

"Look, sweetheart. Didn't I take care of it for you? So there was a slight hitch—big deal!"

Christine stopped pacing and blew more smoke into the air. She opened the window a crack and gazed out.

"Some hitch! A judge charged with conspiracy to steal his own car?"

"Don't worry. Everything will work out fine."

She was still at the window and was not aware of Carmine until he grabbed her and spun her around. His hands gripped her arms so tightly that she was unable to move. Her cigarette fell to the floor and he ground it into the carpet.

"Hey, that's an expensive carpet," Christine said.

"I think the problem with you is the goddamned apartment. Look at it! Everything is rotting. It smells like shit, too."

"I don't care. I'm not fixing it up. Even this place they left to Caroline."

"I set you up in a beautiful apartment and you're worrying about this shithole?"

Christine stepped back from Carmine into the center of the living room and lit another cigarette. She then extended her arms upward in an imaginary welcome.

"I'm home, Daddy," Christine said.

"You're sick. Your father fucked you up when he was alive and he's fucking you up from the grave."

"You're fucking me up, too, Carmine. What about your wife? You're still living with her."

"Don't change the subject. Tomorrow you go to the lawyer and drop the lawsuit. Let's settle this thing once and for all. You do what you're supposed to do."

"Don't I always?"

The sarcasm in her voice was too much for Carmine. He reached out and seized her neck. He slapped her face—first on one side and then on the other.

"How did I ever get mixed up with a broad like you?"

Twenty-nine

Paramount Mercedes was on Coney Island Avenue in Brooklyn. The street was lined with Toyota, Ford, Chrysler, Honda, and other Dealers. The Mercedes showroom offered a coffee bar and none-too-subtle overhead lights that were strategically placed so that they shone like spotlights onto the impeccably clean newest models.

When Norman walked into the showroom, he wore a bright multicolored Hawaiian shirt that Barbara had given him. The shirt was so outrageous that she had bought it for him as a joke, but he liked it and wore it, weather permitting, at every opportunity. Norman did not look like a man who could afford a $70,000 car. Consequently, no salesman bothered to approach him.

Entranced with the beauty of the cars, Norman strolled about the various models, opened a door here and there, and took pleasure at the quiet click of it closing shut.

Finally, a salesman approached him.

"We have a wide selection of previous-owner models," the salesman said.

"I came to see the manager. These cars are so beautiful I couldn't resist taking a gander at them."

The salesman pointed his finger in the direction of the rear of the showroom and marched away.

Sol Finkelstein was on the phone and waited a while before he acknowledged Norman. Anyone who approached him without being accompanied by a salesman was either not a customer or, more irritatingly, a customer who had a complaint.

"What can I do for you?" Finkelstein asked when he finally hung up. He was an obese man, and his jacket hung carelessly on the back of his chair. He reached for a Rolaid and popped one into his mouth. He considered offering one to Norman but then decided against it. Norman's loud shirt had struck again.

"I need some information about a car that was bought here."

"That's confidential information."

"Police business." Norman took out his old badge and flashed it.

"You have a subpoena?"

"Yeah," Norman said. He took a twenty-dollar bill from his Hawaiian shirt and gave it to Finkelstein.

Thirty

"It's nice to see you, again, Miss Palmer," Lucy Sparrow said. She could not resist adding, "I'm glad you didn't have to break *this* appointment."

"I did call. Is that why Miss Danzig is making me wait?" Christine opened her purse and took out a pack of cigarettes.

"Of course not. She'll be with you in a moment."

Christine fumbled through her purse. "Do you have a match?"

"We have a No Smoking policy in this office."

"You told me that the last time. Do you have a match or not?"

Lucy fished in her drawer. She found a book of matches and handed it to Christine. She dug down into her bottom drawer and came up with an ashtray.

"Thank you." Christine lit her cigarette and took a deep drag.

"That's a pretty outfit you're wearing."

"Thank you," Christine said, as if a compliment from the help was irrelevant.

"No, really. I think it's stunning."

Christine wore a yellow two-piece business suit with matching pumps. Her blonde hair was slicked back into a bun, and she wore a black scarf around her neck—less for contrast them to hide the black and blue marks left by Carmine.

A man on crutches emerged from the inner offices.

"Miss Danzig handles personal-injury cases?"

"It depends. Mainly we have a litigation practice."

When Barbara was ready for their conference, she came into the outer office to meet Christine.

"Doesn't she look stunning?" Lucy said.

"That's her favorite word for the day," Barbara said, and led Christine into her office.

"You look stunning, too," Christine said. She appraised Barbara, who wore a pinstriped suit with a ruffled blouse. "I love your hair color."

"Nothing like a good color rinse," Barbara said.

"It looks natural to me."

Barbara sat Christine in the same chair that had been occupied by Justice Simmons.

"Do you mind if I smoke?"

"Of course not. Paying clients can always smoke in my office."

Christine puffed away on her cigarette.

Barbara looked at Christine through the haze and tried to imagine what Caroline Simmons was like. The judge had said that they were identical. Did this one have a mind to match her beauty? It didn't seem that way. But, then, why had their parents made such a peculiar will? Was Christine the wild one and her sister the sedate, more solid one?

Barbara had decided to keep the will contest case—at least for now. What she had not decided was whether she would disclose to Christine that she was also representing Simmons in the criminal case. There wasn't any hurry.

"Since your mother and father were killed in a small plane crash, the exclusion clause in their insurance policy comes into play."

"So I've been told. That was the policy where I was the sole beneficiary?"

"Yes."

"So I get nothing?"

"As far as the insurance company is concerned. When they died together, the common-disaster clause of their mutual wills became operative."

"You're talking about the residuary clause?"

"I guess I'm not the first lawyer you've consulted," Barbara said.

"No, you're not. I understand that if there were no will that Caroline and I would share equally in the ten million. But my parents set up a trust in the will so that my money goes to Caroline—and she decides how much money she'll dole out to me."

"Well, it's a little more complicated than that—and not that bad."

"What are my chances of breaking the will?"

"To be frank, not good. Your father did put some language in the will explaining why he was creating the trust for your benefit. We may be able to establish malice."

"Yes. That would describe my father—but it really doesn't matter anymore."

"Why do you say that?"

"I've decided to drop the lawsuit."

"You know, weeks ago, I asked you if you wanted me

to negotiate a settlement, but you told me not to. Why did you come to me in the first place?"

"I came to you because I heard that you were a ballbuster at trial, and I wanted to break the will."

"And my reputation helped?" Barbara had been used before, but it did not make her less angry.

"It sure did."

"You've made a deal with your sister, haven't you?"

"You think I'm trying to cheat you out of a fee?" Christine said.

"It's been tried before."

Christine snuffed out her cigarette. "Send me the goddamned bill."

"That's not the point, Miss Palmer. I was your lawyer and you went behind my back."

"Bullshit," Christine said. "You lawyers talk ethics all the time and then sit up nights figuring out how to double-cross somebody."

"Seems like the pot is calling the kettle black."

"Screw you! I'm getting as far away from you people as I can." Christine rose and ground her cigarette into the rug. "And send me the bill for that, too!"

"What's the zip code for hell?" Barbara asked.

Thirty-one

The Bellmore Hotel was on Park Avenue and affected a kinship to the Waldorf-Astoria by displaying the national flags of visiting dignitaries. Its plain facade and simple canopy suggested old money, and the tuxedo-clad doorman did not diminish that image.

Norman's jacket was soaked. His dripping umbrella left a trail of water along the marble floor of the lobby. Norman stood to the side patiently as the clerk at the front desk registered a man. When the clerk had completed his task, he slid over to Norman.

"Is she in?"

"Do you have a subpoena?"

"Another one? This is the fifth time I've been here."

"One is required for each visit," the clerk said.

"This better be worth it." Norman folded a twenty-dollar bill and stuffed it in the clerk's breast pocket. "Now, what about Caroline Simmons?"

"She's in and out so fast that she's hard to catch. She's doing an awful lot of shopping, though. She's always carrying packages. This I'm sure of, she hasn't made one phone call."

"She might have a cell phone," Norman said. He was really getting tired of this twerp. "Who can afford calling from this hotel?"

"Our rates are competitive."

"I'm sure they are. What I mean is—is she home or not?"

"I told you. She's like a phantom."

"You mean she's not."

Norman plucked the twenty dollar bill from the clerk's pocket.

"Call me when she's home."

Thirty-two

Justice Franco, as a courtesy to a visiting judge, had assigned Theodore N. Taylor to a three-room chamber rather than the cramped makeshift chambers that were foisted upon judges with little seniority. In fact, the chambers, on the opposite end of the building, were the mirror images of Justice Simmons's chambers.

The irony was not lost upon Barbara.

"This room looks familiar," she said.

Justice Taylor sat behind the desk. He was an African-American about fifty years old, Barbara figured. He was stocky but not corpulent. His most prominent characteristic was his shaven head set on his thick neck. Football. Notre Dame Tackle. When he looked at you with his deep-set eyes and ferocious stare, there was no doubt about his reputation as a no-nonsense judge.

She and Ray Manning sat adjacent to each other, both opposite Justice Taylor. Sidney Grossman sat on a nearby couch.

"Is it all right if my assistant second chairs the trial?" Manning asked.

"As long as he doesn't open his mouth."

"Your Honor, I object. They're ganging up on my client," Barbara said.

"Where *is* your client?" Taylor said.

"He's right outside. I'd like him to be present," Barbara said.

"His presence is not required. This is only a pretrial conference; his presence is not mandated."

"I'd still like him present."

"He's outside—he's present!" Taylor thrust his face forward and banged his gavel. Barbara had been in many judges' chambers but she had never been gavelled down in them.

Barbara burst into laughter.

"What is so humorous, Miss Danzig?"

"Come on, Judge. Lighten up."

"What did you say?" Taylor rose so rapidly from his chair that it startled Barbara.

"What I meant was that this is just an informal conference and everyone is too serious."

"I demand the same decorum, whether on the bench or in chambers."

"If my client's rights are involved, then I think he should be present."

"He is present! He's outside."

"Outside is not inside."

"You know I'm not going to tolerate this, don't you?" Taylor rose. It was then that she realized he was wearing his robe. She had never seen that before either. Courtroom, yes—but in chambers? It was going to be easy to provoke this judge into error. Error that would require reversal on appeal—*if* Simmons was convicted.

As if reading her mind, Taylor said, "There will be no error in this trial."

Barbara almost jumped when he banged the gavel again. This time he broke the glass top on the desk. Taylor sat back down and scotch taped the long crack in the glass.

"Can we get to the business at hand?" Taylor said, as if the repair was another matter he had successfully concluded.

"You're going to have to control her, Your Honor," Manning said.

"You starting, too?"

Manning avoided Taylor's glare. He unbuttoned his jacket and reflectively plucked at his green suspenders.

"Please make a note. We have been assigned Room 721 as the courtroom."

"Why that's . . ." Barbara said. That courtroom was the same one in which McCauley had been tried.

"You have some objection?"

"No, Judge."

"Well, that's a first, isn't it? No objection?" Taylor half smiled to show he was a pleasant man and then thought better of it.

"The People are ready for trial, Your Honor," Manning said.

"Am I correct that the District Attorney himself is going to try this case?"

"Yes, sir. We've been ready for the past month."

"And you, Miss Danzig?" Taylor said.

"I know that Your Honor is only visiting here."

"And what is that supposed to mean?"

"Just that I'm aware of the inconvenience to you, and . . ." Barbara paused and decided not to finish the sentence.

"Don't you concern yourself about my inconvenience, young lady."

"I prefer to be called counselor."

"You'll find out, Judge, she ain't no lady."

"And you will find out, Mr. Manning, that I ain't no gentleman. I will not tolerate bickering or snide remarks—from either of you. Is that clear? I want jury selection to commence next Thursday."

"The D.A. says he's ready," Barbara offered, "but he's not."

"You're telling me when I'm ready?" Manning said.

"Judge, the People cannot be ready until they have supplied the defendant with all of the *Rosario* material."

"She's gotten everything she's entitled to, including the statement by our principal witness. We have complied scrupulously with the requirements of *People v. Rosario.*"

"How about the notes made by the arresting officer? We never received those. That's *Rosario* material also."

"This is a joke. What notes? You want to know the description that the detectives gave when they arrested your client?"

"I want everything we're entitled to. How do I know what the arresting officer wrote in his report?"

"You'll have it this afternoon," Manning said.

"What about complying with *Brady v. Maryland?*"

"You see what she's doing, Judge? She knows perfectly well that there are no exculpatory statements of any kind."

"Our investigation hasn't been completed yet."

"She's had ample time, Judge. This is the old stall tactic."

"I have reason to believe that the district attorney is hindering our investigation. . . ."

"That's a damned lie," Manning said.

". . . by secreting a material witness."

"I resent these wild accusations, Judge," Manning said.

"Does the prosecution intend to call Caroline Simmons as a witness?" Barbara asked.

"Maybe. Is the defendant waiving the spousal privilege against confidential communications?"

"That's the point, Judge. How can I know that if we can't find her?"

"Maybe you should hire a better investigator," Sidney Grossman said.

Taylor threw up his hands. He had a light complexion and his face reddened, but he was not blushing.

"You better keep your assistant on a leash if you want him in the courtroom," Taylor said.

"I have a right to interview her," Barbara said. "And I can't do it when the D.A. has her stashed away."

"We're not hiding her, Your Honor. Miss Danzig knows exactly where Mrs. Simmons resides."

"I'm not going to spend the rest of my life listening to you two haggle. There will be no more delay. Next Thursday!"

"Really, Judge. There hasn't been any delay in this case. I need a little more time."

"Next Thursday—or your client will be in jail during the trial, judge or no judge."

Barbara jumped up. This was no act. The red in her hair almost matched the flush on her cheeks.

"That is the most odious threat I have ever heard! I want a court reporter in here, right now! I want this on the record!"

"I'll decide what goes on the record, young lady." Taylor leaned back in his chair. He smiled at his small triumph. Two could play the same game. He could get her goat, too.

"Sit down, Miss Danzig."

"Is this all off the record?" Barbara ignored his direction and remained standing.

"Of course."

"Then I can tell you that you are a sexist son of a bitch and I demand that you recuse yourself."

"Nine-thirty sharp on Thursday," Taylor said, and spun his chair around.

Thirty-three

"I've heard of someone being given the back of his hand, but this is the first time I've ever been given the back of a chair," Manning said when they were outside the chambers.

Barbara motioned to Justice Simmons, and he followed her down the hallway. Manning and Grossman trailed behind on their way to the central elevators.

"What was all that yelling about?" Simmons said.

"It was nothing. We were just setting the ground rules. Feeling each other out."

"Do you do this all the time?"

As Manning passed by, he could not resist a chuckle.

"How to win friends and influence people...."

"I'm not interested in influencing enemies."

"Hey, Barbara, I'm not your enemy," Manning said.

"Ms. Danzig—that's my name."

"Maybe *you* should lighten up," Grossman said.

"Why don't you tell your attack dog to shut up," Barbara said.

Manning touched Simmons's arm.

"Perhaps we should talk a little," Manning said.

"I don't talk in hallways," Barbara said. Mistake. There would be other cases. Why was she getting angry with Grossman? As the chief assistant district attorney, he wielded substantial power if not influence. Grossman assigned cases, consented to pleas, and, when necessary, arranged for polygraphs of defendants. He was the one who often determined whether an indictment should be dismissed. Yes. Grossman could make her life much easier and here she had told him to shut up. She looked at him for some sign of animosity but could discern none. No. Grossman was a "don't get mad, get even," kind of man. Barbara considered making a conciliatory remark but then decided against it. It would be too obvious. There was always later. She knew that he liked cleavage. Maybe the next time, when she knew they were going to meet—at a Bar Association dinner or Christmas party—she'd wear a low-cut dress and sidle up to him.

"We've made many a deal in courtroom corridors, haven't we, Barbara?" Grossman said. He winked. It was a too-friendly wink.

"He wants to talk about a plea," Barbara said to Simmons as if the possible were impossible.

"Come on, Greg. I hope you realize that there is nothing personal in this," Manning said.

"That's the laugh for the day," Simmons said.

"I have a job to do. If you're interested in a plea, I would give it serious consideration," Manning said.

Simmons turned his back and started to walk away, but Barbara stopped him.

"Like what?" Barbara asked.

"Well . . . Attempted Insurance Fraud," Manning said.

"To cover all counts in the indictment?"

"Of course."

"Let's see, that's an E felony. Up to three years in jail," Barbara said.

"Oh, I would recommend no jail time."

"Only disgrace and disbarment," Simmons said.

"You have to understand. More than half the car thefts in New York City are arranged by the cars' owners. The insurance companies have been pressuring me to make an example of you."

"In other words, if you can get a judge convicted of the crime, then it will trickle down to John Q. Public," Barbara said.

"You make it sound like a vendetta," Grossman said.

"Isn't it? It sounds like selective prosecution to me."

"I don't care what you think: all I'm asking is, 'are you interested in a plea?'" Manning said.

"How about a dismissal of the indictment and a public apology?" Barbara said.

"I made a serious offer. Not something to joke about."

"Oh, I'm not joking. You drop the charges and we won't sue you for malicious prosecution."

"That's ludicrous."

"Is it? How's your sister, Agnes?" Barbara took Simmons by the arm and walked away. She stopped and turned. "Hatred is a terrible basis for prosecuting a person."

"You can burn in hell!" Manning was livid. Grossman grabbed his arm.

"You sure play hardball," Simmons said. "We had

better take the judges' elevator. I think Manning was about to slug you." Simmons led her to the elevator.

"Isn't the first rule of advocacy," Barbara said, "to get your opponent so angry that he can't think?"

"You have a knack for that."

"That's the difference between men and women, and that's why women make better lawyers than men."

"Am I to get a classic Danzig observation?"

"You heard?" Barbara said.

"Only by reputation."

"Okay. It's more than cultural. It's historical. Homo sapiens developed, diverged, and specialized. Men hunt, women nurture. So men, as aggressors, strike out when they're angry—women talk. You have never heard of a woman 'sputtering with rage,' have you?"

"You are an extremely bright woman, Ms. Danzig."

"Thank you, Your Honor. I'm good at talk but bad at concealing my emotions."

"Is that cultural or historical?" Simmons said. He smiled.

"Now, you're making fun of me." Barbara felt herself blush. Damn. Just like a teenager.

"But only with respect."

"Speaking of respect . . ." Barbara returned to business. "That Taylor is not giving you any. I thought all judges knew each other."

"I met him once at a convention, but we never spoke."

"He's a nasty son of a bitch," Barbara said.

"But he's a fair judge," Simmons said.

"It really doesn't matter, I have ways to deal with him," Barbara said.

"You're going to end up being held in contempt."

"When we're in court, and on the record, I'll be as sweet as sugar. Meanwhile, just relax. Play a little golf.

. . . Incidentally, the memorandum you wrote for the omnibus motion was brilliant."

"Why, thank you, Ms. Danzig."
"Call me Barbara."

Thirty-four

Barbara was glad she had kept her appointment with Dr. Reich. He never complained when, on short notice, she would cancel the appointment, and unlike other therapists, he didn't charge her for the missed meetings. In fact, he never sent a bill for the times—and they were innumerable—when she would telephone him at all hours. Gershon was more than her therapist. He was her friend. So it was that she would give him little gifts designed to make him laugh. A swagger stick to "match his personality." A monacle for "her Prussian." A copy of *The Prince* by Machiavelli, in German.

For his part, he would talk about different things despite them having little to do with therapy. Or did they? Gershon Reich was a sly one.

She still had the recurring dreams. They were lucid dreams, in that she challenged herself to stay asleep but always found herself forcing herself to wake up. Whether it was flying straight into a cliff or racing down twisting corridors, the dreams all ended the same way—her waking too frightened to know the outcome.

If sleeping was a part of life, then waking seemed to be a contradiction. How was it that she could be such a successful human being during the day and such a failure when sleeping?

"That's the secret, Barbara," Gershon Reich said. "You're not a failure. When you sleep you're preparing yourself for the day."

"Are you saying that if I were a clerk in a store that I wouldn't have nightmares?"

"No, you'd probably just have different kinds."

"Thanks a lot, Gershon. You're a big help."

"No, listen. It's a paper I'm writing about sleep and why we dream."

"Freud beat you to it." Barbara looked at him curiously. What the hell. Gershon was entertaining.

"Barbara, he didn't have enough scientific facts to back him up. He was satisfied with just trying to interpret dreams. Not *why* we dream. For example, what did he know about oxygen deficits? Nothing!"

"And you're a physiologist?"

"Listen. When you're awake, you're like a sprinter who uses up all his energy and is exhausted after running full speed for a hundred meters. You need time to recover. To catch your breath. To replenish the oxygen you've expended. Time to process the wastes from every cell in your body. And that is why you sleep—because, during your waking hours, like the sprinter, you're producing more waste that your body is capable of handling. Deprive a person of sleep, and he becomes psychotic. In effect, the poisons overwhelm his nervous system."

"I hope you're not including this in my hour," Barbara said.

"Always a joke. Let me finish. The brain is not like an automobile that can be shut off. But like the automobile stopped for a red light, the brain 'idles' while we sleep. What we dream is what we are. A farmer dreams about his problems and a lawyer dreams about his problems. The dreams are a review of what we have experienced and a preview of what we can expect. It's like a violinist warming up. Experimenting with the notes of life, warming up for tomorrow's symphony. Lamenting yesterday's mistakes and hoping to correct them by future action. Learning. And the violin responds to the ear—if the ear is acute."

"And the strings are not broken. Is that where you get the term 'high-strung,' Gershon?"

"Always a joke?"

"No, really, Gershon, that is very poetic."

"To tell you the truth, I stole a little from Shakespeare," Reich said.

"Not Freud?"

"*Romeo and Juliet.* Where he says, 'True, I talk of dreams, which are the children of an *idle* brain, begot of nothing but vain fantasy.'"

"Can we get back to my therapy now?"

"We never left. Did you learn anything from my rambling?"

"Not much of value. So you think that my daytime attempts at control are really a reflection of my fear of failure?"

"Why not? You're a woman competing in a field traditionally recognized as the province of men. Notice that even as a lawyer you didn't go into a safe area, like corporate law. You chose to be a trial lawyer. What did you tell me it was?"

"Vicarious combat, but Gershon, forget about all your bullshit, I need your advice. I think . . ." Barbara hesitated. "I think I'm falling in love."

"That's nice," Reich said.

"Is that all you can say?"

"Barbara. My little sweetheart. You don't want advice, you want approval."

"Sometimes I think you're a demented gnome!"

"I'm not your father. I'm your therapist. I don't give advice to the lovelorn." Reich twisted his mustache.

"Please, Gershon. I'm serious."

"Does the poor sap know what he's getting into?"

"I don't think he even knows I care."

"So tell him."

"I can't," Barbara said. "He's my client."

"You're not falling for that crooked judge, are you?"

"You *are* a demented gnome." Barbara lunged at Reich and slapped his face.

"My God! You are falling in love."

"Oh, I'm so sorry, Gershon. I didn't mean it." She embraced him and held him. Then she began to cry.

Thirty-five

The Brooklyn and Manhattan Trial Lawyers Association golf outing, though usually held in the spring, had been repeatedly postponed by the weather, so they renamed it the "Fall Classic." The location remained the same—the Richmond County Country Club in Staten Island.

"I know where it is," David Leibowitz said.

"Knowing where it is and getting there are two different things," Simmons said.

"We traversed the Verrazano Bridge rather well, I thought."

"David, try not to straddle the lanes."

"Would you like to drive, Your Honor?"

"Here, you turn here." Simmons reached out and turned the steering wheel sharply.

They exited the Staten Island Expressway and eventually came to Todt Hill Road. Unfortunately, it was narrow and winding. David steered gingerly with an occasional assist from the judge.

"I hope you play golf better than you drive."

"Worse. You know the Talmud has something to say on almost any subject, but there's not one word about golf."

"Your wife must have been surprised when you told her you were playing golf," Simmons said.

"Leah was more surprised when I told her that I was driving you. She tells the children, 'What's to worry? Your father will smash the car and then that Judge Taylor will *have* to give the adjournment.'"

"We don't need an adjournment, you know. It's a ploy of Ms. Danzig."

"Yes, I'm aware of that."

"She liked the memorandum we prepared."

"Didn't do you much good," David said.

"I told you that Taylor would never dismiss the indictment. He's on the hot seat, too."

"What do you think of Ms. Danzig?"

"I'd hate to be married to her."

"Not pretty enough?"

"It's not that. She's extremely attractive."

"Not bright enough?"

"It's not that, either."

"Then what is it?"

"She makes a wonderful lawyer, but with her mouth she would drive a man crazy."

"But I like her," David said.

"I like her, too."

David managed to turn in to the Richmond County Country Club parking lot without hitting the chain-link fence but drove perilously close to its edge.

The parking lot was located off Todt Hill Road and was strategically placed so that the clubhouse, the 1st tee, and the 18th green abutted. David, who had never been to the golf course, was awed by the view. He looked down from the parking lot toward the immaculate greens and tree-lined fairways that sloped precipitously from the parking lot.

"Wow."

"And wow to you," Simmons said. David wore plaid knickers and knee-high socks.

"Don't laugh, Judge, until you see my golf clubs. I borrowed them from Rabbi Wasserman."

Justice Simmons wore white slacks and a crisp white Izod shirt. His golf clubs were also top-of-the-line, his five-hundred-dollar "Big Bertha driver," protruding from his kangaroo skin bag.

At the starter's hut a number of lawyers gathered to sign in. Several came over to greet Simmons.

"We have a package of golf balls for all the players, Judge." Bob Bellard was one of the more competent lawyers practicing in Brooklyn.

"I'm going to need them. I missed the last outing, you know." Simmons smiled.

"It's all a crock, Judge. We're all for you."

"Thank you, Bobby."

"We have hats for you, too." He handed David a red baseball cap with the inscription "Brooklyn and Manhattan Trial Lawyers Assn."

The starter checked his chart and then his watch. Simmons, not sure whether he would be shunned or embraced, enjoyed their extravagant greetings.

"You're up next, Judge. Your bags are on the cart."

"Who else is in the foursome?"

"They're already on the tee," the starter said, and turned to set up the next group.

Barbara was waiting for them at the tee. Norman,

like Babe Ruth coming to bat, swung several clubs to warm up.

Barbara smiled. Her smile was so engaging that anyone to whom it was directed was obliged to smile back. As they approached, she waved and then returned to her stretching exercises. She touched her toes and then twisted her body in warmup, with a golf-club set behind her back and cradled in her arms. If there were any doubts as to her figure, which was usually hidden in business suits, they were dispelled by her pink slacks and snug fitting blouse.

"Surprised?"

"Nothing about you surprises me." He gazed at her as she continued to stretch, and then added, "Well, almost nothing."

"Say hello to my Uncle Norman."

Norman smiled, showing his missing tooth. He wore his Hawaiian shirt but eschewed the red cap for his blue Brooklyn Dodgers cap.

"Hello, Uncle Norman." He turned and then introduced David.

"Uncle Norman is my investigator," Barbara said.

"The man behind the mirror. All this time and we never met," Simmons said.

"You should feel complimented. She always keeps me separate from the clients."

"My uncle is too judgmental. He thinks that he's the lawyer—always giving advice. I have to keep him in his place."

"David, can we switch bags? I'd like to ride with the judge."

"Of course," David said.

"Don't touch my bag," said Norman. "I put my Glock in there."

"You brought a gun to a golf course?" Barbara said.

"I take my gun to bed with me!"

"I'm not going near that one," Simmons said.

"Can we please tee off. We're holding everyone up already," Barbara said.

"What's the hurry? It's going to be a long day," Norman said.

David teed up. He swung with an unpracticed arc, bending his arm. The ball dribbled off the tee.

"You have to keep your left arm straight," Simmons said. He took a practice swing to demonstrate. When Norman teed up, his swing showed the same unfamiliarity with the game as David. His ball also dribbled off the tee.

"At least we're both in the same direction," Norman said.

Barbara motioned to Simmons to proceed.

"Gentlemen before ladies," she said. "You might have to teach me, too."

Simmons placed the ball down and threw up some grass, to check the wind direction. His swing was smooth and professional. The ball shot from the tee, straight and far down the fairway.

"What a wonderful shot!" David said.

"I'm glad we switched bags," Norman said.

Barbara then stepped up and, with the same fluid swing, struck the ball, sending it not as far, but just as straight and splitting the fairway.

"Beautiful. I'll bet an awful lot of lessons went into perfecting that swing," Simmons said.

"Wait until you see me putt," Barbara said. She replaced the club in her bag.

"I'd rather watch you swing."

She was, as Mac the cop would have said, "poetry in motion."

"You stroke the ball pretty well, yourself," Barbara said.

"Rich little girls take lessons," Simmons said.

"And underprivileged boys develop their swings by caddying for rich girls?"

"This *is* going to be a long day," Norman said.

Barbara took the passenger seat in the golf cart and waited for Simmons to come aboard.

"I love when a man drives."

"I find that hard to believe, Ms. Danzig."

"I told you, call me Barbara, Greg."

The twosome traversed the course, from fairway to green, each playing well. An occasional missed putt resulted in a bogey. Simmons had a double bogey when he three-putted a green. Barbara took a seven when her ball rolled into a water hazard. The competition was friendly but keen, and they lost themselves in the game.

The inept others were having just as good a time as they hacked away from rough to fairway and back to rough. David continuously laughed as Norman told joke after joke.

"David, you're wonderful. You laugh at all my jokes."

"I don't hear many jokes," David said. "And those I do, I can't remember."

Their ineffectual play afforded Barbara and Simmons an opportunity to idly chat, as they waited for Norman and David to catch up.

When Barbara replaced her lost ball with a yellow one, Simmons laughed.

"What's so funny?" Barbara said. "You never lose a ball?"

"No. No. Barbara. It's the yellow ball. I was laughing at the yellow ball."

"What's wrong with a yellow ball? It's a regulation ball."

"I pictured Caroline playing with a yellow ball. She hates the color yellow more than her sister loves it. Caroline hates yellow so much that she won't even take a yellow cab."

"Doesn't she have platinum blonde hair like her sister?"

"Caroline draws the line there. She's a bug on naturalness. She wouldn't think of dying her hair, although she has quite a collection of wigs—but no blonde ones."

"Are you one of those gentlemen who prefer blondes?"

"Auburn is lovely. Where did a nice Jewish girl like you get red hair?"

"My mother has red hair and she got it from the Cossacks."

"Is this another Danzig classic?"

"Maybe. Do you want to hear?"

"Sure."

"In Russia when the Cossacks invaded a *shtetel* in a pogrom, they killed all the men and raped all the women. The women became pregnant. Their children were brought up as Jews. Jewishness is determined through the mother, not the father. So the Cossacks with red hair transmitted their red hair to the Jews."

"It's an interesting theory."

"It's precious when you think about it, because in the next pogrom, and the next, Cossacks killed their own children."

"So, through the centuries, the more pogroms, the more red hair?" Simmons reasoned.

"Exactly."

"The things you learn on a golf course!"

"You asked for it. What about you? Do you still love your wife?"

"It really doesn't matter. She hates me."

"Love and hate go together like a horse and burning carriage, eh?" Barbara said.

"I've made mistakes."

"What did Shakespeare say? 'Heat not a furnace for your foe so hot that it do singe yourself,'" Barbara said.

"Yes, *Henry VIII*. He also said, 'Love thyself last: cherish those hearts that hate thee,'" Simmons said.

"You *were* the class poet!"

He looked at her curiously and then smiled. "You checked my credentials that thoroughly?"

"As much as I could."

"Well, I checked you out, too—*Vassar* girl," he said.

"And I still can't figure out why your wife has such animosity—are you leveling with me?"

"Absolutely, Barbara. Remember. 'He is secure and now can never mourn a heart grown cold'—Shelly!"

"That's nice, Greg, but I have to know how your wife thinks and feels, and how you think, too. So Caroline hates yellow and she hates you. What do *you* hate?"

"I hated being a caddy."

"Being a caddy tells a lot about a young person," Barbara said. She took out her putter and lined up her putt.

"The only thing it indicates is that I was poor."

"I don't know. It shows ambition. Energy. Industriousness. It explains a lot—like you probably worked your way through school."

Barbara stroked her putt and sunk a twelve footer.

"Poor is poor. There's no glamour in it."

"My parents were well off, not rich, and I was brought up with, you know, private schools, exclusive summer camp—but sometimes I think I missed something."

"You missed nothing."

"I missed proving that I could have made it without a silver spoon. You made it that way, didn't you?"

"Therefore, rich is better than poor?"

"You're really a smartass. How did you ever get to be a judge?"

"I married a rich girl," Simmons said.

Barbara raised her putter in mock attack, and he backed off. He, too, waved his putter as in a duel.

"What's going on here?" Norman called out. "Can't I leave you alone for a minute?"

David and Norman looked slightly ragged as they drove up. Neither of their golf balls were in sight, but Norman nevertheless parked their cart by the green.

Norman took his putter and dropped his ball two feet from the cup.

"Uncle Norman!"

"Don't break my concentration," Norman said. "I'm playing imagination golf. I lost my ball after I hit a great shot out of the woods. So I'm imagining my next shot, and this is where it landed." Norman took careful aim and struck the ball. It stopped on the rim of the cup.

"See, God punished you," Barbara said.

"You should have kept playing imagination golf," Simmons added.

"I knew it. I knew it! She's contaminating him already," Norman said.

Thirty-six

Jimmy Four Eyes Riley was neither Irish nor bespectacled. His grandfather had been a prizefighter and had changed his name from Realla to Riley at a time when fight promoters paid more money for Irish boxers. "Like Willie Pep. He was Italian," his grandfather had said. Unlike Willie Pep, the great prizefighter, Jimmy Riley the elder had never lasted more than two rounds with any fighter of consequence.

The nickname Four Eyes was bestowed upon him by his friends in appreciation of Jimmy's keen sight. At one time, he was recorded as having 20/5 vision. The inheritance of his grandfather's aggression coupled with this extraordinary gift of sight dictated Jimmy Riley's occupation. He was a contract murderer.

Riley prided himself on his thoroughness. "Leave nothing to chance and always have a way out," he told those few who knew that he was not a pizza parlor owner. "And have a good cover, like mine." Riley was athletically built and kept trim by jogging five miles daily. His dark good looks were often obscured by a ski mask, but when the occasion called for it, he would adopt an appropriate disguise.

When Jimmy Four Eyes turned into the parking lot at Richmond County Country Club, he was dressed like any ordinary golfer. He wore blue slacks with a white sport shirt and white golf shoes. He wore skintight golf gloves on *both* hands. The Lincoln was stolen, but Jimmy had been assured that the license plates had also been freshly stolen from another Lincoln. Given the number of Cadillacs and other expensive cars in the lot, he was satisfied that it was the right car for the job.

Riley parked at the farthest end of the lot and leisurely alighted. He took a golf bag from the trunk and glanced around. Perfect timing. The early golfers had not finished, and the late golfers had already arrived. There was no one to see Riley disappear into the thick brush.

He moved through the undergrowth and picked his way to the spot he had selected when he had cased the place. He cleared away the bushes to insure his field of vision, and looked down into the valley that overlooked the 18th green. The terrain sloped precipitously from the hill to the green—a hundred yards. It was far enough away so that only the most wayward ball would be hit near him and close enough to make his task a piece of cake.

Riley saw several golfers putting out, and he rearranged a few branches to enhance his concealment. He unzipped the large pocket in the golf bag and removed a polished case. He assembled a rifle and attached a scope to it. He knelt and took a practice aim at the 18th green. Bang, *Bang,* he imagined, as he caught a golfer in the crosshairs of the telescopic sight. Riley checked the rifle and made a slight adjustment on the scope. He took off the red baseball cap he was wearing, sat back on a log, and waited. The cap did not have "Brooklyn and Manhattan Trial Lawyers Assn." written on it.

Thirty-seven

Clothing hung neatly in the open walk-in closet of the bedroom. Christine grabbed dresses here and there and scattered them onto the unmade bed. She took a large suitcase from the top of a closet and threw it on the bed.

Carmine Miano, with his arm stretched across the doorjamb, remained motionless.

"Don't take any clothes," he said.

"Where the hell are my cigarettes?" Christine barked. She found them under a skirt that had been thrown onto a night table. She lit one and paced the room. "Where the hell is an ashtray?"

"I said you shouldn't take any clothes! You thick or something?"

"I'm not going empty-handed, Carmine. Besides, I told the lawyer I was leaving. How would it look if I left without taking any clothes?"

"I'll dispose of them for you."

"You're really good at that, aren't you?"

"You're really aggravating me."

"I told you that I was frightened, but that doesn't mean anything to you. You're making me do things that scare me, and you just stand there and give orders."

"You're a spoiled bitch. When there's a little pressure, you fold up like an accordion."

"I'm not from Mulberry Street."

"What's that supposed to mean?"

"I'll draw you a picture," Christine said. She bent over the bed to close the suitcase and her skirt tightened around her hips.

Carmine looked at her buttocks and her well formed legs. He tiptoed to her and seized her before she could turn around. His hand reached into her yellow silk blouse and caressed her breast.

"Christ, not now, Carmine." She struggled but he held her tightly. They fell onto the bed. The suitcase and its contents spilled to the floor.

"You're going to rip my skirt!"

"Yeah."

In one motion, he raised her skirt and took her from behind. It was quick and it was furious, but Christine was not an unwilling participant. She turned and kissed him, first on the lips and then down his neck, all the while clutching his hair.

"You're going to rip my blouse," she said.

"Yeah."

Afterward, Carmine returned to the doorjamb as if nothing had happened. He adjusted his clothes and watched Christine as she picked up the suitcase and resumed packing.

"Better fix your hair," he said.

Christine looked in the vanity mirror. After a few

quick brushes, her hair seemed presentable enough for her. There were new bruises on her body.

"Why are you so rough? You know how sensitive my skin is."

"You don't know what rough is."

"Oh, I forgot. The great mastermind from the streets."

"What I know they don't teach in your fancy colleges."

"You have a lot to learn, too."

"Christine, I'm warning you. Don't fuck with me."

"Well, smart one. Now that you've engineered things, what are you going to do if they call me as a witness?" Christine asked.

"Number one—why should they call *you*?"

"And number two?"

"That's why you're disappearing for a while."

"It's very funny, but it seems that I'm the one who has to do everything."

"I'm doing plenty. Then there's number three . . ."

"Well . . . do I have to wait all day?"

"There ain't going to be a trial," Carmine said.

"Yeah, sure. You bribed the D.A. and the judge."

"Don't have to," Carmine said.

"I don't want to get any deeper into this." Christine bit her lip. "You're really scaring me now."

"Then don't ask questions and do like you're told."

She had to open and close the suitcase twice, to stuff a dress and a slip in, before she was finally able to close it. She tested the weight and found it heavy. She looked at Carmine still standing there, wearing what she called his "mobster's grin." It looked like a smile but he would show no teeth. How appropriate. His lips were sealed.

"Are you sure you have everything?"

"I'm sure." She lifted the suitcase from the bed and looked at Carmine. The bastard was still smiling.

"How about these . . . bubblehead?" Carmine took her keys from his pocket and dangled them.

She struggled with the suitcase and dragged it along the floor. When he was within reach, she snatched the keys from his hand and dropped the suitcase.

"You really aren't going to help me."

"No. And we're not going to see each other until this is over."

"Carmine, I don't know how I can go through this without you."

"I'll be around."

Christine bent to pick up the suitcase, but the sight of her half-buttoned blouse was too much for Carmine. He swept her up and she allowed him to carry her back to the bed.

"Carmine, you're an animal!" she said.

Thirty-eight

It was a long day. As with most lawyer-sponsored golf outings, there was a disproportionate number of "duffers." Their clumsiness and insistence upon searching endlessly for lost balls contributed to the backing up of foursomes at each tee. By the time Barbara's group had reached the 18th hole, the sun cast long shadows across the fairway.

Most of the time Barbara and Greg split the middle of the fairway with their tee shots and were far ahead of Norman and David.

"They're perfectly matched," Barbara said. She looked back to see David coming from the woods. Norman repeatedly swung his club until the ball popped out of the rough.

She waved to Norman, who held his club over his head, triumphantly—but still one hundred yards behind them.

"Is that my ball?" Simmons said.

"You're sweet, Greg. You know damn well that you out-drove me by thirty yards."

"Yes, but you're killing me with your putting."

Barbara checked the scorecard.

"You're beating me by five strokes. You make a practice of beating women?"

"Only in golf," he said.

"How about your wife?"

"If holding her arm while trying to avoid her kicking me constitutes 'beating,' then I guess I beat her."

"Think this is a six-iron shot?" Barbara said, calculating the distance to the green. "Your wife filed for a divorce pretty quickly after she left. I have to tell you, I still don't buy your explanation."

"Was I selling it to you?"

"I'm not sure. I think you're a very complicated man, Mr. Justice Simmons. Do you think your wife has a boyfriend?"

"I really don't know."

Barbara hit her six iron, taking just the right amount of turf. The ball hit the green and bit—twenty feet from the pin. She bent down and replaced the divot that she had made in the fairway. "What about her sister?"

"Christine? She has a mobster for a boyfriend. That was one of the reasons why her father put her money in trust—she only gets the interest and can't touch the principal."

"What about the plane crash? It seems strange that both of them should be killed."

"No, Harold Armbuster Palmer was an avid pilot and a golfer. He liked to be called 'Hap,' like General Hap Arnold. Flew jets in the Korean War and it did him in."

"What do you mean?"

"He took risks. Loved them. Bad weather was a challenge to him. So the night Hap was coming from Hilton

Head, it was raining and they hit some electrical lines. Plane exploded. End of story."

Simmons swung his nine iron and the ball arched high and true. The ball bit and spun back. It stopped five feet from the pin.

"That's the way to end a round!" She clapped.

"Thanks."

"Mrs. Palmer must have been a beautiful woman. Her daughters are stunning."

"I thought you hadn't found Caroline."

"We haven't, but they're twins, aren't they? I met Christine."

"Yes, of course. I'm glad you told me about her."

They stopped by the green and watched as Norman bumped out the rough and careened into the fairway.

"When you slept with Christine, could you tell the difference? Come on, tell the truth."

"The truth is that I think it was a mistake to play golf with you."

"I don't," Barbara said.

Norman and David were close to each other and to the green. Luck followed them as each hit his ball into the giant sand trap that abutted the 18th green.

"How's your score, Norman?" Barbara asked.

"Thank God numbers are infinite," Norman said.

The bunker was so steep and deep that David and Norman had to hit blindly. Norman raised his head to check the flag position and then disappeared back into the sand trap.

Jimmy Four Eyes Riley took careful aim—and paused. He cleared a bit of brush but remained well concealed.

Barbara and Gregory watched as Norman swung.

There was a shower of sand, and the ball landed within inches of the cup.

"Leave it to Norman to get the best shot of the day," Barbara said.

The crosshairs of Riley's rifle scope alighted on Norman as he emerged from the trap and then shifted to Simmons. Piece of cake.

"Hey, Judge. That's a gimmee."

"It sure is," Simmons said. He bent to pick up the ball just as David peered over the sandtrap.

It was like an old Three Stooges skit. A tragic one. One goes to slaps the other. The other ducks, and the innocent one is slapped. So, too, with David. As Simmons bent to pick up the ball, Jimmy Four Eyes Riley fired. The bullet struck David squarely in the forehead. The force of the bullet sent David backward into the sand killing him instantly.

Norman ran to Barbara, and the three of them dove into the bunker. Barbara landed on the body of David and screamed when she saw that the sand was wet with his blood.

Norman crouched and raced for his cart.

"Norman, get back here, you fool!" Simmons cried.

Norman, however, was already at his golf cart. He unzipped his bag when another round ricocheted off the cart. He took out his Glock and fired. He then zigzagged up the slope and fired repeatedly.

Jimmy Four Eyes saw this crazy man running at him and was tempted to bring him down with another shot, but the guy was a moving target. This was no longer a piece of cake. Now bullets were whistling past him. Riley dropped his rifle and ran from the bushes, leaving behind the golf bag.

Although no longer in Norman's range, he bolted into

the car and sped from the lot. In his haste and without caring, he rammed into several parked cars.

Norman, near the top of the hill, out of breath and out of bullets, stood there and listened to the sounds of the crashing cars. He walked slowly back. Barbara was cradling David. Reflexively she was cleaning his face, using her tears to wipe away the sand and blood.

"He killed David. Oh, Uncle Norman, he killed David."

"We'll get the son of a bitch," Simmons said.

Thirty-nine

Dusk found the forensic team still searching for evidence. It was abundant. There was the rifle, the golf bag, even cleat marked footprints. The hunt for bullets was slow and difficult because the slug had entered David's forehead and exited. It was finally located deep in the sand.

The parking lot was aglow with the flashing lights of the emergency vehicles and the several tow trucks that were hauling away the damaged cars.

The EMS people eventually placed David in a body bag. When they folded the gurney into the ambulance, Simmons had to be restrained.

"There's no use in you coming with us, Judge," an EMS worker said. He had given them blankets, which they had wrapped around themselves. Barbara was in a police cruiser. The door was open, and she sat sideways with her feet on the ground. Simmons paced back and forth.

"I'm cold," Barbara said.

"Who's going to tell his wife? My God! I have to see Leah!"

"Who knew you were playing golf today?" Norman asked.

"Someone tried to kill me! I don't believe it. David, what have I done?"

"You can't blame yourself, Greg. The killer is to blame, not you."

"He didn't want to play. He never plays golf. I made him drive me!"

Sanford Fox from Homicide was in charge. From the moment he arrived at the parking lot, he took over the investigation. His team isolated the skid marks and the paint implanted by the getaway car. He attended to the details and recorded his observations in his pocket tape recorder.

Fox sipped a can of Diet Coke. He was small for a cop and looked smaller because of his heavy-set frame.

"No prints. The rifle and scope together must have cost three thousand. He left everything. Maybe we can trace the golf clubs, but I'll bet that everything was stolen," Fox told Norman.

"You have to know who the gunsmith is. That's one hell of a weapon."

"No. They're artists, but they don't exhibit their work," Fox said.

"It was a professional hit. No doubt about that, Sandy."

"The son of a bitch even wore golf shoes. Did you see the cleat marks in his footprints?"

"It's a trademark hit," Fox said.

"You mean you know the guy?"

"This thug likes to work in costumes, but you know, we have to catch him in the act."

"I would have thought that for this kind of a job they would have imported someone from out of town."

"Nah, they can be pretty arrogant," Fox said.

Barbara still wrapped in the blanket, walked over to Fox. "I want police protection for Judge Simmons," she said.

"That's not my department, Ms. Danzig."

"Make it your department, Detective Fox! My client was the obvious target of a hired assassin."

"Just a minute. I have to explore every possibility. It was David Leibowitz who was killed! Maybe he had enemies."

"That's absurd!" she said.

"These guys don't usually miss."

"He did this time. He took a shot at me, too, and missed," said Norman.

"Yeah, Norman. I heard that you went charging up that hill like you were still in the Marines."

"Look, Detective, can you have someone drive me to David's wife?" Simmons said.

"I took care of that, Judge. I got on the horn about an hour ago. I had an officer pick up Judge Franco. He went there. I figured that you're in no shape to do anything."

"I guess you're right. But that was my job."

"Your job is to stay alive. Don't you understand? Someone is trying to kill you," Barbara said.

"Or us," Norman said.

Like a magnet, both Simmons and Barbara turned to stare at Norman.

"I think we'd better talk," Norman said.

Forty

It took little persuasion to convince Simmons that he should not go home that night.

"I thought it would be safe here. But we're not safe from starvation," Norman said. He peered into Barbara's almost empty refrigerator. He closed it, and then opened it again in mock disbelief. He poured himself a glass of skim milk and found a few biscuits in the pantry. He had taken off his shirt and wrapped a comforter around himself. It trailed after him as he walked back to the living room in his stocking feet.

"I don't know why you two don't make yourselves more comfortable," Norman said. Simmons and Barbara, still wearing their golf clothes, sat at opposite ends of the brocade sofa.

Barbara called Gershon at his private number, but he wasn't home. She left a message with his service—he'd return the call, he always did.

The decor surprised Simmons. It was quite unlike

Barbara's office, inner or outer. It was not an appropriate time to observe these things, but the mind did not necessarily concentrate on what was often the most important matter before it.

Barbara's apartment, except for the usual modern appliances, such as a sleek bread-making machine and convection oven, was furnished in a warm manner. The long sectional sofa, covered in a white silk brocade, and the wing chair were set in front of a fireplace. *That* was an anomaly—a fireplace in an apartment on the Upper East Side! It was a nonworking one, but nevertheless gave a cozy feeling to the living room. The several paintings that hung on the wall, mostly originals, were bucolic scenes in the style of the Hudson Valley School. His eyes darted from paintings to Barbara to Norman, who was meandering about the room munching on a biscuit, and trying to hum at the same time.

"Uncle Norman, will you stop eating and shut up! You've kept us in suspense long enough. What did you find out?"

Norman placed his glass on a small end table and stretched out on the wing chair. He put his feet on the ottoman opposite the judge.

"First she tells me to shut up and then she tells me to talk."

"What did you find out?" Simmons said.

"Find out? I found a puzzle. That's why those shots could have been meant for me and not the judge."

"For God's sake, Norman, that's paranoid!" Barbara said.

"What would you say if I told you that the Mercedes that was stolen from your driveway was not your car?"

Norman dunked his biscuit into the milk and waited for it to be absorbed.

"You do it every time, Norman. Will you please finish the story."

"Don't be so impatient." Norman wiped the milk from his mustache.

"Judge, the car that was stolen had your license plates, your insurance certificate in the glove compartment, and your golf clubs in the trunk. The Mercedes was identical to your car in every way, but it was not your car. The vehicle identification numbers were different."

"This was a tag job?" Barbara said. "How could that be?"

Simmons knit his brow.

"Yeah, Judge. You wouldn't know anything about these things. VIN numbers are placed in secret places all over new cars—even under them. Professional thieves change them whenever they can find them. In effect, they 'tag' the car. This was a very sloppy job. The last number of the VIN of the Mercedes now at the Precinct is 1304. The number on the insurance certificate was 9567. I checked with Paramount Mercedes. . . ." Norman turned to Simmons. "That's where you bought it, right?"

Simmons nodded.

"Their records show the VIN ending with 9567. I'll bet that their numbers match the numbers on your registration certificate."

Simmons took out the registration from his wallet.

"Now check the numbers against the numbers from Paramount." Norman took out his pad. He flipped to the designated page and gave it to Simmons.

Simmons examined both papers. His eyes shifted back and forth as he compared the numbers.

"It's . . . 9567."

"I thought so. Now all we have to do is figure out what it all means."

"You're terrific, Uncle Norman!"

"That isn't all. The Mercedes with the 1304 number that was stolen from your driveway was reported stolen the week before." Norman took back his pad and read from it. "The car belongs to a stockbroker."

"Not William Scharf?"

"No, my sweet, a guy by the name of John Fadule," Norman said.

"Who's William Scharf?" Simmons said.

"Just a friend. That would be too much of a coincidence. He owns a Mercedes."

"Now, who's getting off the subject?" Norman said.

"You're saying that someone stole my car, replaced it with a stolen car, put my license plates on it, and then stole the stolen car?"

"Wait a minute. Who said that your car was stolen?" Barbara asked.

The look on Simmons's face was unmistakable.

"Caroline!"

"Maybe. . . . Did you drive the other car the day before it was stolen from your driveway?"

"Yes. That means that Caroline switched cars and gave the thief the key. Doesn't that prove my innocence?"

"You did make a claim for the insurance money," Barbara said.

"But it wasn't on my car."

"Manning will say that's why you had the car stolen. Greg, it seems that your wife is not satisfied with just a divorce!"

"I tried to talk to your wife, but she's like a phantom—she's never at home," Norman said.

"She shops during the day. Trying to build up living

expenses for the divorce proceedings, I guess. I must confess, however, that she always shopped during the day—before we were separated. I spoke with her yesterday morning."

"Did you tell her that you were playing golf today?" Norman asked.

Simmons's face flushed, and his body uncoiled as he leaped from the chair. "Christ, she doesn't want him ruined. She wants him dead!" Norman said.

"Of course!" said Barbara. She smacked the side of her head as if to wake herself up. "Disgrace, Divorce, and Death. Inheritance without Equitable Distribution."

Simmons seized the remote phone and punched in numbers. He circled the room as he waited for a response.

"Take it easy," Norman said. Simmons ignored him.

"Are you insane . . . ?" Simmons screamed into the phone.

Barbara reached out to touch him, but he pulled away.

"Yes, David is dead. . . . Bullshit. You didn't have to hear it on television. I want some answers from you. . . . What about? . . . Yes. The key, the car, the attempt on my life . . . don't play dumb with me. This is murder!"

Norman tried to flag down Simmons as he moved around the room.

"Let me talk to her."

Simmons nodded but continued to speak.

"You better do something about the boyfriend. . . . Christine . . . yes. What am I supposed to believe?"

Simmons held the phone to his ear and then, after a moment, put it down.

"She hung up on me."

"Norman. First thing in the morning, we're getting a

court order to inspect the car. No more unofficial visits to the pound. Do the police know about the switched cars?"

"They haven't a clue, if you'll pardon the expression," Norman said. "I figure it's another thing we can spring on them."

"True. Manning is in too deep to just give up."

"David's death has put a whole new spin on this, Greg," said Barbara.

"Yes, it has," Simmons said. "The question is, what can I do about it?"

"Leave it to the police," Barbara said.

"We *are* dependent on them, aren't we?" Simmons was now calm. "I'd better go home," he said.

Barbara made a little mental note. From hurricane to placid in seconds.

"Didn't Detective Fox advise you not to go home tonight?"

"Look at me," Simmons pointed to his golf outfit. "I have to shower and pick up clothes. David was an Orthodox Jew, remember? He has to be buried within twenty-four hours."

"You had better stay. It might not be safe."

"It's kind of crowded in here, isn't it?"

"Norman was just leaving."

"I was not," Norman said.

At two A.M. Dr. Reich returned her call. It was ironic that, for the first time in weeks, she had been fast asleep. He listened patiently as she related to him the day's trauma.

"I'm with you anytime you need me, Barbara."

"I know that, Gershon. Gershon?"

"What?"

"I love you, you little Nazi."

"You're supposed to," he said.

Forty-one

Carmine Miano's bedroom was sumptuously furnished. The dresser, vanity, and four-poster bed were in rococo style. A mirror covered the entire ceiling.

The phone rang several times before Carmine awoke. He turned away from his sleeping wife.

"Yeah?"

When he heard Christine's voice he bolted up.

"Are you nuts? I told you never to call me here. How'd you get this number?" he said in a harsh whisper. "I did not give it to you, goddammit . . . yeah, it's probably tapped. . . . Don't say your name. . . . I don't want to hear it. . . . No, we can't meet. . . . I did what? That's a lie."

Carmine's voice began to rise. His wife turned and pulled the silk sheets over her.

"I'll take care of things the way *I* want, not your way! Stop being hysterical. You crazy. . . . I'm a legitimate businessman. . . . I don't have nobody killed. . . . I told you, don't fucking call me here again!"

Carmine hung up.
"Who was that?" his wife asked.
"It was a wrong number," Carmine said.

Forty-two

It seemed fitting that it should rain on the morning of David's funeral. Friends, relatives, and other mourners rushed up the steps to the synagogue and out of the rain, carefully stepping away from the casket that had been placed outside the front doorway. It was a simple pine box, made in the prescribed way, without nails.

Leah had decided that services should be in the synagogue instead of a funeral home. The dead, being basically "unclean," were barred from the temple.

Justice Judith Eissner entered and interposed herself among the others as more people crowded into the synagogue, but she was gently reminded to step aside.

"The women's area is upstairs," one of the members of the synagogue said.

"And right where they belong," Justice Greenberg said. "Separate and apart!" Justice Eissner hesitated, but only for a moment, as the member took her arm and led her to the women's section in the balcony. "She can't open her hypersensitive mouth about that one!" Greenberg said.

Simmons was escorted to a small waiting room. There he embraced Leah Leibowitz. David's father, Chaim, with lapels torn from his suit, in mourning, stood by, not knowing whom to comfort first. His mother was near collapse, as was Leah. The children sat there bewildered. Rabbi Wasserman, a rotund, usually cheerful man, seemed as destroyed as everyone else.

"Your Honor . . ." His voice failed him.

It was Leah who continued. "I would like you to say the eulogy."

"I will commence the ceremony, but Leah wants you to do it," the rabbi said.

"I loved David," Simmons said.

"We all did," said his father.

"His death will not go unavenged, I promise you."

"I don't want revenge," Leah said. "I want my David." She clutched the handkerchief that was wet with her tears.

"You have to be brave for your children," David's mother said.

"Do you have a Bible, Rabbi, one in English?" Simmons asked.

"Of course." Rabbi Wasserman took a book from the shelf and gave it to Simmons.

The synagogue was filled with people. The decor was simple—the Jews were not permitted graven images. The Torah itself, double scrolls sheathed in a rich purple velvet covering, had been taken from its Ark and set out on a small lectern.

The casual murmuring of the people who had come to pay their respects ceased when the rabbi entered, followed by Simmons and the family. They sat in the first row as Rabbi Wasserman strode past the railing and walked to the pulpit.

He surveyed this unusual gathering of people. Congregants, judges—some wearing their robes—uniformed court officers, lawyers, friends, and family.

"I look out and see all of you, some prominent and others humble, all gathered here to pay your last respects to our beloved David Mordecai, who was struck down in a most cowardly manner, in a most untimely manner, in a most horrible manner. Leah, with your children, I ask you to look around and see the tribute that is being paid to David, a man of greatness. Yes, greatness.

"Greatness is not measured by time, nor by mere secular achievement. It is measured by the devotion that one person bestows upon another. By that standard, this young man—kind, gentle, attentive, brilliant—I could go on and on, piling adjective upon adjectives and they would all be consistent with the same conclusion. This young man, struck down long before his allotted time, was a great, just man. Who can say more about another human being?

"David was called by the Almighty for reasons that are unfathomable to us all, which we are unable to question. . . ." He spoke for another twenty minutes, going over in detail David's accomplishments, both educational and religious.

"Leah," he said finally, "I have no words to explain this calamity, except to say that your loss is truly a loss to us all."

Rabbi Wasserman nodded to Simmons, who went to the pulpit.

"I am Gregory A. Simmons, a Justice of the Supreme Court of the State of New York. David Leibowitz was my law clerk. I have been given the honor of speaking on behalf of David. . . . Leah, to you and your children and to David's parents, you have my most profound sympathy."

Simmons fumbled with the Bible he had carried with him to the pulpit. He paused for a moment, as if he were gathering strength to continue.

"A law clerk is required to be a lawyer. And I used to refer to David as my lawyer! We were close, intellectually and professionally. We would argue constantly over some point of law, and I can still hear him saying, 'Judge, you know my position and I know yours. If I can't persuade you, then there is nothing more I can say. So you make the decision even if I think you're incorrect.' And then he would clasp his hands and purse his lips—in that studious manner of his, you'll remember, and add slyly, 'Even if you get reversed by the Appellate Division.' He was as devoted to his wife and family as he was to his work. He integrated his religion into his daily life. At lunchtime, he would eat kosher food with his friends. He could always round up the ten Jews required to form a *minyan* and, there in the courthouse, discuss the Talmud.

"I used to tease him and call him a 'juggler' because he was able to handle so many matters at the same time. Whether he was preparing a memorandum for me or arranging a meeting with the elders in the synagogue, he did everything with skill and alacrity." Simmons looked down at the Bible and opened it to the page he had marked.

"As Rabbi Wasserman spoke, I thought, in this holy place, of what passage could describe my sense of loss. And it came to me that it was written in the Book of Samuel, that when King David was brought news of his son's death, he went up to his chambers and wept. And as he went, he said, 'O my son Absalom, my son, my son Absalom! Would God I had died for you, O Absalom, my son, my son."

Simmons closed the Bible. He dabbed his face with his handkerchief.

"Goodbye, David. My son, my son."

Simmons left the altar. He did not return to his seat. Instead he rapidly walked down the aisle and out the door.

His secretary, Elaine, followed him.

"My God, Judge, there's not a dry eye in the balcony. You were magnificent!" Elaine said.

"Isn't it odd, Elaine? You can be sad and happy at the same time. I had to make a good speech—for David. And yet it felt so good to stir an audience outside a courtroom."

"Aren't you the wicked one!" Elaine Trezza said.

Forty-three

"For what it's worth," Zangara said to Sandy Fox, "we have the thief who stole the judge's car at Rikers Island."

"How come he didn't make bail?"

"He can't. We're holding him as a material witness."

"That's pretty cute. He can make bail on the auto theft, but he can't make bail on the insurance fraud case," Fox said.

"It wasn't hard to convince Judge Taylor that Ragazza was a material witness. He's a key part of the case against Simmons, and the D.A. wanted to make sure that we kept him in jail until it was time to testify."

"Is he talking?" Fox asked.

"Singing like a canary, but I don't trust him."

"And you think there's a connection between the two cases?"

"Who knows? Something is going on," Zangara said.

"If I have time, I'll check it out."

"I thought that we might work together on this one."

"Thanks for the tip, but this is a homicide investigation," Fox said.

"I'd really like to help out."

"Stay in your own backyard," Fox said.

The murder had occurred on Staten Island. Zangara was out of Brooklyn. Different jurisdictions—but it would look good on his reports that he explored every possibility. Fox did not expect to accomplish anything by interviewing Ragazza, but he had to go to Rikers Island anyway on another case. He recognized Ragazza immediately.

"Rags Ragazza—burglary, three or four years ago, right?"

"I ain't talking to nobody but Zangara."

"You gained a little weight. It must be getting tough to squeeze into those second-story windows."

"I don't do those jobs anymore."

"Oh, I forgot. You graduated to stealing expensive cars. I graduated, too, Rags. I'm not in Burglary anymore. I'm in Homicide."

"So what do you want from me?"

"Who you working for?"

"I did the job for the judge."

"I know what you told Zangara. What I want to know is who are you working for?"

"Simmons."

"I wouldn't get my hopes too high about the deal you worked out with Zangara, because I'm breaking it."

"My deal's with the D.A."

"That was before murder was involved. Now tell me who you're working for."

"I told you everything," Ragazza said in his squeaky voice.

"Let me mention a few names. Maybe that will help your memory. Miano?"

Ragazza shook his head.

"Fratello?"

"Who? I don't even know the name."

"I'm sure you don't," Fox said.

"You trying to get me killed?"

"I'm just trying to understand the players," Fox said.

"I was locked up when that guy got killed."

"Oh, so you know who we're talking about?"

"I read the papers," Ragazza said.

Fox rose as if to slap Ragazza. He saw a Correction guard nearby, thought better of it, and sat down. He straightened his tie.

"Who put out the contract on the judge?"

"I was wondering about that myself. It don't make sense—unless it was someone else they were after. Killing a judge brings a lot of heat."

"Killing his law clerk doesn't make it lukewarm, either."

"Maybe they were trying to embarrass the golf club. Like a sudden-death playoff. Get it? Sudden death!"

"I didn't come to Rikers to hear your dumb jokes, you little shit," Fox said.

"You cops are all alike. No sense of humor."

Fox looked at the Correction officer, who nodded at him. Fox reached across the small table that separated them and lifted Ragazza from his chair.

"Where can I find Jimmy Riley?"

"Four Eyes? I don't know. In his pizza parlor on 18th Avenue, I guess."

"This looks like his work, doesn't it?"

"Whaddaya talking about? He makes the best pizza pie in Brooklyn."

Fox threw Ragazza back into his chair.

"Keep your ears open—maybe we can make a better deal for you."

"I ain't no rat!"

"Once a rat, always a rat," Fox said.

Forty-four

Three men in dark clothing clustered about the chain link gate to the parking lot next to the 66th Precinct.

One clipped the chain with large pincers, while the others followed him into the lot. The gate creaked slightly, but the noise was lost in the sound of the heavy falling rain. They crouched and went in different directions until one spotted their target. He signaled and the three men converged on the 2005 Mercedes.

"Damn, it's all wet inside." One of the men opened the driver's side door and got behind the wheel.

"Of course, it's wet, you schmuck. It don't have a window."

The other two men pushed the Mercedes out of the parking lot and into the street.

A tow truck pulled up. Without haste, the car was hooked up and then pulled onto the flatbed truck.

A police officer just coming off duty waved to them.

"Hell of a night to be out," he said.

"Yeah, they always seem to break down at the wrong time," one of the thieves said.

Forty-five

It was a terrible way to obtain an adjournment. But even Taylor could not be so callous as to force them to trial immediately after David's murder. A conference was held in chambers, and after discussion, despite the disapproving look on his face—tight lips, unblinking eyes, and prominent veins on his forehead, Taylor granted the adjournment.

"You have a week. That's it!"

"Perhaps two weeks would be more seemly," Manning said.

"That's decent of you," Barbara said. "And the time will be chargeable to the prosecution?"

"Of course."

The speedy rule again. The trial had to commence within 180 days of the arrest, but any adjournments requested by the prosecution were not counted. Why was Manning being so generous? Two weeks might not be enough.

"Make it three weeks and charge the defendant for

one," Barbara said. "If it was not for the attempt on Judge Simmons's life, I would be ready to go to trial tomorrow. The sooner the trial, the sooner he's vindicated."

"You have information about the murder of David Leibowitz?" Manning asked.

"You want me to do your job?" Barbara said.

"See, Judge, how she slips these little things in?" Manning said. "We were talking about an adjournment."

"Two weeks!" barked Taylor.

"Why are you favoring the district attorney, Judge? He merely has to ask for something and he gets it."

"You'll find out that I don't play favorites, young lady—and I won't be provoked!"

"Three weeks will be fine, Your Honor," said Manning.

"All right. Three weeks, but no more adjournments. Do you understand?" He hit the desk with his gavel.

"Sure, no favorites. You could have fooled me." Barbara saw that the glass top on the desk had been replaced. "Careful you don't break the glass," she warned.

With the theft of the Mercedes from the police lot, the district attorney's office was thrown into confusion.

An investigation was launched, and accusations of incompetence went up and down the chain of command—from the precinct captain to the police commissioner, himself. Manning was particularly vehement on the lapse in security.

"They steal heroin from the property clerk, cars from the pound—what is going on with the Police Department?" Manning asked the Commissioner.

It fell to Zangara, in Auto Theft, to investigate. If there was any physical evidence, it had been washed away by the rain.

"Why the hell do we have to examine for tire tracks?" Tracy complained.

"Put in the report—no tire tracks found. Put everything in the report." When they found a footprint in the mud, Zangara had a cast made of it.

"How do we know that it's not a cop's foot?"

"We don't, dummy. We're going to show the captain that we're thorough."

"What about the clipped chain?"

"Bag it. It can tell us a lot."

"Like what?"

"That they didn't pick the lock," Zangara said.

"Jack, you're kidding!"

"Think so? Somebody's making us look bad, Marty. It's time we kicked a little ass."

Forty-six

"Stolen right out of the police lot—the brazen bastards!" Manning said.

The phone to his outer office rang, but Manning ignored it. He was wearing his red suspenders. Grossman took it as a color code. Red for office, green for court. Red could also signify explosiveness.

The business of the district attorney's office went on as usual even during the rare times that Manning was personally trying a case. The thousands of indictments, the investigations, the trials, the dispositions—like time—waited for no man. Decisions continued to be made, and the four-hundred-odd assistant district attorneys went about their own work. They interviewed witnesses, responded to the omnibus motions and attended to the many details required to dispose of their inventories, by trials or pleas.

The pressure on everyone, especially upon Sidney Grossman, the chief assistant, was enormous. He was the point man in the army of the Office of the District Attorney.

"Yes, the point man," Grossman would often say. "When things go wrong, you point to me!"

Grossman sat in an armchair and turned his head as Manning circled around him.

"Can we trust Zangara? Can we trust anyone on the police force?" Manning held a sheaf of papers.

"It's not like it used to be," Grossman said.

"Damned unions. Infect everything—even the police."

"It's the times, Ray."

"That's bullshit. Just like this report!" Manning threw the papers onto his desk.

"There was a time when you ordered a cop to shut up, he'd button up. Now, if you say anything to them, they report you for interfering with an investigation."

"Then how are we going to keep this thing quiet?"

"My advice is to ignore it." Grossman tugged on his beard. It was the sure sign that he was giving his best advice. "We don't have an obligation to advise the defendant of the theft. We have photographs and the original police reports. We really don't need the car to proceed."

"Danzig is sure to find out that it was stolen."

"Even if she does, so what? We don't drag entire cars into court every time we try a vehicular homicide case. We use photographs to show the impact damage."

"So we shouldn't worry any more about Danzig finding out?"

"I think we should worry about the Leibowitz murder. They have to be related."

"You know what I think, Sidney? I think Simmons hired an assassin to fake a hit and that the jerk killed Leibowitz by mistake. If I can prove that, I'm going to prosecute Simmons for murder. What do you think of that?"

"It's an interesting theory."

"Did you know that his father was a drunk? They didn't have a pot to piss in, but they were always putting on airs. Descended from the kings of Ireland, they claimed."

"I went to Brooklyn College with him. He was Phi Beta Kappa," Grossman said.

"I'll give him that," Manning said. "I didn't say Simmons was dumb. He's as smart as they come."

"How is your sister, Agnes?"

"Why did you ask that?" Manning said.

"You know, Ray, sometimes you're very funny. I can't ask about your sister?"

"Sure you can, Sidney, but it seems strange. Especially after that crack by Danzig. Do you think she's trying to drag Agnes in to get to me?"

"She was just fishing," Grossman said.

"But how did she know?"

"Simmons told her, naturally. He's the prick."

"Told her what? That she's still teaching in Catholic school?"

"No, that you don't have any use for Simmons," Grossman said.

"Maybe you're right—he doesn't know how right he is."

Grossman looked at Manning and was satisfied that he had deflected the district attorney's suspicions. He was not prepared yet to tell Manning that he had ordered one of his detectives to trail Simmons—and that it had led right to Agnes's door.

Forty-seven

"Greg, I have to see you," Agnes Manning said.

"I don't think it's a good idea."

"Listen, you son of a bitch, you get over here right now," she said and abandoned the sweet-tempered schoolmarm facade.

Agnes Manning was 43 years old. She had the Manning face, with the long Irish nose and the flat rosy cheeks. She had become slightly plump, but was still nicely proportioned.

They had dated before Gregory Simmons married, but he had made the mistake of having an affair with her. The passion had long since dissipated, but, nevertheless, she retained possessory rights. To keep him at heel, she had not been above calling Caroline anonymously. If that did not work, she would fabricate crises to force Simmons to come to her.

It was not yet two A.M. when Gregory drove up to the small two-family house. It was a rented car—at least he did not have to worry about any telltale license plates. Agnes lived on the ground floor, its entrance discreetly set in the side with a stairway leading to the upper floor.

The chance of anyone observing him was remote, but Simmons still looked around before knocking. He paused for a moment and waited as a car parked down the street. Could it be that someone was following him? They had tried to kill him once. Why not again? He fingered the .38 revolver he had taken with him.

Agnes was dressed in a loosely tied housecoat. She opened both the screen door and her arms. She was not wearing a bra.

Simmons pushed her arms away.

"What is so important?" he demanded, stepping inside.

"Greg. I'm going to end this nightmare for us."

"And how are you going to do that?" he said.

"I've decided to tell Ray about us."

"You're crazy, Agnes."

"Don't you see how simple it is? When Caroline gets her divorce, we can get married."

"And your brother is going to dismiss the indictment?"

"He can't very well put his future brother-in-law in jail."

"Agnes, you really are sick. If your brother ever found out about us, he'd hound me to death. Not only would he press with the trial, he'd indict me for adultery—and there hasn't been an indictment for adultery in a hundred years!"

"I love it when you get angry."

Agnes came close to him and put her arms around his waist.

"Aren't you getting a little bit horny now that Caroline has left you?"

"Agnes. It's two o'clock in the morning, your brother and Caroline are out to destroy me, I've been suspended from the bench, and you want to have *sex?*"

"I love you, Greg." She raised her arms to his neck.

"I'm telling you, Agnes, what we once had is over," he said, but allowed the embrace.

"I know you love me, Greg." She reached down and felt him stir.

"That's not love, Agnes!" Simmons pushed her away. He pushed a little too hard, and she struck her head on a picture frame. "And I'm not going to put up with any more of your emergencies."

"My God, you should be indicted for assault!"

"Agnes, you're a sweet, wonderful person. Why can't we be civilized with each other?" He sounded sincere.

"*Civilized?* You're so naive, Greg. If I had been civilized, Caroline would still be in your bed."

"Stop playing the femme fatale. The letters and phone calls I easily explained. They were a pain, but they had no effect."

"Oh, didn't they? I hired a male escort service for Caroline. It didn't take much effort to lure her. It cost me a fortune, but she never rejected one of them." Agnes laughed. "Success every time! You didn't know that, you chump. Dear, unfaithful Greg. She must have enjoyed getting even. I arranged to watch a couple of times. She likes to do it doggy style, doesn't she?"

"You're evil, Agnes."

"I'm not the one who sold his soul—or should I say sold out—for a judgeship. How many people did you step over to get where you are? How many trusting old ladies did you cheat out of their life savings, not to mention deflowering a young girl and then dumping her to marry a rich woman?"

"You know very well that those are all lies."

"All?"

"Goddammit, so you were a virgin! That was twenty years ago. You make it sound like I'm the only villain."

"Yes. Yes. Life does make villains of us all, doesn't it!"

She clutched her housecoat at the lapels and held the door open for him.

"I'll call you tomorrow," Agnes said.

Forty-eight

The Apache Social Club was a storefront off Mulberry Street where Alex Fratello conducted his business. His businesses included loan-sharking, gambling, pimping, drugs, and, occasionally—when the score was big enough—a little burglary. His main business was shipping vehicles to South America along with selected body parts, all of which were stolen. Alex's was a small mob family with the right to operate in Brooklyn and sections of Manhattan.

Fratello was a portly man. His slicked-back hair had turned to gray. "It's *steal* gray," he often said. His voice was gruff, as befitted a boss who employed one hundred and fifty soldiers and a man who could kill on command. You did not cheat Fratello. He liked to consider himself a businessman—able to make the necessary concessions when required. "I'm a reasonable man," he would continually say. It was this image of himself that made him amenable to the visit by Sanford Fox.

"My man!" Fratello said, when Fox entered the store. He motioned to Fox to approach.

Fratello sat at a back table. Several men sat at other tables playing pinochle.

"I'm not your man," Fox said. He flashed his badge.

"I know who you are. You think you can just walk in here without an okay?"

"I have a little problem, Mr. Fratello."

"Hey, call me Alex. We're all friends here." He waved his hand. "Vince, get the detective a drink. What you like?"

"Diet Coke," Fox said. He sat opposite Fratello.

"What's your problem?"

"There's bookmakers on the street. Hospital workers are complaining about loan sharks. Hookers are pestering citizens."

"Why you talking so tough? That ain't nice."

"I want the killer of David Leibowitz."

"What's that got to do with me?"

"Jimmy Four Eyes."

"Who?"

"You know. Your goombah who runs the Pizza Parlor."

"Oh, that Jimmy! He don't work for me."

"Somebody hired him. You see, Fratello, that's life," Fox said. "One person does something wrong and you end up paying for it. It's like when a doctor cuts off the wrong leg and the hospital has to pay for it."

"So, I deliver to you a guy—any guy—and finger him as the killer just so you won't put on the heat?"

"Not just any person," Fox said.

"Are you for real? Even if I was who you say I am, why would I rat on anybody?"

"I heard you were a businessman. A reasonable man."

"With all due respect, Detective, screw you. You come in here and threaten me? You're a little late. I got F.B.I. agents watching this place twenty-four hours a day."

"So you have problems and I have problems. Maybe we can help each other out. I'm only interested in the homicide."

"Yeah. Sure, I only wish. I'll tell you one thing. You're following the wrong people. Everything is mafioso with you guys, but take a hint, follow the broads."

"The broads?"

"Yeah. The girls. The twins. Everybody thinks one's an angel and the other's a witch, but I hear one's no better than the other. Yeah. As they say, *cherchez la femme*."

"How many languages do you speak?" Fox tucked his mouth downward and nodded as if he were impressed with Fratello's language skills.

"Hey, Vince, forget about the fucking Diet Coke," Fratello called out.

Forty-nine

Parallel investigations, like parallel universes, often collide. This evening was no exception.

    Zangara and Tracy approached just as Norman came through the revolving door of the Bellmore Hotel.
    "She's still not home," Norman said.
    "Who?" Zangara asked.
    "Come on. You can't talk to Caroline Simmons anyway. She's still married to the judge. You ever heard of 'privileged communications'?"
    "You're getting to sound like a lawyer," Tracy said.
    "We've just been to the other one's apartment on Riverside Drive. It looks like both of them skipped." Zangara shook his head. "We're chasing goddamned will-o'-the-wisps."
    They were congregating near the entrance to the Bellmore when Sanford Fox drove up.
    "Look who's here," Tracy said, "the foxy one!"
    Norman went to the car and leaned in. "She's not home," he said.

Fox alighted and stretched his legs. He surveyed the scene.

"Pretty ritzy neighborhood," said Fox.

Zangara took Fox aside and walked him a short distance away so that Norman was out of earshot.

"So, you *do* think that there's a connection with the Simmons case?" Zangara said.

"Of course," Fox said.

"You interested in making headlines tomorrow?"

"What do you have in mind?"

Fifty

The SWAT team attacked in the early morning. The truck, fitted with a battering ram, smashed through the garage door of Tony's Body Shop on Utica Avenue. The team wore blue flak jackets and steel helmets and followed the ram. The men carried M-16 rifles and shotguns. They quickly spread out through the garage.

The brightly lit body shop was crammed with a number of automobiles, all in the process of being dismantled. The workers scurried around, ducking behind the cars, but were quickly rounded up.

Zangara and Fox, followed by Tracy, sauntered in. They wandered through the garage and inspected the stolen cars.

"The Mercedes ain't here," Tracy said.

"That car was unrecognizable a half hour after it got here."

"I'm not used to this. Why don't we kill somebody so I feel at home?" Fox said.

"Then who would carry the message to Fratello?"

Zangara nodded to the SWAT team, and the arrested workers, hands cuffed behind their backs, were paraded past him.

"Stealing from the police is like smoking. It's hazardous to your health," Zangara said in a booming voice.

Fifty-one

Fox found Jimmy Four Eyes Riley at his pizza parlor. It had rained again. Despite the bad weather, Riley's store was filled with customers. Some sat at banquettes eating their pies, while others waited in line for their orders. Six workers were busy behind the counter. One flipped and stretched the dough. Another prepared a pie with tomato sauce, mozzarella, and, finally, olive oil. Others were engaged in taking the pizzas in and out of the ovens. Their long-handled wooden shovels dumped the cooked pizzas into cardboard boxes—ready for delivery.

Riley was at the cash register.

"Jimmy Riley?" Fox said.

"Best pizza in town," Jimmy Four Eyes replied. "Real brick oven. Who can make pizzas with those shitty electric ovens?"

Fox displayed his badge.

"I'm from Homicide."

"Wonderful—like I couldn't spot a cop from a mile away."

"You been in Staten Island lately?"

"Not in years," Riley said.

The customers seemed to crowd around Fox. Not threatening, but curious, straining to hear the conversation. Jimmy Four Eyes, however, glared at them and they backed off.

"You with Miano last week?"

"Who?"

"You sound like an owl," Fox said.

"Hey, I'm a taxpaying citizen. You can't come in here and strong-arm me."

"Is that what you think I'm doing?" Fox said.

"Don't tell him shit," a young customer said. "He got no warrant."

Fox grabbed the youngster by his shirt collar and pulled him close. "Go to medical school, kid. It's a lot healthier."

"Come on, Detective. He's my cousin. He didn't mean nothing," Riley said.

Fox pushed the teenager away.

"Where's Miano now?" Fox said. He remained calm, his voice low and steady. Not that he expected a reply, but harassment was better than doing nothing.

"I ain't seen him in a week," Riley said.

"Tell him to call me. I have a few questions I want to ask him." Fox took out his card and handed it to Riley.

"Find him yourself!" Riley tore the card and threw it at Fox.

Fox peered over the counter.

"Are those mouse droppings I see in the corner?" he said in a loud voice. "When was the last time you were inspected by the Board of Health?"

Fifty-two

Miano ran numbers for Fratello. It was a much larger responsibility than it appeared because he was required to supervise twenty-five people in the collections and pay-outs.

Miano was not a "made man" in the sense that he would be allowed to run his own businesses, independently, but through his ambition, industriousness, and loyalty, he was climbing the mob's corporate ladder.

If one could create new sources of revenue or make a "score," that is, a sudden onetime money maker, so much the better.

Miano was not in hiding, but he was not staying too long in any one place, either. He drove the streets in his white Cadillac de Ville and collected the take.

"Where you been?" a runner said. "The Boss wants to see you."

That was it. He had been told—and it would be quickly reported. The worst, most dangerous way to lose your position—and perhaps more—was to ignore a command. In the paranoia of the streets, it was a true sign of defection.

Miano stopped his rounds and sped to Manhattan. He was sure that the telephone call would beat him there.

He stopped off in front of the Apache Social Club and honked his horn. Louie the Lover came over to the car.

Louie was so named because he was particularly ugly. His extreme buck teeth and beetle eyes were set in a face that had been ravaged by chicken pox. As was so often the case, nicknames were studies in contradiction or cruelty. Yet there was no hard or fast rule, since a handsome man might also acquire the nickname Lover. Sometimes, one had to be familiar with the history before making a determination as to the appropriateness of the name. Such was the case with Sammy the Snake, Charlie Chuckles, and, of course, Jimmy Four Eyes. There seemed to be a decided preference for alliterative nicknames.

When Louie leaned into the Cadillac, he said, "Geronimo." The mob had an inclination toward code words, the better to confuse the wiretaps—which they never did.

"Geronimo" meant that Fratello was at Beni's Turkish Baths. Miano immediately went there. Beni's was located on Avenue B off East 12th Street and looked like any ordinary tenement house with stores on the ground floor. Miano double-parked and handed a street kid a ten-dollar bill.

"Watch the car," Miano said.

The weather-worn sign over the doorway hung on a broken chain, like the proverbial sword of Damocles. It menaced all who dared to wrongfully enter. Miano, showing an easy familiarity with the place, entered and went to a locker. He disrobed, placed a large towel around his waist, and stepped into the steam room. The escaping steam fogged his vision for a moment.

The steam room was empty except for Fratello, who was completely wrapped in towels and smoking a fat cigar.

"You're fucking up, Carmine," Fratello said. He waved the cigar as though trying to separate the steam from the smoke.

"Bear with me, boss. I got everything under control."

"I don't need meetings with homicide detectives."

"They're just fishing around. They don't know anything."

"I don't need raids on my places of business, either."

"I just had a little bad luck."

"Your bad luck is costing me money," Fratello said.

"I talked to Howie the Hump. The chop shop's been moved to Buffalo Avenue, and we're only going to lose three days," Miano said.

"Why did you have to steal from the police?" The question was couched in criticism.

"I was correcting Ragazza's mistake. We're scheming for a ten-million-dollar score," Miano said.

"Trying to kill a judge isn't a good score. And then to kill by mistake is even worse. Somebody is getting very sloppy."

"You remember we had to switch the car, so I figured if we got the judge out of the way, then everybody would forget about the car. That didn't work, so I figured . . ."

"You figured." Fratello raised his hand as if to slap Miano. "That's the trouble with you young ones. You *figure* but you don't *plan*. You *react* instead of *act*. The cops are all over us. Wiretaps, electronic devices, informers! We have to be creative, too. Why the hell do you think I'm meeting you here? Goddammit, I hate steam rooms!" Fratello threw down his cigar in disgust. A shower of embers lit up Miano's feet.

"They ain't getting me, boss. Three times they tried, and three times I been acquitted."

"They only have to get you once to put you away for life. Once those guys decide they want you, they don't stop until they get you."

"That'll never happen."

Fratello shook his head in disbelief. Was there a connection between arrogance and stupidity? "You know what the weak link is, don't you, Carmine?"

"Ragazza? I can snuff out that punk any time. Even from jail."

"No, the weak link is your cock." Fratello wished he hadn't thrown down the cigar. He waved his arm, as if still holding it. "The broad, Carmine! She's not built for our kind of loyalty. Faithful? Sometimes. Loyal? Never! If they put pressure on her, she cracks. And when she does . . ."

"It was *her* scheme in the first place," Miano said. "She's the least of my worries."

"I hope so, for your sake," Fratello said.

Fifty-three

Barbara and Simmons were in the corridor near the door to the courtroom, and though their voices were hushed, it was obvious that they were arguing. Several times she pulled Simmons down the corridor, away from any spectators.

The trial was about to begin—almost.

Taylor, as was customary, scheduled the last pretrial conference in the courtroom. Motions *in limine,* pre-marking of exhibits, and other ground rules would be set down prior to the actual trial. It was not a time to argue.

"I told you, I don't want to win on a technicality," Simmons said.

"That's bullshit, Greg! A win is a win. We can win on the corroboration issue alone. Besides, how can you commit a fraudulent insurance act if it wasn't your car that was really stolen?"

"And how are we going to prove that now that the car has been stolen again?" Simmons said.

Barbara put her finger to her lips and glanced around to confirm that they were not being overheard.

"They don't know that we know. I'm going to move for a dismissal on the ground that they haven't complied with the order of discovery," Barbara said.

"I don't want you to do that. Why can't I make you understand? I'm not like an ordinary person. If I'm not completely vindicated, I'll never be able to return to the bench without everyone thinking I was guilty and got away with it because I had power, and money. I have to prove my *innocence,* not my lack of guilt!"

"You don't understand my problem," Barbara said. "This isn't Talmudic law. They don't need two witnesses. They only need one. Breaking down Ragazza won't be easy. He's not only a professional crook, he's also a practiced liar. It's your word against his—and at this point I'm not sure whether I want you to testify."

"If a jury believes a thief and not me, then we're all in trouble."

"No. *I'm* in trouble," Barbara said. "That's why all this nonsense about a victory with honor is just that—nonsense."

"We do have another witness, don't we?"

"You mean your wife?"

"Yes."

"Who knows what she'll say? We can't interview her until we find her, and Norman can't find her."

"Your Uncle Norman can't be much of a detective. I had dinner with Caroline last night."

"You did?" Barbara furrowed her brow. She hated to show surprise.

"After what happened to David, you didn't think I was going to stand around and do nothing! There's no doubt in my mind that I was the real target."

"What did she say?" Barbara looked around as if the assassin could hear them.

"She denied everything, of course."

"Then what?" Barbara said.

"We had a few drinks and I calmed down a little. I think she wants to reconcile. I pretended that I wanted it, too."

"Guaranteeing that she'll be a friendly witness?" Barbara did not bother to conceal the sarcasm in her voice.

"We're dealing with vicious people here, Barbara!"

"So you took her home and slept with her?"

"You don't think much of me, do you?" Simmons said.

"I'm sorry."

"Reconciliation doesn't mean that I slept with her. We merely talked. Besides, I think I'm falling for someone else." Simmons reached out and touched her hand.

"Did you tell her that?" Barbara said. She did not move her hand away.

"You don't know me, but I'm a one-woman kind of man."

"One woman or one at a time?" Barbara said. If tongues could really be bitten to take back words, Barbara would have severed hers. "I have a great knack for saying the wrong things, don't I?"

"We're both under a lot of pressure." This time, he squeezed her hand.

"Whenever you're ready," Sharon, the court officer, said. "Judge Taylor is almost finished with reading the motion papers. Is the district attorney here yet?"

As if on cue, Manning and Sidney Grossman came charging down the corridor. Manning nodded perfunctorily, brushed past Barbara and Simmons, and marched into the courtroom.

Simmons paused at the door. "Don't push your motion to inspect the car, and don't ask for a dismissal—yet. If things become really desperate, we can always have Norman testify," he said.

"That's pretty smart for a judge! *Now* you're beginning to think like a defense lawyer." There was no way she was going to allow anyone to bring this man down. Disgraced? By the time she was through with him, she'd have the governor appointing him to the Appellate Division. He was so damned naive, though. She'd have to work on that.

"But I can't be the villain in this. Do you understand?"

Barbara nodded.

"No, Barbara. Tell me you understand!"

"That's the fifth time you've said that. I'm not dense, you know." Simmons waited for her to answer.

"I understand," Barbara said.

Fifty-four

Norman walked down Riverside Drive and tried to picture how it must have been before all those grand old buildings had been built. The view across the Hudson River was spectacular, but, oddly enough, the view from the Jersey side was far more picturesque. New York could not see New York. The terrain was hilly and sloped sharply toward the river. It must have been around here during the Revolutionary War where George Washington crossed the Hudson to escape the British army. Once into Jersey, the pursuit was over. The English had not dared to follow into hostile country. It was odd. People were still fleeing today to Fort Lee, Paramus, Hackensack, and other New Jersey enclaves of imagined safety.

The lobby of the apartment building resembled a 1920s movie theater, with ornate rococo plaster carvings and stucco walls. It was being restored to its original condition and gleamed with gold leaf. The only concession to the times was the thick glass doors and the security desk manned by the concierge.

"Christine Palmer is gone. I don't think she'll be back," the concierge said.

"Why not?" Norman said.

"Went to Vegas—for good," he said. "I think her sister forced her out. Put this co-op up for sale."

"How much is she asking?"

"Two point five million, I think. You have to ask the realtor," said the concierge.

"What are the chances of taking a peek at the apartment?"

"Without a search warrant?"

"Is a subpoena good enough?" Norman said. He reached into his pocket and gave the man a twenty-dollar bill.

Norman followed the concierge to the duplex. The curtains were drawn and Norman picked his way through the living room. He swiped his fingers along a table, leaving a clean mark in the dust.

"This place looks like shit." He sneezed. Damned allergies.

"I can't open the windows, for obvious reasons," the concierge said.

"Yeah, I know," Norman said and sneezed again.

The concierge trailed behind Norman as they toured the rooms. The upstairs bedroom was in disarray. The floor was cluttered with bedsheets, pillows, and various articles of underclothing.

"What the hell is all this with yellow clothes?" Norman said. He looked into the walk-in closet that was filled with clothing, much of it yellow. "Christ, she even has yellow panties." He stooped down and picked up the panties.

"Please don't touch anything."

"It sure doesn't look like she's left for good," Norman said.

"No, it doesn't."

Back in the lobby, Norman gave his card to the concierge, who did not accept it until it was joined with another twenty-dollar bill.

"You'll call me if she comes back?" Norman said.

Fifty-five

On the morning of jury selection, and before Manning went to court, Agnes Manning insisted on seeing her brother.

"What is it, Agnes? It's a very busy day for me."

"Yes, I know. I came to wish you luck." Agnes wore a flowered silk dress with a high neck and ruffles that hid her double chin. Her eye shadow and deep red lipstick seemed more appropriate for evening than morning. Agnes caught her brother's disapproving look.

"Thank you," he said.

"You don't like it," Agnes said. She turned quickly and her skirt swirled about her.

"No, you look very attractive. . . . Agnes, will you please tell me why you're here."

"They're saying that you're persecuting Greg."

"Who's saying that?"

"I have ears," Agnes said. She twisted a curl of hair about her finger.

"I thought you'd be happy about my nailing your ex-boyfriend."

"And if you don't?"

"Then I'll find something else."

"I really don't want that, Ray. I still love him, you know."

"That's exactly why I'm going to get him."

"Wouldn't it be funny if after all these years he gets a divorce and we marry."

"He'd have to marry you from jail—because that's where he's going."

"No, he's not, Ray. Greg's going to get off."

Ray Manning went to his sister and embraced her. He took her face in his hands and gazed at her. "Even if he were acquitted, he wouldn't marry you, Sis. Why can't you accept reality? You can't *force* someone to marry you. There are no more 'shotgun weddings.' "

Agnes kissed Manning, lightly, on the lips.

"Ray, is it true that there hasn't been a prosecution for adultery in a hundred years?"

"That's a funny question."

"But is it true? Is it still a crime?"

"Yes."

"And why is that, Ray. Aren't you sworn to uphold the law?"

"If we enforced that law, then half the people in the State of New York would be in prison."

"But you could—if you wanted to?"

"Agnes!" Manning's face flushed. "What are you telling me!"

Fifty-six

The panel of fifty prospective jurors sat in the courtroom. The clerk spun a hollowed-out drum that contained cards with their names written on them. He called the first fourteen names and they took their place in the jury box. As each name was called, the clerk put each one's card in a slot on the jury board and then handed it to Justice Taylor.

Jury selection in the case would last for two days, as each side searched for the predisposing attitudes of these strangers. Since the charges against Gregory amounted to a class D felony, Barbara would only be allowed ten peremptory challenges.

"There's no *Batson* issue here," she said more to herself than Simmons.

In the good old days, a peremptory challenge meant that if a defendant could not find a reason to excuse a juror, he could challenge that juror because he didn't like his face, his tone of voice, his evasions, or his background. In other words—for no reason. The case of *U.S. v. Batson* said that you could still excuse a juror for no reason, unless that reason was racial. The decision was extended to include gender and then, coming full circle, nationality and so forth.

"Pack the jury with Irishmen," Simmons said.

"We'd have to go to Dublin for that," Barbara said.

Justice Taylor asked preliminary questions but stopped and glared at Barbara.

"Can't talk in school," she said softly.

"Please, Ms. Danzig. I think this is important enough for you to pay attention." Taylor banged his gavel for emphasis.

The initial questions were addressed to the fifty jurors. Jury selection was important business. Barbara knew that a case was often won or lost there. It was the time to establish a rapport with those in whose hands the life, liberty, and future of Gregory Simmons would be placed. It was important business and to be handled delicately. That did not mean, however, it should be humorless. Laughter was another tool that Barbara would use.

When Taylor asked if there was "any reason whatsoever" why any juror could not serve, a Mr. Piscatelli raised his hand. "My wife is not exactly sick," said this elderly prospective juror.

"What does that mean, exactly?" Taylor said.

"She's in an old-age home. If I don't visit her every day, she'll think I have a girlfriend."

"How old are you, Mr. Piscatelli?"

"What did you say?" He cupped his hand to his ear.

"I said, how old are you?"

"Oh, I'm seventy-nine." The other jurors burst into laughter. "And I don't hear too well either, Your Honor."

"You're excused, Mr. Piscatelli."

As he rose to leave, Barbara turned to the audience.

"And give my regards to your girlfriend."

"I will, ma'am," he said. More laughter.

"Ms. Danzig, please. You don't seem to appreciate the gravity of this proceeding." Taylor used his gavel again.

"Oh, I do, Your Honor. Just trying to have the proceedings fit the crime."

This time Taylor banged his gavel harder. "I'm not going to ask you what that is supposed to mean, but I will not tolerate your disrupting this trial."

"Your Honor, I resent that. What is this, guilty until proven innocent?"

"I'm warning you, Ms. Danzig." This time he waved the gavel instead of slamming it on the bench.

"I'm sorry, Your Honor. I want the record to be clear that I am in no way disrupting this trial."

"It's perfectly clear, Your Honor, that is her precise intention," Manning said.

"All right, Jurors, you can see what kind of trial this is going to be," Taylor said.

The clash between lawyers and judge always stirred excitement. When the jurors learned that this was the trial of Judge Simmons—the famous one in the news—many tailored their answers in such a manner that they would be selected.

Justice Taylor continued the litany of questions as Manning and Barbara made notes. Each waited his or her turn to personally address the jurors in the box.

Do you know any of the lawyers or anyone in this case? Do you know anything about this case? Does anyone know the defendant? Has anyone heard of him? The newspapers? Television? Can you be fair and wait to hear all of the evidence before reaching a verdict? Do you own a car? What kind? What is your occupation? Are you married?

What does your spouse do for a living? Are you or any of your relatives in law enforcement? Can you be fair? What neighborhood do you live in? Were you ever the victim of a crime? If not, was any relative a victim? What kind of crime? Burglary? Robbery? Assault? Car theft? When? Did they apprehend the criminal? Was there a trial? Can you be fair? Has anyone ever served on a jury before? Was it a civil or criminal trial? Without telling us the result, did you deliberate? Can you be fair? Can you be fair?

The day grew as long as the questioning, and eventually most of the panel of fifty jurors were excused, many "for cause"—that is, they were disqualified for some serious reason, such as bias.

"I had a car stolen, and the insurance company gave me peanuts," one prospective juror said. "They caught the guy, but the police let him go. Illegally obtained evidence, or something.... *Fair?* I'd hang them all!"

"My mother reported a burglary. The burglar was caught red-handed with her jewelry. She couldn't get it back until after the trial. Then the cops said they lost it," another juror said.

By the end of the day, six jurors had been chosen. Barbara had used up seven peremptory challenges and Manning had exercised only five of his.

The next day, the tedious process continued. A new panel of fifty jurors was called and each juror took his or her turn in the jury box and was questioned, first by Taylor, then by Manning, then by Barbara.

At one point, a particularly beautiful woman, one Mary Nancy McNamara, was questioned by Manning and announced in effect that she was gay "and proud of it." She shook her long blonde tresses and smiled a smile that was dazzling. Her high cheekbones accentuated her deep, widely spaced brown eyes. She was smartly dressed in a long gypsy skirt and blouse and her earrings jangled when she snapped her head in curt answers.

"My sexual orientation is really irrelevant," Ms. McNamara said. "People seem to think that because of one's sexual preference they are going to corrupt the world. I can be fair. I can listen to all of the evidence. If the person is guilty, then that's how I'll vote."

Sharon nodded ever so slightly, as if she were cheering the juror. After each "round," when all the questions had been asked, the Court Reporter along with Taylor, Simmons, and the lawyers, retired to the rear corridor so that the final selection could be made—out of the presence of the jurors.

Each side stated its objections "for cause," and Taylor overruled every one of them.

Barbara wanted Mary McNamara on the jury. She calculated that Manning would not challenge McNamara if he believed that Barbara didn't either.

"But, Judge, she's a lesbian," Barbara said.

"So? She indicated that she could be impartial," Taylor said.

"How can she be impartial when she's partial to women?" Barbara replied.

"It's getting late and we have at least two more rounds to go. Preempt or not?"

"I need more challenges, your Honor." Discretion. Judges have the power to allow additional peremptory challenges.

"You're not getting them, Ms. Danzig. Make your challenge—now!"

They took turns exercising their challenges, and when it was over, Manning had not challenged Mary McNamara. She was the sole woman. Of the eleven men on the jury, five were African-American, three were Hispanic and three were Caucasian. Three alternates were also chosen. The reserves. The jurors who, in effect, sit on the bench ready to pinch-hit in the event of an emergency.

Barbara recognized that she had to condition the jury immediately.

She was not afraid to slip in questions that would achieve her objective despite it being legally perilous.

In the Simmons case, she wanted the jury to consider that the punishment—the ruination of a respectable judge—was disproportionate to the crime charged.

"If a person was guilty of, say, spitting on the sidewalk, and you knew that the punishment was five years in prison would you convict that person—even if they were guilty?"

Manning leapt to his feet to object.

"Ms. Danzig!" interrupted Taylor, "that is a flagrantly improper line of inquiry! I will instruct the jury as to what the law is, and they must swear to follow it even if they do not agree with it." He addressed the entire panel. "The jury is a fact-finding body. Punishment is reserved for the Court."

"Your Honor, with all due respect, I believe that my client has a constitutional right to have a jury evaluate punishment relative to the crime charged."

There it was. The nasty secret of the judiciary. Jury nullification! The Court could only instruct the jury on the law but if the jury disobeyed—there was no recourse. Double jeopardy would prevail.

"You have my ruling, Miss Danzig. It is a time-honored one." Taylor said.

"No, my position is time-honored. In 1776, all the persons involved in the Boston Tea Party were found not guilty. All! An American jury refused to convict them even when they confessed to their act. It is unfair that a jury's power is hidden from them."

"Miss Danzig, you are in contempt of court. Your persistent speeches in the face of my rulings are disruptive of this trial." Taylor motioned them to approach and indicated for the Court Reporter to memorialize his decision at a sidebar. "At the completion of this trial, I will determine your punishment, but I promise you this: If you plan to continue with these tactics, you had better bring your nightgown with you."

Barbara wanted to say, "I sleep in the nude, Judge," but she realized she was on the record.

Fifty-seven

When court adjourned, Simmons took Barbara to Orlando's, a cozy bistro on Montague Street, down the street from the courthouse. There was a small bar to the right of the entrance and tables to the rear.

Instead of paintings, a ledge ran along the wall and upon it were perched miniature marionettes of Orlando, the Sicilian knight, and his cohorts in various positions of battle against their archenemies, the Turks.

They both ordered martinis. Beefeater. On the rocks with a lemon twist. Extra dry. The waiter, a pleasant little man, though perhaps a bit obsequious, quickly delivered the drinks. He placed a plate of bruschetta on the table. The garlic bread was soaked with olive oil and covered with diced tomatoes.

"I used to come here for lunch," Simmons said.

"I know. I used to come here, too—and watch you."

"Watch *me?*"

"Sure. If I ate in the same restaurant as you, I would know when to leave for the afternoon court session," Barbara said.

"Pretty smart, aren't you?"

"I thought jury selection went well." Back to the business at hand.

"You're a sly one, Barbara. I think your red hair came from an Irishman, not a Cossack."

"Why do you say that?"

"You know perfectly well. Ms. McNamara. A lesbian, and 'proud of it.' "

"I think she's going to be an excellent juror. She has a different lifestyle and courage. She's not afraid to bend the rules. We need someone like her."

They fell silent for a moment as the waiter delivered their second martini. He left the empty glasses. It was easier to keep count.

"Oh, I agree," Simmons said. "It's the motive that I'm not sure I approve of."

"You mean, Sharon, the court officer?"

"Exactly. I could see your mind working. If the jury is sequestered, they'll have to stay at a hotel overnight and she's the only female juror—you're putting temptation in their path. You're setting up grounds for a mistrial based on jury misconduct," Simmons said.

"I must say this, Greg. Under your cosmopolitan veneer, you're really a homophobic sexist. Just because Ms. McNamara is gay does not mean she's a person of loose morals."

"That's a nice speech. Now tell me that the thought of jury misconduct never crossed your mind."

"As a tactic? Yes. As a probability? No. You toss the balls in the air and juggle as many as you can." Barbara sipped her martini, but she still felt no buzz. Too much adrenaline.

"To me, that's devious, and I don't like it. No tricks. And that's why I have to testify. You said it before. It's my word against Ragazza's. I think this jury would want to hear me," Simmons said.

"To hear what? To hear you say that you didn't do it? You can't testify, anyway. Manning would tear you apart with innuendo." Barbara reached down and retrieved her briefcase. She pulled out a computer printout and rifled through the pages. "Why didn't you tell me that you knew Ragazza?"

"What are you talking about?"

"Five years ago you took his plea to grand larceny." She read from the printout.

"I did?" Simmons appeared surprised.

"The larceny was an automobile. A Mercedes, no less. He could have been sentenced to seven years—you gave him probation," she said.

"I was sitting in the calendar part, then. Hundreds of cases a day. I must have taken a thousand pleas in the last five years."

"Eight hundred and twenty-three," Barbara said. "Do you remember why you didn't give Ragazza any jail time?"

"Of course not! I probably sentenced him to probation because it was his first offense."

"No, it was his second."

"I'll have to check my files. I don't remember the cases I had last year. Does the district attorney's office know?" Simmons said.

"They were the ones who gave me the information. It was part of Ragazza's confession. They were obliged to give it to us."

"What do you think?"

"I think that it would be suicide for you to testify," Barbara said.

"I think that it would be suicide *not* to testify.

Manning will make it look like Ragazza is my bosom buddy," Simmons said.

"We still have plenty of witnesses. You should feel complimented. All of your colleagues want to be character witnesses."

"I'm really going to be indebted to them, but you know that they can only testify as to my reputation and that kind of testimony is all so stilted." Simmons shook his head. He mimicked:

"How long do you know Justice Simmons—have you had an opportunity to speak with his colleagues? Have you formed an opinion as to his truth and veracity? What is that opinion? Excellent, you say? Why, that's excellent! Christ, I think character witnesses are the worst kind of witnesses. It's like the last act of a desperate man. We can't rely just on character witnesses."

"We're not. Your wife is going to testify."

"Caroline?"

"That is, if Uncle Norman can ever find her. He should be here soon. I left a message for him to meet us."

Barbara started on her third martini. She was beginning to feel it. The computer sheets went back into the briefcase after Simmons had examined them. She noticed that he was keeping up with her, drink for drink. Was he as tense as she? Barbara sat back and studied him. He seemed so perfect. Why would Caroline divorce him? She never would.

"Tell me, Greg. What do you think of Brancusi?"

"He's all right."

"And Giacometti?"

"Is this a test?" he asked.

"Just curious."

"When it comes to sculptors, I prefer Henry Moore. Especially his marble figures of women with holes in their bellies." He laughed, and the dimples seemed even deeper.

"*Now* who's the sly one?" asked Barbara. The third martini was definitely affecting her.

After a time, Norman arrived. He looked at both of them, then looked at the glasses on the table. He sat down without comment and ordered a drink.

"Dewars on the rocks."

"Well?" Barbara said.

"Christine has flown the coop, but I got Caroline." Norman said. "Boy, is she pissed off at you, Greg!"

"What did she have to say?" Barbara slurred her words, but her mind seemed sharp enough.

"She wouldn't talk to me. Just kept ranting about the judge, here. 'Fancy man,' she called him."

"I guess your cute little ploy at reconciliation didn't work," Barbara said. "It's a good thing you're a judge because as a lawyer you stink. As a client you're even worse!" She tossed a martini olive at him in disgust.

"The important thing is—did you serve her?" Simmons said.

Norman looked at him. Simmons was not slurring his words. The only evidence that he had been drinking was a slight flushing of his face.

"Yeah. I served her. That made her even more angry. She'll testify, all right, but God only knows what she's going to say."

"Don't you worry about that, Norman. The more hostile she is—the better," Barbara said, as if anger was a necessary preparation for battle.

Fifty-eight

The trial of *People v. Gregory A. Simmons* was about to begin in earnest, and the television crews once again converged on the courthouse.

Arrangements had been made for a large courtroom to accommodate the spectators as well as the reporters. The courtroom was the same one, Part 8, in which Reginald McCauley had been tried—and the newscasters, on the steps of the courthouse, were quick to note that irony in their reports.

The corridor was filled with spectators struggling to enter the courtroom. Basil, the same huge court officer, blocked the door, repeating the mantra, "The courtroom is filled. You have to get here earlier."

Inside, the clerk waited until the lawyers were seated before he allowed the jury to enter. Everyone then rose as he delivered the proclamation that accompanied the entrance of Justice Theodore N. Taylor.

The jury was sworn and Taylor read his preliminary

instructions to the jurors. Taylor spoke first of the order of trial.

"The district attorney will make an opening statement and will be followed, if the defendant so chooses, in the making of an Opening Statement. The People are the plaintiff in this case and have the burden of proof. The district attorney must present all of his evidence. When the evidentiary phase of the trial is completed, the parties will make closing statements. In the summations, we reverse the order, so that the defendant sums up first and the district attorney, last. Thereafter, I will charge you on the law and you will then deliberate. That is the order of proof.

"Your verdict will be based upon the competent evidence before you. In other words, I determine what evidence you may hear. At that point, your job begins—because you must weigh all this competent evidence and determine wherein lies the truth. The tests you use in weighing this evidence are the same tests you use in your everyday lives. Just use your common sense.

"Lastly, I must caution you that you are not to speak to anyone about the trial. Not wives, friends, or relatives. Not witnesses, lawyers, litigants. No one! And that includes your fellow jurors. You'll have plenty of time to talk when you retire to deliberate. Don't visit any place that you hear about during the trial. And if anyone tries to influence you in any way, you must report it to me immediately.

"Before you deliberate, I will explain the law to you and remind you of several of the matters I have just discussed."

Taylor closed his notebook, looked at the clock on the wall and banged his gavel.

"Opening statements at two o'clock." Taylor gathered

his papers, rose, and was about to leave by the rear door, when he saw that he had dropped a paper. He glanced around and satisfied himself that no one had noticed that it was a marked-up copy of the daily racing form. He had plenty of time to go to OTB before lunch.

Fifty-nine

Before Manning could begin his opening statement, Barbara objected. He had walked to the jury box with the indictment in his hand.

"Are you picking up where you left off, Ms. Danzig?"

"Judge, are you telling me that I am not permitted to object? If you are, I'll sit right down, now."

"It is your privilege to object." Taylor turned to the jury and smiled. "It's the *bickering* I object to."

"There is bickering, and then there is bickering." She smiled.

"It just sounds that way to some people. I am merely objecting to Mr. Manning telling this jury what the law is. I thought that was Your Honor's task."

"Ms. Danzig, you know perfectly well that I have a right to read the indictment to the jury," Manning said. He held out the paper and waved it at Barbara.

"You can't tell the jury the law. You'd tell it wrong, anyway," Barbara said.

Taylor banged his gavel and stood up.

"Counselors! There will be no arguing between lawyers in my courtroom. If you have anything to say, address the Court. I don't want you to speak to each other, not even to say 'good morning.' I will not tolerate this behavior!"

"He can read the indictment, but Your Honor shouldn't tolerate his telling the jury what the law is in this case," Barbara said.

"You may read the indictment, but I will explain to the jury what constitutes a fraudulent insurance act," Taylor said to Manning.

Taylor sat down and leaned back. He was quick to anger, but he was also quick to cool off. The lawyers should know that to control the courtroom, sarcasm was a tool available to him, too.

"I don't allow the lawyers to speak with each other in my courtroom. Once it happens, they tend to forget about their clients and end up squabbling like a bunch of children." There! That will fix them. You had to jump on them as soon as the trial began. It was like the tough teacher. There was always time to mellow.

"That was uncalled for, Judge. I object."

"You can object all you want, Ms. Danzig, but we're going to move this case along." Taylor said. He smiled for the jury. "Please proceed, Mr. Manning."

Manning picked up the indictment and read it to the jury. He occasionally stressed a word for emphasis.

"Count One of the Indictment reads, 'On the ninth of October, 2004, in the County of Kings, Gregory A. Simmons committed a fraudulent insurance act by attempting to wrongfully take and obtain property with a value in excess of three thousand dollars, to wit, by submitting a written statement to the Cosmopolitan Insurance Company, claiming the alleged theft of his 2005 Mercedes-Benz automobile, such act constituting the crime of insurance fraud in the third degree.' The People will prove, beyond a reasonable doubt, each and every element of this crime."

Manning kept his opening statement simple. He did not want to give away his entire case, but he did speak at length about his key witness. He had tried to ameliorate that weakness in his case in jury selection, by extracting a promise from each juror that he or she would not "compare reputations" but compare the facts. "We have other proof, some of it circumstantial, but the judge will tell you that!"

Barbara sat and feigned boredom as Manning droned on. He had not given a bad performance and had sneaked in a few items that he would never be able to prove. She would obtain a transcript of the openings and remind him of his failures in summation.

She did interrupt his opening statement when he struck his fist repeatedly on the jury rail and said, "We must send a message to all those persons, high and low, who by their thievery cause us all to pay. Who do you think pays when a false report is made? You. You and you! The insurance company is defrauded and we are defrauded. Our insurance rates go up, and respect for society lessens. The message must be loud and clear and can only come by your finding this defendant, guilty!" Manning pointed at Simmons.

"Judge, if the district attorney wants to send a message, he should call Western Union," Barbara said. It was old Samuel Goldwyn but good enough for chuckles from the spectators. To Barbara, it was perfect timing.

Manning had completed his opening statement but she had had the last laugh.

"Is that an objection, Ms. Danzig?"

"It sure is, and I would like an instruction that the jury disregard the last comment of the district attorney."

"Yes. The jury will disregard that," Taylor said. "Ms. Danzig . . ."

Barbara went to the jury rail slowly. She enjoyed the sound of her high heels clicking in the hush before she spoke. She carried no papers and had decided to make it short.

"If it please the Court, Justice Taylor," Barbara looked up at Taylor who nodded "and members of the jury. What brings us here today is the triumph of bad over good. It is simply the case of a prominent man who was unfortunate enough to have his automobile stolen. It was a Mercedes—and that made him a target because he didn't own an inexpensive compact. If any of you members of the jury did what Justice Simmons is accused of, do you think you'd be here today? No. Justice Simmons is here today because he's a judge. A brilliant, highly regarded judge, as you will learn. There is only one reason why Justice Simmons is here today, and that is because he was unfortunate. His misfortune continued—do you know why? He was unfortunate enough to have the thief apprehended by the police! Imagine that. The police finally catch a thief and they put the victim on trial. You see the sole basis for this indictment is that a convicted felon, a two time-loser, a career thief, cut a deal for himself when he was caught red-handed stealing the judge's car.

"He tells the cops, 'Look, I'm a low-life, a nothing. Why put me in jail when I can make headlines for you?' And the police—and the District Attorney for whatever personal reasons . . ." Barbara turned and pointed, palm up, at Manning and slowly repeated "... for whatever personal reasons, took the bait and persecuted—I mean prosecuted—a man who has dedicated himself to the law." Barbara watched as Manning flushed.

"I object, Your Honor," Manning said.

"Sustained."

"What, Your Honor?" Barbara said.

"Sustained."

"Well, anyway, you will not be determining innocence here. No court, except perhaps in Scotland, allows that. And that is because only God can look into a person's heart and determine innocence. Our meager system can only determine whether a person is 'not guilty beyond a reasonable doubt.' And doubtless Justice Taylor will explain that clearly and succinctly. But I'm going to ask you for something more at the end of the case. I want you to find Justice Simmons not guilty and also innocent! *Then* there will be a message sent that trumped-up charges cannot be made by every crook who steals a car and is looking to save his skin!"

"If you want to send a message, use a fax," Manning said. There were no chuckles from the audience.

"Is that an objection, Mr. Manning?"

"Yes, sir."

"Sustained."

Barbara walked back to the counsel table and spoke in a stage whisper—loud enough for the first row but soft enough to elude Taylor's ear.

"No sense in sending a fax to the district attorney's office—his shredder is working 24 hours a day."

"I resent that!" Manning said.

"Resent what?" Barbara said and gave Taylor her innocent look.

The first witness for the People was Sol Finkelstein, the fat manager of Paramount Mercedes. The tables had been turned on Sol, and his motto, "Treat Them Like Shit," was now being applied to him. He had received a subpoena *duces tecum.* That meant he had to testify and bring all his records into court. The district attorney, the police—everyone was shitting on him. Not even compensation for the time lost from work. At least he had gotten a twenty from that investigator, Norman. From the D.A. he got bopkis—nothing. They promised him mileage. And that's what he got—carfare. He would tell the truth, but he sure as hell was going to show how unhappy he was.

"By whom are you employed?" Manning said.

"You should know. You subpoenaed me."

"I have enough trouble with lawyers, Mr. Finkelstein. Just answer the question," Taylor said. The bench was to the right of the witness box and elevated, so that when Taylor banged his gavel, Finkelstein was startled.

"Paramount Mercedes."

"What is your position there?" Manning asked.

"I'm the manager."

"And how long have you been so employed?"

"The defense will stipulate that the witness is an expert on the value of a 2005 Mercedes," Barbara said. "I have no objection to him expressing his opinion that the value of the Mercedes exceeds three thousand dollars."

"Value is one of the elements of this crime, and I told this jury I would prove each and every element of the crime," Manning said. He looked at the jury and then turned to Barbara. "I don't want you to agree with me on anything, Ms. Danzig!"

"Mr. Manning!" Taylor said.

"I apologize, Your Honor. This is my witness, and I

would like to conduct my direct examination in my own manner."

"Judge, I merely wanted to move things along. The defendant is willing to concede that this witness is an expert. In addition, we are willing to stipulate that Justice Simmons purchased his 2005 Mercedes at Paramount Mercedes and that it was valued in excess of three thousand dollars on October ninth. With that stipulation, I would have no cross-examination and the trial would be expedited," Barbara said. She waved her arms grandly and bowed slightly to Manning.

"Well?" Taylor asked.

Manning thumbed his green suspenders as if he were thumbing his nose.

"And how long have you been so employed?"

The audience erupted into laughter, and Taylor struck the gavel pad with his gavel.

"I've been with Paramount for ten years," Finkelstein said.

"This key, which has been marked as People's Exhibit 3, can you identify it?" Manning took the key from his table and gave it to Finkelstein, who examined it.

"Yeah, it's the factory key to a Mercedes."

"I object," Barbara said. "And I move that answer be stricken."

"On what grounds?" Manning said.

"I don't have to tell you the grounds. I only have to tell the judge."

"Then tell me, Ms. Danzig. That does seem like a spurious objection."

"I don't make those kinds of objections, Judge. I object on several grounds. First of all, he might be an expert on car value, but it hasn't been established that he's a locksmith. What does he know about keys? Furthermore, he manages a showroom, not the factory. And lastly, he said that it's a key to a Mercedes. What Mercedes? If not the one at issue, then it could be any Mercedes. Therefore, his testimony would be irrelevant on that ground, alone. I want a voir dire to see if Mr. Finkelstein ever went to a German factory to check out how Germans make keys. Maybe he speaks German. That's where they make the cars, isn't it?"

"What's a voir dire?" one of the younger court enthusiasts asked. They had been lucky enough to walk up the seven flights of steps—undetected, and thus gain timely entrance to the courtroom.

"To hear and to say," said the other buff. "It's an interruption of a witness' testimony to see if he's qualified to testify."

"You a lawyer?"

"Nah, I'm a retired plumber."

"And you know all this from listening?" the younger one said.

"Quiet!" the clerk called out.

"Shhh—watch her. Danzig is just trying to disrupt the trial—keep Manning off balance."

"Quiet. If you can't be quiet I'm going to clear the court," Taylor said. "No voir dire, Miss Danzig."

"What about my objection?"

"Your objection is sustained. And no speeches, please."

She had won the ruling, but Taylor knew that he had been had. He had asked her the basis of her objection, and she had told him! Chalk one up to Danzig. He'd get her for that—later.

"Can we have the court reporter read the last question and answer, Judge? She's made me forget where I'm at," Manning said.

Taylor nodded and the court reporter read it back.

"All right, Mr. Finkelstein, this is the key to a Mercedes." Manning retrieved the key and held it up. "Can you tell me which one?"

"No, the number has been punched out, but it's the key that comes with the car."

"And how would you know that?" Manning said.

"It was in the car when the guy was arrested, wasn't it?"

"And how would you know that?"

"It's got a tag on it that says People's Exhibit Three." Finkelstein smiled broadly.

"Yes, it does, doesn't it," Manning said. "We'll establish how we obtained the key by another witness."

Manning sat down.

Barbara began her cross-examination. She dangled the key from her fingers.

"Mr. Finkelstein, this is a key to a Mercedes, correct?"

"Yes."

"And you can't say which Mercedes, right?"

"I told you, lady. The numbers are punched out."

"And isn't that what you recommend should be done by every new owner?"

"Yeah. That way, if it's lost it can't be duplicated, except by us."

"So your showroom keeps a record of key numbers?"

"Sure. We make a new key when a customer loses his."

"That happens often, doesn't it?"

"All the time."

"That key, the one you make. You call that a factory key, don't you?"

"Yeah." Finkelstein was starting to look uneasy.

"And who has access to those records?"

"We keep the books under lock and key." There were chuckles and Finkelstein looked around, confused by the unintended humor.

"You mean in your computer?"

"It's a secret password."

"But it is available to your staff?"

"They're hand-picked. I trust them all."

"All? Ever have a theft? Ever fire anyone?"

Barbara sat down. To show her contempt, she did not demand an answer. It was a multiple-part question anyway.

Norman had objected to her tactic.

"It's too much of a gamble," he had said.

"It's no gamble at all. It's like boxing, Norman. I feint with the left and deliver the haymaker with the right. First I show that key—although a factory key could have been stolen from the showroom—then show that the key fits a Mercedes that was never bought at Paramount. I have reasonable doubt both ways! After all, how could Greg give Ragazza a key to a car that wasn't bought at Paramount?"

"That still doesn't explain how Ragazza got the key," Norman said.

"I don't have to explain that," Barbara said. "All I need is reasonable doubt!"

The next witness scheduled was Jack Zangara, but he would have to wait.

"Nine-thirty, tomorrow," Taylor said to the jurors. "I

must caution you again, as I shall every time: You are not to discuss this case with anyone, and if anyone approaches you improperly, you are to report that to me immediately." He swept up his papers, careful to include all of them. He would later learn that his crystal ball had been defective today. Every horse he had bet on had lost.

Sixty

Trials were improvisational theater. There is no brilliant performer speaking wonderful words written by a Shakespeare or a Bernard Shaw; there is only the prepared lawyer, with his or her wits, improvising. That was why, after the recess, Barbara returned to her office to prepare for the next day and, hopefully, catch up on several other cases that were approaching trial.

"That was a good piece of cross-examination," Norman said.

"It was okay," Barbara said. She did not look up but continued reading. Her reading glasses, a recent concession to diminished sight, hung at the end of her nose.

"Norman! For Chrissake, will you get out of here!"

Norman left, but as if to get reinforcements, he returned with Lucy Sparrow. He and the secretary stood motionless in front of her desk as Barbara refused to acknowledge them.

After a moment, Barbara threw her glasses to the desk and shook her head in despair.

"Boy, are you strung out," Lucy said. She was holding a sheaf of phone message slips.

"You people are not going to leave me alone, are you?"

"Your mother's been calling—she says you've been avoiding her."

"Please, Uncle Norman, the least you can do is handle your sister!"

"She's your mother," Norman said.

"Call her and tell her I'll call her later, okay? Now is there anything else that is so important?"

"Bill Scharf has been calling you for the last week." Lucy held up the slips.

"Billy Scharf is the last person I want to speak with!"

"He's on the phone now. He says he's going to tie up every one of our phones until you talk to him," Lucy said.

Barbara gave Lucy her "you told I was in" look.

Lucy shrugged. "He's holding on line four."

"Give me one reason why I should talk to him." Barbara said.

"I'll give you *fifty thousand* reasons."

"Maybe a hundred thousand," Norman said.

"He just recommended a client in a stock fraud case," Lucy said.

"White collar crime is where the money is, Barbara. Legal Aid can handle the muggers and the burglars."

"Yes, I know. Simmons isn't the only case in the office."

Barbara punched the number and lifted the receiver.

"Hello, Billy. . . . I'm really busy. . . . I have no time. . . . You're at Michael's? . . . Don't you dare! . . . All right, just for a drink, but it has to be short. . . . Yes . . . in five minutes."

Barbara hung up and brushed back her hair.

"I hope you're all satisfied. I smell a rat here."

"Not me, dear niece."

"Not me, dear boss," Lucy said.

"It's only for a minute. I'll be back. As you doubtless heard, Billy Scharf's at Michael's Restaurant."

Barbara went outside to the elevator and descended to the lower-level restaurant of the Woolworth Building. Too smart. Billy had—or was it they—had arranged that Scharf be only "an elevator away." If he actually said that, she'd scream.

She walked briskly into Michael's. Scharf, along with a double Beefeater martini, was waiting for her.

Michael's Restaurant was vast and seemed like it was cut from the bowels of the earth. Not that it was foreboding. On the contrary, it was pleasantly decorated with English style wood paneling. What gave the restaurant its cavernous feeling was the way it was constructed—artfully, winding around the enormous pillars that supported the once-tallest building in the world.

"I can only stay a minute," Barbara said. She took a significant slug of the martini. She looked at Scharf, then looked at the drink—and downed it. What the hell!

"Well, hello," Scharf said. "You've been avoiding me."

"I've been busy." She signaled the waiter to bring another martini.

"I've been busy, too. Decided money isn't everything. Going to the New School for classes."

"That's wonderful," Barbara said. The second drink arrived. This time she sipped it.

"Ask me about Brancusi."

"I really can't, Billy," Barbara said. She took another sip. This time it was longer. *I can't do this. I have work to do. Trial tomorrow.* She was tired and hungry.

Scharf, as if reading her mind said, "You want a bite to eat?"

"I really have to be going." She looked at her watch. It was eight o'clock already. Couldn't have been here more than a few minutes. Had she been working that long in the office?

"Stay a while." He touched her hand. "Let's have another drink." He waved to the waiter.

"No. I have to go." Barbara said. She finished the martini.

"Why are you acting like this?"

She rose to leave and then sat down. Two martinis without food were doing their part to loosen her tongue. May as well get it over with. No more bothering her. No more phone calls.

"Billy, you're sweet—a bit obtuse—but you're sweet and I'm really fond of you, but I'm really interested in someone else." There it was. Barbara said something she had not even said to herself.

"That judge?"

"Yes."

"Christ, Barbara, that's like an actress falling in love with her leading man. That isn't even puppy love."

"I didn't say I was in love. I said I was interested."

"That judge has to be nuts, you know. He probably did have his car stolen."

"You know, Billy, that's beneath even you."

"Yeah, anyone who would marry Caroline Palmer has to be nuts."

The third martini came but froze in her hand.

"You know Caroline Simmons?"

"Barbara! I used to bounce around. I know Caroline. I know Christine. Everybody thinks that Christine Palmer was the wild one. Let me tell you, in her single days, Caroline was just as wild. Kinky. They're gorgeous. Absolute knockouts. You know what they used to love to do?"

"What?" Barbara said.

"They loved to switch. Tried to fool me into which one I was fucking. I played along, because to me it didn't much matter. They were both great."

"What are we talking about." Barbara's voice was cold as if Scharf had betrayed her. "It couldn't have been recent?"

"You kidding? It's been years—but I followed their careers."

"I'm sure you have," Barbara said.

Sixty-one

The trial did not begin until 10:30 in the morning and Taylor sharply rebuked the tardy juror. It was Ms. McNamara.

"The trains broke down and I couldn't catch a cab," she said.

"Everyone else was here on time. The next time you're late, you're out! Do you understand that, young lady?"

Everyone knew, except perhaps the jury, that Taylor's threat was an empty one. As a duly chosen juror, she could only be replaced on consent or if there were good cause. Being late once or twice did not fall under the category of "good cause."

When the trial finally resumed, Detective Zangara took the witness stand. He was dressed in a wrinkled navy blue suit and unpressed shirt. It was as if his bulging eyes were not the product of a thyroid condition but caused by his tight shirt collar. As he spoke, he kept putting his fingers to his neck to loosen his green tie. Unlike the sky and the trees, he was not color coordinated.

Manning's direct examination took Zangara through the night of the arrest and how Ragazza was turned over to him.

"Did you have a conversation with Anthony Ragazza?"

"Yes."

"What did he say to you, and what did you say to him," Manning said.

"I object, Judge. That's hearsay."

"The objection is sustained," Taylor said. He turned to the jury. "A witness can relate what he said but not what the other person told him."

"As I said, we spoke with Mr. Ragazza after he was arrested. We advised him of his rights and he voluntarily gave us a statement."

"I object," Barbara said and directed her attention to Zangara. "Jack, you know better than that, don't you?"

"Ms. Danzig!" Taylor said.

"Judge. He's not only saying that the statement was voluntary, but he's testifying indirectly as to what someone said to him. Besides, it's a conclusion. I move to strike the answer."

"Sustained. Strike that portion of the answer dealing with whether Mr. Ragazza's statement was voluntary."

"And that it's hearsay?"

"It's stricken! You want me to strike it twice?"

"Do what you think is right," Barbara said.

"You're really trying my patience, Ms. Danzig."

"I'm sorry, Your Honor. It was not my intention to instruct the Court or to anger it," Barbara said.

"I'm sure of that." Taylor banged his gavel. "Now, can we get on with the case?"

"But you did inspect the stolen vehicle?" Manning said.

"Yes, thoroughly."

"Jack . . ." She stretched out his name. "Thoroughly?" *We'll see about that.*

"Ms. Danzig, please stop addressing the witness until it is your turn. And not by his first name."

"We're old friends, Your Honor."

"Yes, I understand your reason for the familiarity," Taylor said.

Manning sat down and nodded to indicate that he had no further questions. He had taken a chance by having Zangara testify about the Mercedes, but it had to be done. Sidney Grossman was right. We never bring the entire vehicle into the courtroom. Zangara's testimony regarding an inspection should be enough.

Barbara went to the rear of the well and leaned against the rail that separated the audience.

"Detective Zangara."

"Yes?"

"Do you mind if I call you Jack. Jack?"

"Be my guest, Barbara."

The spectators laughed, and Jack Zangara smiled broadly.

"Now, Jack, you made an inventory search of the vehicle didn't you?"

"Yes, I did."

"And what did you find?"

"May I look at my notes?" Zangara reached into his pocket and pulled out his small memo book.

"Let's see . . . flashlight, air compressor kit, first aid kit, golf clubs . . . that's about it." He snapped the pad closed.

"Weren't the golf clubs in a bag?"

"Oh, yeah, the clubs were in a golf bag."

"And that was it, right?"

"Those are my only notations."

"Golf shoes?"

"They were probably in the golf bag."

"Probably?"

"Yeah, like the golf umbrella." Zangara's voice took on an annoyed tone. Testifying was one thing. Being made a fool of was another.

"You didn't inventory that, either, did you?"

"No."

"Did you inventory the irons and woods?"

"No."

"So you don't know how many irons there were and how many woods?"

"No. And I didn't inventory the balls, either."

"That's all right, Jack. I'm not concerned about balls."

Several spectators giggled, and Taylor struck with his gavel, again. "Come on, Miss Danzig."

"I'm just trying to establish the extent and accuracy of the police investigation, Your Honor."

"We all know what you're trying to do. Just get on with it." Taylor said.

"Detective, in your *thorough* inventory search, did you note an insurance certificate in the glove compartment?"

"Yes." Zangara began to stir uncomfortably.

"But you did not note that in your inventory?"

"I didn't consider it property to be inventoried."

"Did you record the vehicle identification number?"

"Yes, I did."

Manning was squirming in his chair and glared at Grossman, who, for his part, had his head down and was shuffling papers. What had they missed? Zangara screwed up. That had to be it—or had he sold out?

"I mean the VIN listed on the insurance certificate?"

"No, I did not," Zangara said. *She knows.* But what else was there? If only he had had another chance to look at that damned car. Norman had been too curious. What had he found?

"I object," Manning said. "This is all clearly irrelevant."

"Yes, counselor. Where is all this going?" Taylor said.

"Subject to connection, Judge. I have a good-faith basis for asking these questions."

"I'll allow it, but I warn you, I may order it stricken if you have misled the Court."

"So you do not know whether the VIN number of the automobile matched the VIN number on the insurance certificate?" Barbara said.

"Why shouldn't they?"

"Because, perhaps, they are different? It's easy enough to check, isn't it?"

"No, it's not," Zangara said. *So that was it! She knows the car was stolen and now her damned uncle is going to lie about his inspection. Could that be?* But he had never known Norman Horowitz to pull a fast one like that.

"And why is it difficult to check, Detective Zangara?"

"Because the car was stolen."

"We know that, don't we?" Barbara said. "Isn't that the charge?"

"No, the *stolen* car was stolen."

"Stolen?" Barbara milked the moment by dragging out the question. "Stolen? Stolen from where?"

"From the police parking lot."

243

The spectators broke up with laughter and it was some time before order was restored. Taylor, for his part, gave up banging his gavel and threw it down on the bench.

"This is the sleaziest trick I've ever seen. I object! I object!" With some people the blood rushes to the head. With Manning, it made his pocked nose turn purple.

"Object to what?" Barbara shouted at Manning, "that the car was stolen from the police?"

"I want to see both counsel in my chambers right now!" Taylor roared.

Sixty-two

Taylor took the private judges' elevator to his chambers and waited for the others. Manning made it a point to take a public elevator separate from Barbara and Simmons, although Grossman managed to avoid his boss by squeezing on with them. Manning would be yelling at him soon enough.

Grossman prepared his plan of attack for Manning. First, he would argue that this business of the theft from the police was only a collateral matter. But, then, was it? Danzig didn't usually shoot from the hip—she only made it appear that way. He'd recommend another extensive internal investigation, this time into who leaked the information? It wouldn't be the police, Grossman figured, they would be too embarrassed from the last one. It would be a witch hunt, of course, but then someone had to pay and it sure as hell wasn't going to be him.

Taylor was still in his robe when they entered into his chambers. He was bristling.

"I have never, never encountered two such undisciplined attorneys. Never!" Taylor was not speaking, he was sputtering. The spray of his saliva caught in the sunlight that shone in from the windows.

"It's his fault, Judge. He brought it on himself." Although not invited, Barbara sat down in a chair. Losing her temper was a tactic for her. Obviously neither Manning nor Taylor had much training.

"She's a sneak," Manning said.

"Mr. District Attorney. How dare you not advise the Court that the subject matter of the crime has been stolen!"

"Alleged crime," Barbara said.

"Don't be so smug, young lady. I'll deal with you later."

"I asked to inspect the car. That was my right, and he pussyfooted around. I can tell you, Judge, car or no car, I can prove that the Mercedes stolen from my client's driveway was *not* the car he reported stolen."

"You don't have to prove *anything,* Ms. Danzig," Taylor said. His lawyer mind softened his animosity to Barbara. This was an interesting development.

"I know that, Your Honor, but I'm going to prove it anyway." Barbara said.

"How are you going to do that without the Mercedes?" Taylor asked, his curiosity overcoming his indignation.

"My investigator will testify as to his findings. He inspected the car, unofficially."

"Her *investigator?* He's her uncle!" Grossman said.

"He's a competent witness."

"Wait a minute, Judge. This is all a red herring. What's the difference what car was stolen? It doesn't matter if ten cars were stolen! Simmons reported a theft. It's immaterial whether he owned the car or not." Grossman said. He turned to Manning, who was nodding vigorously.

"That's what *you* say," Barbara said.

"Are you moving for dismissal?" Taylor asked. It was an interesting issue.

Simmons, who had been standing at her side, leaned down and tugged at her sleeve. She looked up at him, and he shook his head.

"Not at this time. I'm reserving on that, Your Honor . . ." Barbara paused. Greg was probably right. Taylor wouldn't rule on it until he read the memoranda of law he would ask both sides to submit. She might as well throw in her other bomb, while she was at it. ". . . And I'm still waiting to see how Mr. Manning is going to corroborate the testimony of Mr. Ragazza—he's an accomplice."

"That's ridiculous. Mr. Ragazza is not an accomplice. Insurance fraud is a completely different crime from auto theft," Manning said.

"That's what *you* say," Barbara said.

Taylor picked up the Criminal Procedure Law and flipped through it.

"We all know—yes, it's section 60:22—it states that 'a defendant may not be convicted of any offense upon the testimony of an accomplice unsupported by corroborative evidence tending to connect the defendant with the commission of such offense' ."

"Read on, Judge," Barbara said. "The next subdivision states that an accomplice is a witness who may reasonably be considered to have participated in the crime."

"Exactly," Manning said. "Since it's a different crime, Ragazza is not an accomplice."

"Perhaps counsel should submit a memorandum of law on this issue," Taylor said.

"Judge, you've already ruled that Ragazza is not an

accomplice." Grossman smiled broadly and patted Manning on the shoulder.

"I did?" Taylor was now truly intrigued.

"When Ms. Danzig objected that Zangara could not testify about the statement by Ragazza because it was hearsay, and you sustained her objection, you were ruling, in effect, that Ragazza was not an accomplice...." Grossman said.

"... Because an accomplice can always testify to admissions," Taylor said, finishing the thought.

"That's a crock," Barbara said.

"No, that's Talmudic reasoning," Grossman replied.

"It's convoluted, anyway," Taylor said. "You'd better brief the issue."

Sixty-three

Court adjourned early, but Simmons went back to Barbara's office to help with the research. He rifled through Westlaw, searching out precedents and texts. She was surprised by his facility with the computer, but then, again, the more she learned of this man, the less she was surprised.

"I think we have them," Barbara said.

"We're going to beat them at trial," Simmons said.

"You're starting with me again?" She looked at her watch. "Let's get a bite to eat at Michael's."

Simmons stretched his arms. He clasped his hands together and cracked his fingers. "Let's go," he agreed.

At Michael's, they sat at a table that was off to the side and behind one of the Gothic pillars. They each ordered a martini. After a while they fell silent, as if all the legal talk had dried that well.

"Tell me a little about yourself, Greg."

"Like what?"

"You know. Your childhood. Things like that."

"If I told you, you might not think much of me."

"I doubt that very much." Barbara reached out and touched his arm.

"It's strange, but this place reminds me of church. Not that it looks like a church, I don't know what it is?" Simmons said.

"You were a choirboy?" Barbara noticed that he was changing the subject. Just as well. She'd need a good night's sleep to prepare for Ragazza's testimony.

"That was mandatory for all good little Irish boys. I hardly go to church anymore."

"Have you lost your faith?"

"No, just too many sins to confess." Simmons laughed. It was not a happy laugh. "To tell you the truth, I don't particularly like what I've become."

"In what way?"

"Pursuit of money. Pursuit of power. Things like that. There's a certain ruthlessness in life that seems to make villains of us all."

"I've heard you say that, Greg, and I don't understand. I think that as long as you're aware of your shortcomings, you can live a decent life."

"Sometimes one has no options."

"We always have options," Barbara said.

"Do we?" Simmons looked up and then down. A woman was standing by their table. At first, Barbara thought that she was a waitress—because she just stood there. But then the woman cleared her throat, to show that she was waiting to be acknowledged.

"Hi, Greg," Agnes said. "Aren't you going to invite me to join you? This is quite a coincidence."

"Go away, just go away."

"You're Ms. Danzig. I've been at the trial. I must tell you I think you're wonderful. Very beautiful, too."

"Do I have to call the police?" Simmons threatened. It was loud enough for the waiter to come over and take her arm.

"Not very polite, are you? But then you're under terrible tension."

"Madam?" the waiter said.

"Oh, I'm not staying. They have important business to discuss." Agnes brushed away the waiter's arm and walked away.

There was a long, awkward moment before Barbara spoke.

"Well, what was *that* all about?"

"She's been stalking me."

"Have you notified the police?"

"No. I can't."

"That's absurd."

"Barbara, I'm not the angel you would like me to be. I've made mistakes—lots of them. And some I can't undo."

"We all make mistakes, Greg."

"Barbara, have you ever been seduced?"

"Well, in college there was this guy."

"No, I mean really seduced. And then that person wouldn't let you go—or let you forget it. Badgering you, night and day. Year after year. You, afraid. Afraid for your wife. Afraid for your judgeship?"

"Oh, that's so terrible," Barbara said. Her face contorted as if to match the pain in his face.

"It was my fault, too. I dated her before I married Caroline. Then one day, she called me. 'Let's have a drink,' she said. Damned martinis. One thing led to another and I—I slept with her. It was only that once. Damn. It was like that movie, *Fatal Attraction*!"

"Greg! You can't live like this. You have to report it. There are laws against stalking."

"I can't!"

"Why not? The woman is obviously unbalanced."

"I can't, because the woman is Agnes Manning—the district attorney's sister."

"My God! No wonder Manning has such hatred for you."

"That's the least of my worries. Someone is following me. The other night I received one of those emergency 'you better come to my house, or else,' telephone calls from her."

"And you went?"

"Of course I went. I'm in the middle of a trial where I'm fighting for my life. I couldn't take the chance of not going."

"And what happened?"

"Nothing. Precisely nothing. Except when I arrived there, I noticed a car was following me. The car parked when I parked. And then pulled away when I did. I have to tell you, I was terrified. Waiting for a bullet to my head."

"Who could it be?"

"Caroline?"

"Or Christine. Her boyfriend certainly has the means. Is it possible that the sisters have joined in some weird plot against you?" Barbara remembered Billy Scharf's assessment of the twins.

Sixty-four

Mary McNamara was on time when it came for the trial to resume. Justice Taylor, however, was involved in an automobile accident that required him to go to the emergency room of Long Island College Hospital to repair a laceration to his gavel arm. He would have to wear a sling supporting his right arm for several days.

Mary McNamara wanted to send a sympathy note to Taylor, saying, "Your Honor, the jury wishes you a speedy recovery. But if you're late one more time, you're out!" After a spirited discussion, however, they all agreed on the note that read, "Your Honor, the jury wishes you a speedy recovery."

At two o'clock, the trial resumed with the usual packed courtroom. Since Jack Zangara had already testified, he was now permitted to attend the trial as a spectator.

Zangara was surprised to see Carmine Miano sitting in the audience. Carmine was dressed in a gray striped business suit, a white shirt, and a red tie. He was color-coordinated. He stood out because most of the audience was dressed in casual clothes. Sandy Fox could also attend because the homicide detective was not scheduled to be a witness.

"You see who's here?" Zangara asked Fox.

"I arranged it. Miano asked and I arranged it," Fox said.

"I was wondering how he got in." They were both to the side of the courtroom—standing.

"He looks out of place in the spectator section, doesn't he?" Fox laughed.

"I don't get the connection. I know the girlfriend is Simmons's sister-in-law . . ." Zangara said.

"And Ragazza is one of Miano's soldiers."

"So you think Miano is protecting his interests?" asked Zangara. He squinted at the bright fluorescent lights that hung from the ceiling.

"Who knows? I'm only a flatfoot from Homicide."

"I'm going to have to reassess my opinion of you. How's Jimmy Four Eyes?" Zangara said.

"Has a hundred alibi witnesses. I'd like to squeeze Ragazza. He's like a tube of toothpaste. Squeeze him hard and he'll spill everything." Fox gave a quick motion of his hand in imitation of crushing the tube.

"Ragazza is in jail."

"Come on, Jack. These guys know more when they're locked up than when they're on the street."

Ragazza entered the courtroom dressed in a beige sport jacket, cream-colored slacks, white shirt, and brown tie. He rubbed his wrists as the handcuffs were removed. On the walk upstairs from the holding cells to the courtroom, all prisoners were required to be handcuffed and accompanied by two court officers. Union rules! Extraordinary measures were taken to conceal the incarceration of a person from a jury. Rear corridors would be cleared and juries would be confined to the jury rooms while a prisoner was being transported.

The trial was settling into a routine now. The clerk informed the judge when the lawyers and witness were ready. Then the jurors were taken from their jury room and Taylor ascended the bench.

After Ragazza was sworn, Manning began his direct examination.

"Mr. Ragazza, would you tell the Court and jury what you do for a living?"

None of the parties were surprised by the question. A witness's testimony could be diminished by his criminal background. That is, impeached. Rather than have that elicited on cross-examination, Manning made it his first question. See, he was saying to the jury, we're hiding nothing.

"I'm a car thief," Ragazza said.

The audience laughed. This was going to be a good show. Taylor banged his gavel with his left hand.

"That is not funny, young man!"

"But that's the truth, Judge. I'm a professional thief."

Carmine looked at Zangara. He was not smiling, like the rest of the audience.

"All right, Mr. Ragazza. I'm sure that Ms. Danzig will have you explain your criminal record—at length," Manning said.

"I object, Your Honor. Would you please admonish Mr. Manning not to instruct the witness as to the questions I might ask?" Barbara did not bother to rise in making the objection.

"I apologize, Your Honor." Manning smiled and bowed slightly.

"Who's being sleazy now!" Barbara said sotto voce.

"Now, Mr. Ragazza you were arrested on or about October ninth for stealing a Mercedes?" Manning ignored Barbara.

"I didn't steal that car."

"And how was it that you came into possession of the vehicle?"

"Judge Simmons gave me the key." Ragazza anticipated the next question and pointed to Simmons. "Yeah, the judge—there at the table."

"He just gave you the key?" Manning said.

"It wasn't exactly like that. A mutual friend tells me that the judge wants to see me—to do him a favor."

"So I go to meet him at this restaurant—Orlando's, you know, Montague Street. He's very cagey. He's at one table, me at another."

"Then what happened?" Manning said.

"My friend goes over to the table and they talk for a while."

"Did you hear what they said?"

"No, but I saw the judge give him the key."

"And . . ."

"And then my friend comes back. Tells me the deal, gives me the key and the judge's address—and you know the rest."

"So you never spoke to the defendant?"

"Nah, I didn't have to. We go way back," Ragazza said.

"Would you explain that to the jury," Manning said, as if he were uncovering new evidence. Ragazza's acquaintance was a double-edged sword. It was good that Ragazza knew Simmons, but it was bad that it was in connection with his plea to the theft of a Mercedes five years before.

"I took a plea before Judge Simmons. He gave me probation."

"And for this leniency, you felt that you were obligated to him?"

"Objection!" Barbara said.

"Sustained."

"He sure knows how to return a favor," Barbara said, snidely.

"Your Honor!" Manning said.

"You're not helping your client," Taylor shouted. "And after this trial, you may not be able to help *any* client!"

Barbara's task was clear when she finally began her cross-examination. There would be no single club to discredit Ragazza. She started with disdain in her voice.

"So Rags—that's your nickname, isn't it?"

"Yes."

"You're a professional car thief?"

"Yes."

"What kind of car do you drive when you're not stealing cars?"

"I object." Manning said.

"Sustained."

Ragazza answered, anyway. "I like the Camaro."

"But you don't drive the car to work?"

"I don't take the train."

"You have an accomplice who usually helps you?"

"Does Macy's tell Gimbel's?"

"Gimbel's is out of business—like you?"

"Your Honor, will you tell Ms. Danzig to get to the

point." Manning had looked back and seen that several of the spectators suppressed laughter.

"Are you objecting, Mr. Manning?"

"Only to this ridiculous line of questioning, Judge."

"Yes, Ms. Danzig. Can we get on with it?" Taylor seemed to have completely recovered from his outburst with Barbara.

"When you took the Mercedes from the driveway at four o'clock in the morning, you weren't stealing it?"

Barbara walked down the well past the entire jury, and then walked back. Her next series of questions were addressed to the witness, but her eyes were directed at the jury. Her eyes fixed on each juror, one at a time.

"Correct."

"It wasn't your car, is that correct?" Barbara said.

"Right."

"You weren't going for a joyride, right?"

"That's right." Ragazza said. He began to feel uncomfortable. The bitch was parroting his words.

"So you needed a car because your Camaro was broken?"

"Look, counselor, I wasn't stealing the car."

"You mean that you were stealing the car with permission?"

"You might say that."

"And you, a three-time convicted car thief, agreed with Justice Simmons to steal his car at four o'clock in the morning."

"I've only been convicted twice." There were continual chuckles in the audience with each of Ragazza's answers. Taylor banged his gavel several times but only half-heartedly.

"Pardon me," Barbara said. She was not begging forgiveness. "And you didn't make a deal with the D.A. to escape prosecution?"

"I owed the judge a favor."

"I didn't ask you that! I move to strike the answer." Barbara whipped around as if she were going to assault Ragazza for volunteering.

"Strike it."

"So there you were at four A.M. driving this fancy car and, according to the police, traveling at a great rate of speed. Were you rushing home to catch a nap?"

"No."

"Oh, I forgot, you work nights, don't you?"

"You don't want to know the truth, lady! If you let me talk, I can explain it."

"Strike that," Taylor said. He had not waited for the objection.

"So what were you going to do with this expensive car—sell it?"

"Yes."

"And at four A.M., you were searching for a buyer, right?"

Miano sat impassively in the audience. He stared at Ragazza, and this made Ragazza more uncomfortable.

"We were going to split the profits," Ragazza said. He twisted in his seat and rubbed a knot he felt in the back of his neck.

"You owed the judge a favor, but it was still going to cost him?"

"Well, I was gonna get the car."

"So, you knew that the judge was going to make a claim on his insurance, didn't you?" Barbara asked.

"I didn't know that he was going to make a claim with

his insurance. I figured that he might, but it was none of my business."

Manning sat back and smiled.

"Now, I didn't ask you that, did I, Rags? You know better than that. You're not only a professional thief, but you're a professional liar, aren't you?" Barbara said. She did not for a moment indicate that the answer had disappointed her.

Barbara knew that Ragazza was aching to testify about this "friend" at Orlando's. If Ragazza knew Simmons, it was plausible that the defendant—judge or not—had committed the crime. The "where there is smoke, there must be fire" syndrome. If Greg hadn't committed the crime, then why had he been arrested?

"Now about this imaginary friend of yours," Barbara said. She held her breath. She hadn't received notice of any other witnesses to testify besides the police. She hoped to call the bluff. "This imaginary friend, does he have a name?"

"He wasn't imaginary!"

"*Wasn't?*"

"He's dead. . . ." Ragazza said. The audience buzzed with laughter, and Taylor banged his gavel.

"Snuffed out by the Russian mafia. He was a good guy!" Ragazza added.

"What was his name—just for the record, just for posterity."

"Rothstein. Arnold Rothstein."

"The famous gangster?"

"Nah, he's dead, too. I think this was his great-grandson."

"You have a wonderful network of friends, Rags."

"I'm a crook, but I ain't no liar."

"That's a double negative, Rags. You don't know what that is, do you?"

"Objection."

"Sustained," Taylor said. "The jury will disregard all this nonsense about grammar...."

"And the failure to respond to the questions, too?" Barbara said.

"Counselor!"

"This witness knows very well how to answer questions, but he's insisting on putting a pack of lies before the jury—regardless of the questions."

"I'm warning you, Ms. Danzig. No more speeches!"

"So, at four A.M., while you were out looking for a buyer, did you have anyone in mind?" Barbara said.

"I didn't have nobody—I mean *anybody*—in mind."

"Weren't you going to drive it to a chop shop, where it would be disassembled and its parts sold?"

"No."

"As a matter of fact, Caroline gave you the key, didn't she?"

"Who?"

"You know. Caroline Simmons. The judge's wife."

"I don't know what you're talking about."

"You *do* know Carmine Miano, don't you?"

"Yeah, slightly." Ragazza looked at Miano and then looked away.

"Isn't his girlfriend Christine Palmer, the sister of Caroline Simmons?"

Manning propelled himself from his chair. "I object. This is outrageous!"

"And isn't it a fact that you were hired by the soon-to-be-divorced Caroline Simmons to steal the car from the judge?"

"Outrageous! Thoroughly outrageous! She can't do that, Judge!" Manning said.

Barbara's voice had risen, and she pointed to Ragazza. She had asked the questions quickly and dramatically because she knew that the objections would be sustained by Taylor. She would say that she had a "good-faith basis" for asking the questions, but in truth, she was tossing balls in the air again, hoping no one would notice the ones that dropped.

"I have no further questions!" Barbara said.

Manning had some questions on redirect. He wasn't through yet. He was not going to roll over and play dead. Grossman, who had continued to second-seat Manning, was frantically passing him notes. When the district attorney personally tries a case, he had better win. It should be airtight. The prestige of his office—*his* prestige—was at stake. The newspapers would never remember the efficient way he ran an office with a budget of millions of dollars, but only whether he was effective as a trial lawyer. He looked crossly at Grossman. His chief assistant should have protested more strongly when he had decided to handle the case himself. He saw that many in the audience were assistant district attorneys, come to watch the show. In effect, to judge him. He made a mental note for Grossman to chase them back to work.

Meanwhile, he had to rehabilitate Ragazza as best he could. The wife issue was a Danzig curveball. He should have expected something like that. Blame somebody else. Someone not on trial. After all, Danzig merely needed "reasonable doubt."

"There is no doubt in your mind that Gregory Simmons gave you the key and told you to take his car?" Manning said.

"As I said. He didn't personally hand me the key, but I saw him give it to Arnold and Arnold told me the address. He also told me the date and time."

"So in your mind, you were not stealing the car."

"I object, Judge."

"Overruled."

"I'm telling you. We made a deal."

"When you saw the defendant at Orlando's, was there any question that you knew him?" Manning asked.

Barbara did not jump up. That would have given the question too much importance, and she had to deflate the moment. Why had Manning waited so long? He had delayed introducing the old calendars as exhibits. It was real evidence. Something that the jury could touch and feel. Something they could examine! Maybe Manning wasn't such a bad tactician.

"I object, Your Honor. Know? In what sense? A biblical sense? An intimate sense? In a public sense?"

"In any sense," Manning said.

"I still object, Your Honor. Justice Simmons is a public figure. Most everyone knows him. May we have a sidebar, Judge?"

Barbara saw that Manning had picked up the old calendars that documented Ragazza's appearance in court for his prior conviction. Had to head Manning off. Sidebar.

"Outside. In the corridor," Taylor said.

Hmm. Maybe Taylor was not such a bad guy after all. A stickler, yes. Dumb? No. Barbara realized that he was aware of what was occurring and wanted to make sure that the jury did not overhear the conference.

The court reporter had to drag his chair to the rear corridor before he could begin the transcription.

"Ms. Danzig?"

"Judge, he's impeaching his own witness."

"I have a calendar here. An official record. That's admissible."

"For what purpose? To show that Ragazza committed a crime?"

"No. To show that the defendant knew Mr. Ragazza. She opened the door, Judge. She was the one that asked about his prior convictions." Grossman was pulling at Manning's sleeve, but Manning ignored him.

"I did not," Barbara said. "He's the one who said that Ragazza had a criminal record!"

"Tell me, is this witness going to testify that he personally knew the defendant in another context, or will it be limited to the taking of a plea five years ago?" Taylor said.

"I'm not sure, but I think it's limited to the record," Manning said.

"Then I renew my objection, Judge. It's collateral, cumulative, and a disguised impeachment of his own witness," Barbara said. She saw the uncertainty in Taylor's face and added, "And it's highly prejudicial. You let this in, Judge, then every judge who's ever accused of a crime by a crook will be a target."

"It's an official document," Manning said.

"I'm going to allow both the question and the document, Mr. Manning. And I'll allow you, Ms. Danzig, to recross. I think that the jury should make the determination as to the extent of knowledge, if any."

It was a close issue, Barbara thought. Resolved against her but made without rancor. She'd have to be less provocative with Taylor. Perhaps it was time for the sugar.

"I respect that ruling, but I still object for the record," she said.

"As is your right."

"Buttering up the judge?" Manning said.

"You're as bad as she is," Taylor said. Quick as a flash, he turned on both of them.

"I take that as a compliment," Manning laughed. It was good to win.

"And I take it as an insult," Barbara said. She followed them back into the courtroom and calculated how she would repair the damage.

The old calendar was marked as an Exhibit.

"Tell the jury how you came to know the defendant before you met him in Orlando's Restaurant."

"Objection," Barbara said.

"Sustained."

"Tell the jury how you came to recognize the defendant when you saw him at Orlando's Restaurant?" Manning said.

"I took a plea before him for auto theft five years ago. I was guilty, and he gave me a break," Ragazza said.

"So you felt obligated to him?"

"Objection," Barbara said. She rose, then sat down. "Never mind. I withdraw the objection."

"Sure. As I said, I owed him a favor, and besides, I was getting the car."

Barbara kept her recross short.

"You're all heart, Rags. But I want you to think back. Five years ago. How many times did you go to court on that charge?"

"I don't remember—maybe fifteen times."

"You had a lawyer?"

"Yeah."

"And he kept negotiating with the district attorney in what they call 'plea bargaining'?"

"Yeah."

"And you did that until you made the plea agreement with the district attorney?"

"So?"

"Tell the court and jury, Rags. Of the fifteen times you were in court, how many times did Justice Simmons preside?"

"Maybe twice."

"So, the other thirteen times, there were thirteen different judges?"

"Well, once or twice there was the same judge."

"No further questions."

Manning rose.

"The People rest."

"Monday morning—nine-thirty A.M.," Taylor said.

After the jury left the courtroom, Taylor leaned back in his chair.

"Well?"

"The defendant moves to dismiss . . ." Barbara was interrupted by Simmons, who tugged violently on her arm.

"Will Your Honor reserve on any motions?" Simmons asked.

"Judge Simmons! You have a lawyer! I don't want to hear another word from you!"

"Barbara. Please . . ."

"My client is afraid that you might grant the motion to dismiss and asks the court to allow us to reserve judgment on all motions until the end of the case." Barbara slapped Simmons's arm to show her annoyance with him.

"This takes the cake for arrogance." Manning shook his head in mock despair. "He's trying to browbeat you,

Judge. Making you think he's entitled to something he's not! He wants a jury verdict? Then let him waive all motions!"

Taylor looked at Barbara.

"The defendant reserves on all motions," Barbara said.

Sixty-five

That evening, Carmine Miano walked into the Apache Social Club. He had a drink at the bar and waited for Fratello to arrive. Instead of sitting, however, Fratello came in and then immediately exited, motioning for Miano to follow.

"Come on, Carmine. Let's go for a walk." Fratello wore a gray silk Armani suit with a blue sport shirt that was open at the collar. A heavy gold chain was around his neck. His maroon loafers were soft Italian leather. He was a muscular man, tending toward fat, and he walked with a swagger, swinging his arms like a sailor who had just been granted shore leave.

Miano, whose attire aped his boss, quickly caught up with Fratello. To his rear, and following, not so discreetly, were his bodyguards. The bodyguards were wearing running suits.

An unmarked van was parked on the other side of Mulberry Street. Fratello waved to it.

"Wave to the fucking Feds. They're taking our pictures. Vince had the place swept yesterday, and we found two more fucking bugs. They got stuff that hears every word we say, even on the street. So mumble when you talk. Now, what's so important that you have to tell me?"

"It went okay. The dummy, Ragazza, stood up all right. I think that fucking judge is going to beat the rap."

"Do we care?"

"I'd like to see him in the joint."

"Why?"

"We can always use top legal talent—for the *coram novis* appeals," Carmine said. "You know, the ones they reverse because the lawyers screw up."

"You sure that's the reason, Carmine?"

"Come on, boss. I was just making a joke."

"Were you? What about the girl?" Fratello turned to the side and spoke into a store window.

The van had started up and trailed behind him.

"I'm staying close to make sure she doesn't lose her nerve."

"I hear you got that homicide dick to let you into the trial."

"Christ, boss, you know everything. Fox is hounding Jimmy Four Eyes but still can't figure out why I'm interested in the trial."

"Just be careful. You better have Modansky there for her tomorrow."

"It's already been arranged," Miano said.

Fratello stopped. They all stopped. They turned, like soldiers doing an about-face, and walked back toward the social club.

The van passed them, made a U-turn, and drove past them again. The Feds were in a harassing mood, as if it did not matter whether any evidence was uncovered. It only mattered that the mob know that they were watching—and listening.

"Wave to the fucking F.B.I.," Fratello said.

Sixty-six

Simmons did not telephone. It was late, but when Barbara opened the door, she did not seem to be surprised. No bullshit like, "What are you doing here?" No banter. She stepped aside. Her eyes never left his.

She wore a long white satin chemise and held a glass of port. He took the glass from her hand and placed it on a table. She just stood there. Wordlessly. Then he kissed her. It was not a violent kiss but a tentative one. One where their lips barely touched.

Barbara backed away, holding him off at arm's length. "Whoa! Not so fast!"

Simmons did not say anything. With one hand he held her waist, and with the other, ever so lightly, he touched her breast.

"You're pretty sure of yourself," she said.

He gazed at her and still said nothing, his hand still moving.

Barbara took his hand and held it. Not resisting. Just putting it on hold.

"I have to make a phone call," she said. "It's very important."

She led Simmons to the liquor closet.

"Make yourself a martini. I'll be right back."

Barbara went into her bedroom. She closed the door and picked up the phone.

"Gershon! Thank heaven you're home."

"Isn't everyone home at two A.M.? Who was killed today?"

"Gershon. Be serious. It's happening."

"What's happening?"

"He's here. Simmons. He just walked in and I'm like a bowl of jelly."

"You're asking me what you should do?" His voice was a mixture of sarcasm and incredulity.

"For God sakes, yes!"

"Then, for God sakes, no! I don't like it. A man rings your bell at two o'clock and you're asking me if you should have sex? The answer is no—no! You hear me, Barbara? Kick the bum out!"

"Christ, Gershon. I'm not asking for permission. I called you because I'm scared. He doesn't know it, but I'm frightened out of my mind. I'm not in control, Gershon. He's the first man I really care about. You understand?"

"You're out of control?"

"Fuck you, you little Nazi."

"Now that's the Barbara I know."

She could just see that little weasel twisting his mustache.

"You're absolutely no help," Barbara said and slammed down the phone.

Barbara immediately hit the redial button. The phone rang several times and the voice mail clicked in.

"Gershon, please. I'm sorry."

Dr. Reich did not pick up.

She dialed again. This time he answered.

"Barbara, you've already made up your mind—so do it. Make believe you're cross-examining a lowlife."

Barbara began to laugh.

"Thank you, Gershon. I love you."

"Don't I always say the right thing? But seriously, Barbara. Go slow. If he's right for you, there will be a lifetime to find out. Sometimes holding out is better than putting out. It makes a man more determined," Dr. Reich said.

Barbara blew a kiss into the phone and hung up.

Finally, but not before she took another deep breath, she returned to the living room—and Simmons. She hoped he would not notice her apprehension. *Come on, Barbara. It's not like it's the first time.* Or was it?

Simmons took her in his arms. He still had not said a word. Perhaps that was the secret. Love was action, not words.

It was like her recurring dream was coming true. Flying around the room. Lifting. Soaring. But those dreams had been nightmares from which she had forced herself to waken. Now she only wanted to lose herself in him. She fought her mind, which was trained in logic and wanted to question everything. Wasn't there a time to suspend thought, abandon judgment? But she was Barbara Danzig. The controller. The one who set the terms. She had been waiting all of her life to tell herself to shut up. *Be quiet!*

"Oh, Greg," Barbara said. There was no groping, tearing, urgency—no animal reaction to spoil the moment. No aggression. There was a pervading gentleness as he lifted her and carried her to the bed—still holding, still kissing. She was only dimly aware of his caresses. A soft delicate touch sought out and found her soul's vital organ—her hidden heart—and subdued it. It was not a surrender, for there had been no battle.

And they made love. And they loved. Passion without words to damage it.

"And now what?" Simmons said afterwards.

"*And now what?*" Barbara repeated. *What the hell did that mean?* Was he just another Billy Scharf?

"I thought this might be a mistake. So soon."

"So soon? I've been waiting for you all my life," Barbara said.

Simmons got up and started to dress.

She looked at him oddly. She did not remember him disrobing. "Barbara, I couldn't help myself."

"Don't ruin it, Greg. Please."

"I'm not sure this was the right thing to do. I said to myself that I wanted you to be sharp and brilliant on Monday, not to complicate things. I didn't want a mushy head."

"Mushy head?" Barbara said. They looked at each other, straight-faced, and then they burst into laughter.

Sixty-seven

Prior to the trial on Monday, all spectators were excluded from the courtroom while Taylor considered whether to allow the next witness to testify.

Caroline had come with her lawyer, Al Modansky, and he sought either to quash the subpoena she had been served or to limit her prospective testimony.

Simmons, Barbara, Manning, and Grossman sat at the counsel table. Taylor read the motion papers and then nodded to the court officer, who stood guard at the back of the courtroom.

Albert Modansky and Caroline Simmons entered.

Caroline was dressed like a young matron attending an exclusive afternoon exhibition at MOMA, the Museum of Modern Art. She wore a tailored blue dress with open-length gloves. Her blonde hair was accentuated by a picture hat that threatened to sail away with the first breeze. She seemed composed, but she clutched her handbag nervously.

Modansky's diamond pinky ring sparkled in the lights as he waddled in beside Caroline Simmons.

"She got Modansky? He's a mob lawyer." Barbara said to Simmons in a low voice. "This confirms the Christine connection."

"He appeared before me once." Simmons said. "He's flashy but good."

Modansky motioned to Caroline, and she sat in the first row. He opened the low swinging door and entered the well.

"Judge, I represent Mrs. Simmons."

"You're not contesting proper service?"

"No, Judge. But she declines to testify."

"On what grounds?" Taylor said.

"Privileged communications, Judge."

Manning rose. "Doesn't apply to me. *I'm* not calling Mrs. Simmons, her *husband* is," Manning said.

"I don't care *who's* calling her. It's spousal privilege. She can't be compelled to disclose any confidential communication made by one to the other during the marriage—and Mrs. Simmons is still married," Modansky said.

"Looks like he's got you there, Ms. Danzig," Taylor said.

"There's no privilege, Judge. We aren't going to ask any questions concerning conversations with her husband."

"Then what is she going to be asked?" Modansky said.

"You'll find out when I ask her."

"It's another red herring, Judge. Nobody committed this crime except the defendant," Manning said.

"If my client is going to be accused of a crime, then she surely stands on her Fifth Amendment right not to give testimony that might tend to incriminate her," Modansky said.

"Good. Let her get on the stand and take the Fifth!" Barbara said. "Wouldn't the jury love that!"

If Mrs. Simmons took the fifth and refused to testify, then Danzig would argue that she hired Ragazza. If Mrs. Simmons did testify, it would probably be on behalf of her husband—otherwise, why would Danzig want her to testify? Was immunity from prosecution too high a price to pay for favorable testimony?

Taylor put on his commiserating face for the District Attorney.

"Well?" He looked at Manning. Taylor found Barbara too aggressive and didn't much like her, but he was starting to appreciate her. She knew how to box Manning in.

"The district attorney will grant immunity to the witness," Manning said.

"For all crimes?" Modansky was pressing.

"For all crimes in connection with this matter," Manning said.

"That's not good enough. It has to be for *all* crimes, known and unknown."

Manning nodded. That bastard Modansky. He was going to have a hard time the next time he tried to cop a plea for one of his *paisanos*.

"The People are confident that the truth will prevail," Manning said. The look on his face contradicted his words.

Sixty-eight

The spectators were unusually silent and strained to hear. The witness spoke in a hushed, hesitant manner. At one point, the juror farthest from the witness raised his hand.

"I can't hear her," the juror said, shaking his head.

"You'll have to speak up, Mrs. Simmons," Taylor said.

Modansky had wanted a chair inside the well, but Manning had insisted that he remain in the gallery. If Caroline was going to testify, Manning did not want it to appear that she was under any compulsion to do so.

Modansky grumbled about being separated from his client but settled for a seat in the first row. He then pushed Zangara over and motioned for Miano to sit on the other side of him.

"You are the wife of Gregory Simmons?" Barbara asked.

"Well, the divorce is not final . . . so you might say so."

"Your husband owns a Mercedes?"
"We own it."
"Please, Mrs. Simmons. Just answer my questions."
"Yes. It is in his name."
"Do you have a key to that Mercedes?"
"No."
"Did you *ever* have a key?"
"He had a key to my car, too."
"You had a Range Rover?"
"I still do."
"So you had a key to the Mercedes?"
"Of course I had a key!" Caroline's voice took a sharp twist of annoyance.

"What happened to it?" Barbara said. Could she be provoked so easily? Bill Scharf might have been right. She wasn't such an angel.

It surely was a puzzle. There just wasn't enough information. The original Mercedes disappeared—that was a fact. So how could Caroline get a key to the second Mercedes, which had been stolen, and then give it to Ragazza? Caroline had to be the culprit! Instinct supplanted logic, and Barbara forged ahead. One of those balls that she was juggling might just bounce up and hit Caroline.

"What happened to the key, Mrs. Simmons?" Barbara repeated.

"I gave it back to him when we separated." Caroline's voice still had its sharp edge.

"Which key did you give back?" Barbara said.

"I don't understand."

"Was it the key to the Mercedes that you and your husband owned, or was it the key to the stolen Mercedes?"

Manning leapt up. "Objection! Objection! Ms. Danzig

is testifying. She's introducing a phantom car! There was no second Mercedes!"

"I told you, Judge, I have a good-faith basis for asking that question."

"You'd better," Taylor said. He rapped his gavel. "I'll listen to a little more."

Barbara leaned toward the witness.

"Didn't you arrange to have your Mercedes stolen, then substitute a second stolen Mercedes and arrange to have *that* one disappear so that your husband would innocently believe it was *his* car that was stolen?"

"Are we in Disney World?" Manning shouted. "She's impeaching her own witness!"

"Sustained!" Taylor banged his gavel, hard.

"There was a dispute over the Mercedes when you separated, wasn't there?" Barbara's voice was calm as if she were in the eye of a hurricane.

"I wouldn't call it a dispute."

"Actually, you fought over possession of the Mercedes, true?"

"False."

"Isn't it true that you felt tricked because Justice Simmons registered the car in his name?"

"I paid for it."

"So you felt cheated?"

"Objection, Judge. How she felt is immaterial."

"I think it's very material," Barbara said. "It goes to her state of mind."

"And I object to what counsel thinks," Manning said. "She's putting the witness on trial!"

Taylor was so engrossed by the witness that he had to be prodded to rule on the objection. When he finally stirred, it was as if he was bothered by the interruption. "Overruled."

"Yes, I felt cheated."

"Do you know an Anthony Ragazza?"

"Objection!" Manning said. "Ms. Danzig's doing it again. She's trying to confuse the issue."

"Overruled. Let's find out." Taylor said.

"Who?"

"Come on, Mrs. Simmons. Where have you been? Ragazza—the man who stole your husband's car."

"I object," Manning said.

"Correction. The man who *took* your husband's car." Barbara said.

"I didn't know his name."

"Whether you knew his name or not, didn't you give Ragazza the key to the Mercedes?"

"Absolutely not!" Caroline turned and looked at Taylor. "Your Honor, I'm not a vindictive person." She opened her handbag and took out a handkerchief, dabbing it at her eyes.

"Am I upsetting you, Mrs. Simmons?" Barbara said. Why the hell was she crying? *This one is a hell of an actress. Wait until I really get started. There's going to be a flood.*

"Please, Ms. Danzig, just ask pertinent questions," Taylor said.

"Mrs. Simmons, isn't it a fact that you gave the key to Ragazza and told him to take the Mercedes from the driveway?" Barbara asked. *That was pertinent enough, wasn't it?* Barbara smiled sweetly at Taylor.

Taylor, however, was not looking.

"No. No." Caroline said. She opened her pocketbook and put the handkerchief away.

"Do you know a Carmine Miano?"

Manning half rose to object and then decided not to.

"Who?"

"You don't know him either? Come on, Caroline, your sister's boyfriend."

"Oh, you mean Carmine?" Caroline pointed to the first row. "I didn't know his last name."

Everyone turned for a glimpse at Miano. Carmine bowed slightly and half smiled in embarrassment. He definitely did not enjoy being fingered.

"Doesn't Ragazza work for Miano as a car thief?"

"Objection," Manning said.

"Overruled." Taylor banged his gavel more in annoyance than to emphasize his ruling.

"How would I know that?"

"Because you arranged the whole theft to embarrass your husband . . ."

"Objection. Objection." Manning was on his feet, but Barbara was waiting neither for a ruling nor an answer.

". . . and ruin his career."

"I gave him back the key."

"Isn't it true that you hired Ragazza to steal your husband's car?"

"How could I?"

"I want an answer and I want the truth!" Barbara said. The moment had come as it occasionally comes, unexpectedly. When the context becomes more important than the content. It didn't matter what the questions were. She was rattling Caroline! Barbara persisted—gazing at Caroline. It was like having a fighter on the ropes and one last blow was needed.

"The truth—Caroline. The truth!"

"The truth is . . ." Caroline fumbled with her handbag to retrieve her handkerchief, but she dropped it. It fell to the floor and its contents spilled out. Barbara bent down to help her gather the various articles that included a yellow wallet and a pack of Marlboro cigarettes.

Barbara stopped cold. Then, as if nothing extraordinary had happened, Barbara put back the wallet and pack of cigarettes that had fallen from Caroline's handbag.

Barbara returned to the counsel table and sat, staring at Caroline. *Oh my God. Oh my God.* Simmons leaned over to whisper to her, but she brushed him away.

"Ms. Danzig, have you completed your examination?" Taylor asked.

Barbara shook her head but did not otherwise move.

"Ms. Danzig?" Taylor looked at Barbara. There was something in her face that obliged him to wait for Barbara to continue.

"When were you born?" Barbara asked. She rose and asked the question as if it was with great reluctance.

"This is stupid. I object," Manning said.

Taylor ignored Manning and leaned toward the witness. Something was happening and he did not want the moment to be interrupted.

"You're an identical twin, aren't you?"

"Yes." Her voice was almost inaudible.

Manning, for his part was now also caught in the moment and he sat down, fingering his pen with both hands.

"Were you born first?"

"Second."

"You're jealous of her, aren't you?" Barbara said. *What was going on? She had to be Christine. If so, where was Caroline? And why the deception?*

"I loved her." Caroline started to sob.

"*Loved?*"

Caroline took out her handkerchief and buried her

face in it. Her body twitched, but there was no sound, only movement—like a volcano about to erupt.

"You're really Christine Palmer, aren't you?"

Caroline looked up and wiped her tears.

Miano rose and started to move to the aisle.

"The man—the one who is leaving—he is Carmine Miano?" Barbara turned and pointed.

"Yes."

"Your Honor. I would ask that Mr. Miano be restrained from leaving," Barbara said.

Taylor motioned to the court officer. Miano resumed his seat.

"Please tell the court your name." Barbara was gentle. Standing. Waiting.

Caroline began crying uncontrollably. Now her whole body shook and she emitted a long poignant wail.

"It was an accident! By God, it was an accident." Caroline's face was contorted with a look of unbelievable pain.

"What is your name?" Barbara waited. The entire courtroom was pin-drop silent. Barbara did not repeat the question. It, too, was there—waiting.

"Christine Palmer. I'm Christine Palmer."

"Where is your sister, Caroline?"

"She's dead. My poor sister is dead." Christine had recovered enough to speak, but her voice, now louder, was still almost inaudible. "Not even a proper burial . . . somewhere in concrete . . . or crushed . . ."

"Tell us what happened," Barbara said.

Modansky bolted from his seat and pushed through the swinging double door. "I object! I object!"

"She's been granted immunity!" Barbara shouted at Modansky.

"Danzig!" Taylor banged his gavel and shouted out

her name. That woman was going to get it from him yet. How dare she?

Several members of the jury looked at Taylor, not understanding what was going on.

"Mr. Modansky is Mrs. Simmons's lawyer—or whatever her name is. . . ." Taylor said.

"I'm sorry, Your Honor," Barbara said and bowed her head so as to look appropriately contrite.

"Sit down, Mr. Modansky. I'm not going to tolerate any interruption from you, either."

Big Al Modansky walked back to his seat. What was he getting excited about? He had suckered the D.A. into granting her immunity for all crimes—known and unknown. She couldn't be prosecuted no matter what she had done. But then there was perjury. That wouldn't be included in the immunity. It was subsequent. He glanced at Miano. Modansky was really angry with him. How the hell can I adequately represent these people if they don't come clean with me?

"But . . ." Modansky objected.

"Sit!" Taylor said. It was like he was commanding a Saint Bernard.

"Tell us what happened, Christine," Barbara continued.

"Caroline called me. I had been very angry about my parents' will. They left her half the money, but Caroline was also given control over my half. She called me and explained that it wasn't her fault and that we should talk. She picked me up at Riverside Drive and we took a drive over the George Washington Bridge. I was surprised that she had the Mercedes, but she said it would be more comfortable. Greg, wouldn't mind, she said." Christine wiped the tears from her cheeks.

"We were driving along—we weren't even fighting. Soon I didn't even know where we were, except that the weather had turned bad. Caroline lost control of the car and struck a tree. The air bag saved me, but the car spun off and struck another tree on the driver's side. I didn't know what to do. It looked like her neck was broken. She was dead. I was sure of that. Her eyes just stared at me. We were alone. There was nobody around. No one to help me. No one. My arm felt like it was broken. There was blood all over me." Christine brushed herself as if just now wiping off the blood.

"I panicked. I thought I was dialing 911 on the cellular phone, but in my confusion, I had called Carmine. He came with a tow truck. And that's when it all started. It would all be so easy, he said. He could get another Mercedes—just like that. Caroline was dead. If I didn't impersonate Caroline, then Greg would inherit all her money and have control over mine, too—because they weren't divorced yet. I was in shock and Carmine was scheming. I was amazed at how quickly he was thinking. All I had to do was to pretend to be Caroline and he would do the rest. The Mercedes was a wreck so he had to dispose of the car, as well as . . . take care of Caroline's body. But the identification numbers on the Mercedes were different, so he had this Ragazza steal the Mercedes before the annual inspection."

Christine pointed at Miano, as if the truth had finally given her the right to be angry. "He did it for the money. Money, that's all he kept talking about!"

She began to cry again. ". . . all for the money."

"But you went along with it," Barbara said.

"You don't understand these people! He would have killed me. Once he smelled money, there was nothing he wouldn't do. The power he has is frightening. He made my sister disappear and tried to kill Greg. If Greg was dead, then there'd be no trial and he wouldn't have to worry about the switched cars. Assassination. Murder. That innocent boy, David, was killed—by mistake. Just correct a mistake. No matter. They even stole the car from the police. They didn't care how complicated it got. I found all this out a little at a time, until I was in so deep that if I didn't go along with the plans, I was going to 'end up in cement'—Carmine said, 'just like Caroline.' "

Christine bowed her head and kept the handkerchief to her face. The only sound was that of her softly sobbing.

Manning did not have to do it. The jury could still, theoretically, have evaluated the evidence, but Manning knew when he was beaten.

"Your Honor. Under the circumstances, the People move that the indictment be dismissed."

Pandemonium is the capital of Hell in John Milton's *Paradise Lost;* this accurately described the tumult in the courtroom. The uproar was deafening and Taylor rose and banged his gavel incessantly. To his surprise, the gavel broke, sending the splintered wooden hammer across the room.

"Order! Order!" Taylor pointed toward Miano, who tried to hide behind the massive body of Modansky. "I want that man taken into custody!"

Two of the larger court officers struggled against the crowd that was now on its feet. Unable to escape, Miano remained seated.

Well-wishers, even strangers, rushed through the swinging double door into the well to congratulate them.

When order was finally restored, Taylor granted the motion to dismiss.

Christine was still seated on the witness stand—head bowed and still sobbing.

Zangara seemed more embarrassed than Fox.

"It's your case, not mine," Fox said. "I got Miano, you got Christine."

"You believe her bullshit? Maybe you better keep her as a material witness."

"It's up to the D.A.," Fox said.

They pushed their way through the spectators.

"What about Christine Palmer?" Zangara said to Manning. "Shouldn't we arrest her, too?"

"We've been waiting for a long time to catch Miano. The witness had much to fear and was obviously acting under duress," Manning said, using generosity to salvage catastrophe.

They stood by the jury box. The jurors had filed out, and the spectators were being eased out of the courtroom.

"What now?" Zangara said.

"Can I borrow your handcuffs?" Fox said. "I left mine in the car. Never figured I'd use them in Court."

Zangara reached behind him and took out handcuffs.

"I always carry an extra pair." Zangara smiled.

Miano sat impassively, flanked by Basil and Sharon.

"You know, Zangara. We work pretty well together. It was fun raiding that chop shop with you. You think you might want to transfer over to Homicide?"

"The hours any better?"

"You don't get any smartass answers from the victims," Fox said.

"It's something to think about," Zangara said.

"Want to come along now? It won't take long to book Miano."

"I'll take a rain check," Zangara said. "I still have some unfinished business."

Sixty-nine

After Taylor departed from the bench, it still took time before the courtroom was cleared.

Barbara was about to hug Simmons, when she turned and saw Agnes standing there.

Barbara touched Gregory so that he turned and noticed Agnes.

"She doesn't matter," Simmons said.

Agnes, like the Biblical pillar of salt, seemed transfixed. Then unlike Lot's wife, she came alive. She smiled and rushed through the swinging double door.

Barbara braced herself, but Agnes instead went to her brother.

"You were magnificent. Winning isn't everything." Agnes said, and kissed Manning on the cheek. She smiled and made it appear that it was her triumph.

Zangara walked back to Manning. He fidgeted until he had the district attorney's attention.

"Yes, detective?" Manning said.

"What about Ragazza?" Zangara said.

"A deal is a deal. Let him go."

"Do you mind if I talk to him first?"

"Be my guest," Manning said.

Zangara walked past Barbara and Simmons. He shook his head as if he were saying that again justice had *not* triumphed.

"Congratulations, Barbara. You pulled another rabbit out of the hat."

"Thanks, Jack. The truth always prevails."

"Yeah, when you have a good lawyer." Zangara laughed and left by the rear door.

Barbara and Simmons were alone now in the courtroom. Sharon stood by the clerk, who was at his desk making notations in the minute book—the official record that would record the day's activity and document the completion of the case. Barbara hugged Simmons, but he did not reciprocate. Instead, he pulled back and held her arms.

"You were good. Real good!" Simmons said.

"Victory with honor. That's what you wanted, and that's what you got," Barbara said. He had a right to be reserved. Courtroom and all. Simmons seemed like an old-fashioned man. She liked that, too.

"Yes. We achieved my objective completely." Simmons smiled slyly.

It was not like Barbara to miss the ambiguous tone. But, then, flushed with success who was looking for ambiguity?

"When I saw the yellow wallet, I was stunned. And then the cigarettes! You knew it, too—didn't you?" Barbara said. Post-mortems were always exciting—when you won.

"Almost as quickly as you," he said.

"It's odd how she fooled you, twice, isn't it?"

Simmons looked at her quizzically.

"Remember when you told me that you slept with Christine, thinking it was Caroline?" Barbara asked.

"Of course!" Simmons said. "We had dinner the other week."

"But Caroline was already dead."

"If I had taken her home that night, I would have realized who she was," Simmons said.

"Are you sure? You didn't catch on until I picked up the cigarettes."

"I was a heartbeat behind you—I guess smoking is hazardous to your health," Simmons said.

"It's a shame about Caroline, though. No burial, No mourning."

"What Caroline and I had was lost a long time ago."

"Still," Barbara said. She touched his arm and looked at him as if she were searching for understanding.

"Dead is dead," Simmons said.

"I guess you're right," Barbara said. "With Caroline dead, you inherit quite a tidy sum." Her eyes brightened and she laughed.

"You'll even be able to pay my indecently large fee. Until then, I'll settle for dinner."

"I'd like to take a rain check on that," Simmons said.

Barbara, who had not bothered to gather her papers from the table, looked at them. Was she being brushed off? She had to do something. Forgetting about order, she began to stuff the file into her litigation bag. What happened? Where was the Greg of last night. *Explain. Don't beg. Don't be an Agnes.*

". . . I thought we had something wonderful going." It was all Barbara could say, and she said it without looking at him.

"It was wonderful and I'll always be indebted to you."

"Indebted?"

"I never made you any promises," Simmons said.

"Promises? You never said a fucking word." It had not taken long for the old Barbara to recover. "You think promises are only words? You think actions count for shit?"

"Don't get excited, Barbara." Simmons looked at Sharon and the court clerk. They were by the desk with their heads bowed, each embarrassed to be a witness to the conversation.

"What the hell did you expect?"

"I'm sorry. I need time for myself. This is all too quick. Perhaps later we can . . ."

". . . Pick up where we left off?" she said.

"That would be nice. You really are a wonderful person and a great lawyer."

"The next thing you'll tell me is that I can get an adjournment from you anytime," Barbara said. Great lawyer. Great lay. There were Agnes, Christine, Caroline, and—besides her—God knows who else. How could she not have seen it? Yes. He had achieved his objectives. Life makes villains of us all? *Justice Gregory A. Simmons, you're a fucking satyr!*

"Please, Barbara, let's not have a scene. Just come to my chambers tomorrow." Simmons held her arms. "Okay?"

"Guess you're right," Barbara said. "The one thing I don't want is to be *mushy-headed*."

Seventy

The holding pen on the third floor held the prisoners who were on trial that day or might be needed as witnesses. At the beginning of the day, they were transported, mainly from Rikers Island to the courthouse, and then returned the same evening. Meanwhile, they sat around on benches, waiting for court officers to take them to the courtrooms. The pen itself was a rabbit warren. Its maze of small cells was designed so that there were not too many prisoners confined in any one cell. The massive exterior door was made of steel and had a little window from which the outside world could be observed by the Corrections Department officers.

Zangara knocked on that door and showed his identification. The correction officer opened the door.

"I want to see Ragazza. But I need some privacy."

"Always happy to oblige," the correction officer replied. "He's in cell four—and he's alone already."

They walked to Ragazza's cell, and the officer opened

the cell door. Zangara went in, and the officer locked the door behind them.

Ragazza was chewing on a baloney sandwich.

Zangara slapped Ragazza's hand and sent the sandwich flying across the room. Bread separated from baloney. It seemed appropriate.

"Hey. That's my lunch!"

"You know what a *schmuck* is, Rags?"

"What you talking about? We made a deal and I kept it."

"Did you, now? Then why do I feel like a schmuck?" Zangara slapped Ragazza's face.

"What's that for? Everybody smacks me. I get kicked by the cops. You, Fox, Tracy. You fucks never heard of police brutality?" Ragazza said.

"I guess you *forgot* to tell me about the switched Mercedes," Zangara said.

"What are you talking about? I just stole the car, like I was told!" Zangara slapped him again. This time harder. "Why you leaning on me so heavy, Jack?"

"You like jokes, don't you, Rags? Why do you hit a donkey with a two-by-four?"

"Yeah, I know. To get his attention." Zangara slapped Ragazza another time.

"Does Jack have your attention now, Rags?"

"Yeah. Yeah."

"I want to know about the other matters you've been dealing with, not the deal with the D.A."

"How would I know? I've been cooped up in jail."

"They allow you phone calls from Rikers, don't they?"

"So?"

"So, you know everything that's going on."

"Not everything," Ragazza said.

Zangara reached back to smack Ragazza again, but this time his hand stopped inches from Ragazza's cheek.

"Now, spit it all out—otherwise a dime can be dropped the other way."

"What do you mean?"

"You know we busted that chop shop on Utica Avenue."

"So?"

"Fratello will be very angry when he's told that you were the one that tipped us off," Zangara said.

"He'd never believe it!"

"He'd believe it if I told him."

The threat was the key that unlocked more than the cell door.

Seventy-one

Barbara was ambivalent about going to court the next day. Didn't common sense tell her she should wait awhile before seeing Greg? Hadn't he said that he needed time to himself? But he *had* told her to see him in chambers.

Fortune, in the form of the court clerk, intervened, when he called her at her office.

"Ms. Danzig? Your client, Richard McCauley? He's been indicted. The arraignment is at two o'clock."

"For what?" Barbara said.

"Not my business. I'm just advising you." The clerk hung up.

The arraignment developed into a farce when both Reginald and Richard McCauley refused to identify themselves.

This time, each had been accused of a separate robbery and despite the D.A.'s efforts to clarify the case, the two only added to the confusion. It would be an easy case because, already, the assistant district attorney had mixed up the fingerprints and the yellow sheets, which showed prior arrests and convictions. In addition, the complaining witness, when confronted with the identical twins—as with the Sackheim case—was unable to tell them apart.

After the arraignment, she decided to go to Simmons's chambers. The bumbling of the district attorney's office had raised Barbara's spirits.

Elaine Trezza sat at her desk in the outer office, again strategically placed so as to block all but the most aggressive visitors.

"Why, hello, Miss Danzig," Elaine said. "I must congratulate you. You were superb!"

"Thank you."

"Justice Simmons isn't in. He should be back in two weeks."

"Oh?"

"This has all been so stressful for him—I would imagine for you, also."

"In two weeks?"

"Yes, first Paris and then Rome."

"He's asked me to stop by today," Barbara said. She stammered, as if she had something to say.

"He must have forgotten. He's off this afternoon for France. Been planning the trip for a long time."

"It has been stressful and he does need time," Barbara said, fishing. Was he going alone? Even now, she considered it might be a mistake. Was he going to surprise her? He had said to meet her—he had said to come to his chambers. Why? It would be adventurous—last minute plans, passport at the ready. Barbara looked at Elaine almost longingly.

"All I know is that he's leaving for France today and

he'll be back in two weeks. He's calling me when they arrive. I shouldn't tell you this, Ms. Danzig, but I'm really worried about him. I've been his secretary for more years than I like to remember, and I've never seen him act so strangely."

"Thank you, Elaine." Barbara walked down the corridor and headed for Orlando's, but not before she called Norman on her cell phone. Dr. Gershon Reich would not be any help on this one. Elaine had said, "When *they* arrive!"

Seventy-two

"Uncle Norman? Did you ever see a judge's gavel break?"

Barbara sat with Norman at a rear table at Orlando's. Silence was needed, not humor, so Norman said little. He moved the several empty martini glasses around the table.

Barbara toyed with a speared olive in her half-finished drink. Norman nursed his scotch. Someone had to maintain a level head.

"Switched drinks, didn't you?"

"What do you mean?"

"An olive instead of a lemon twist." Norman smiled. Innocuousness sometimes helped.

"Not funny, Norman . . . but you know, I never saw a judge's gavel break. It was like a bad omen."

"You should know better, Barbara. You can't get emotionally involved with a client."

"I really thought he was different," Barbara said. The martinis were having no effect.

"He was the bad omen," Norman said.

"No. It's something else."

"You won! Nobody can take that away from you," Norman said.

"Can't they?"

"You're worrying about his paying the rest of the fee?"

Barbara shook her head. Something else. What was it?

"Uncle Norman . . ."

"Yes?"

"Am I a good lawyer?"

"You're a great lawyer, Barbara."

"As great as Clarence Darrow?"

"I never saw him."

"He's dead. How about Johnnie Cochran?" Barbara asked.

"Almost as good."

"And Perry Mason?" The waiter came by with another martini and set it down.

"Maybe you shouldn't have another drink."

"Now that I look at it, Uncle Norman, it was too easy. She broke down too quickly. Don't you see. It was much too easy. And how does a defendant book tickets for Paris—in advance—for the day after he wins the case?"

"Barbara, you're talking like a jilted lover."

"Maybe I am. I was falling in love with him. But now it seems that he was charming me just to motivate me."

"There are some things an uncle can't help you with, Barbara. Why don't you talk it over with your shrink."

"I'm embarrassed. That little Nazi warned me."

"So you eat crow. It won't be the first time."

"Do you really think I'm talking like a jilted lover?" Barbara laughed. "You're quaint, Uncle Norman. I haven't heard that expression in years."

When Jack Zangara entered Orlando's, he looked around until he saw Barbara.

"Been looking for you, Barbara."

"You got a story to tell, too?" Norman said.

"Maybe."

"So sit, already," Norman said.

Zangara motioned to the waiter, who, without being told, brought him a bloody mary.

"Barbara's not satisfied with winning," Norman said.

"Why? Because she thinks she's been manipulated?" Zangara said.

Barbara had been about to chew on the olive she had put in her mouth but stopped. That was something else to chew on.

"You know, they never found the car or the body, and suddenly there's an explanation for everything. . . . But how do you have a serious accident and the boyfriend gets there before the police?" Barbara said.

"And with an identical Mercedes?" Zangara added.

"The mob is pretty resourceful," Norman said. "You can put your order in for a car and they'll deliver it tagged the next day."

"But how do you hit a tree and not damage the license plate?" Barbara said. Zangara took some pills from a vial and washed them down with his drink.

"Isn't that dangerous?"

"What, hitting a tree?" Zangara laughed.

"Come on, Jack. What do you know?" Barbara said.

"Not much, but hey, if you're going to cheat on your wife, what better way than with her twin sister. You can go anywhere—to the best restaurants, to public functions—who would know the difference?"

"But the boyfriend?"

"Ah, there's the problem. Isn't it? A woman just doesn't dump a gangster, does she?"

"Are you saying what I think you're saying?"

"What am I saying?" Zangara said. He had that teasing look that was often comical. It wasn't comical.

"Are you saying that this whole trial was a setup? An elaborate scheme just to put Miano behind bars and out of the way?" Barbara said. Instead of the queen, had she been a pawn?

"Suppose, just suppose, that you have a wife controlling ten million dollars and you're in love—infatuated, whatever—with the wrong sister," Zangara said. "The one who feels cheated out of an inheritance. And suppose the wrong sister has a connection with a mobster she wants to break. How do you get rid of them?"

"*That's* why Simmons kept insisting on a trial, that son of a bitch! The two of them kill Caroline and use Miano to get rid of the body. Then they use the trial to get rid of Miano."

"He ends up with the girl and the money," said Norman. He shook his head at the brilliant deviousness. "And all the while, we're giving him information about the stolen car—so he knew his plan was working. I was a chump, too!"

"His only flaw was that he never figured Miano would try to have him killed," Zangara said.

"Yeah, what about that?" Norman said.

"It didn't matter," Zangara said. "Her confession implicating Miano would hasten his departure, wouldn't it?"

"Yes. And he used me while preaching about ethics and a 'principled defense.' "

"You have to admit, Christine Palmer is one hell of an actress," Zangara said.

"If it's true, then I was a part of their plan all along," Barbara said. "Didn't she retain me on the will case?"

"That, I don't understand," Norman said.

"I had to meet Christine. Yes. Of course, I had to meet Christine," Barbara said. She was becoming more sure now of the deception. "Don't you see, Norman. I had to see her in yellow. I had to see her chain smoking in my office so I could break her when she testified."

"Nobody can plan that far ahead," Norman said.

"I heard once that the Russians planted kids here so that, when they grew up, they would become spies," Zangara said. "Made a movie about it. Kevin Costner, I think?"

"How come you know so much, Jack?" Barbara said. Wasn't this all still speculation?

"Me? I was just supposing. When I see greed and passion together, it's like one and one makes two," Zangara said. "The bells started to go off when she walked in with Modansky. Now, where would a judge's wife find a mob lawyer to represent her? Why would a mob lawyer represent her? So when you pushed her and she revealed the switch, it all made sense. Switched cars, switched women. It was all really interesting," Zangara said, adopting a Charlie Chan accent.

He sure as hell knew more, and he was obviously enjoying having it dragged out of him.

"The loose end here is Ragazza," Barbara said. Suspicion still had not risen to the level of certainty.

"No, he's not. A favor is a favor, or maybe a half million dollars for a few months or so in jail. Miano thinks he needs the second Mercedes stolen to avoid anyone discovering the switch. Christine probably convinced him of that. What he didn't know was that Ragazza intentionally got caught. Meanwhile the rich judge is off to gay Paree—just about now." Zangara looked at his watch.

"How did you know about that?" Barbara said. "Dammit, I just found out!"

"A little birdie told me," Zangara said. "A stool pigeon."

He raised his glass in salutation and then drank the bloody mary.

"What time does the plane leave?" Barbara asked. She, too, checked her wristwatch.

"Just about now. Leaves in the evening, arrives in the afternoon. Time difference, you know," Zangara said.

"If he's on that plane with the sister, I want to shove this glass in his face," Barbara said, brandishing the empty glass. The last martini had finally done its job. Indignant. Vengeful.

"Come on, counselor. You mustn't take the law into your own hands," Zangara said.

"Oh no?" Barbara said. She collected her purse and briefcase, seized Norman by the jacket, and dragged him toward the door. "I'm not going to sit around here doing nothing."

"Barbara, you don't even know if she's with him. Zangara is just giving you the business."

Norman knew that he could neither change her mind nor allow her to go alone—even if it didn't make sense. Damned martinis. Next time, he'd get drunk!

"You'll never get there in time," Zangara said. He was teasing. So what? He had rights, too. Zangara liked Barbara. He liked Norman. It was his investigation that had gone sour. Hadn't he been manipulated, too? Everyone had to pay, even if the currency was only sarcasm. "Maybe the flight was delayed," he added.

"Never know unless you try," Barbara said.

Outside they hailed a taxicab. It was the first good omen of the day. They caught a cab immediately—it was yellow.

Seventy-three

The flight *had* been delayed. It was raining—not so hard as to impede the journey, yet sufficient to back up the outgoing flights.

Simmons was relaxed. He wore casual clothes. Navy polo shirt. Beige slacks. An American traveler. Comfort was not to be sacrificed for formality. He removed his shoes and carefully tucked his feet back as Christine slid by him into the window seat.

Christine also wore blue, a two-piece pantsuit. Her Coach handbag was large and stuffed with easy-to-access toiletries. She leaned down and rummaged through it.

"I think I left my lipstick behind."

"You don't need lipstick," Simmons said. He had noticed the French copilot ogle her when they had come aboard. Christine was stunning.

"Are you happy, Greg?"

"You were marvelous, absolutely marvelous."

"I feel like a monster," Christine said.

"Don't get soft on me now," Simmons said.

"I hated her—but she was still my sister."

"Life makes villains of us, doesn't it?"

"Greg, you must have *some* feelings?"

"Only for you," said Simmons.

He turned her face to him and kissed her lightly on the cheek. He gazed at her. "Your eyes are like silent tongues of love."

"Why, Greg, that's lovely. Especially the part about the tongue." Christine giggled and forgot her guilt.

"And your face is a benediction."

"Did you just make that up?"

"Unfortunately not. It's from *Don Quixote*."

"It's lovely, anyway."

"And appropriate, my darling. No more jousting with windmills. Ten million and free. No splits, no trusts, all ours! That's what money is, you know, freedom. Freedom from the nine-to-five tyranny. Freedom to do what you please, when you please."

"And not answer to anyone." Christine leaned her head on his shoulder.

"Except ourselves," Simmons said.

"I'm worried about Agnes. She's out to ruin your career. Besides, God knows what she knows. She was stalking you—maybe she saw something."

"Don't worry. I took care of that, too."

"How?"

"Never mind, my sweet. No loose ends."

"Isn't Danzig a loose end?"

"No. She's been kissed off." Simmons chuckled at the image.

"I think you made a mistake there."

"Why?"

"She was relentless for you."

"She was supposed to be—isn't that why we chose her?"

"I think you liked her—a little bit."

"She was all right for a tough-talking bitch."

"Did you sleep with her, Greg?"

"Absolutely not!"

"I would have understood," Christine said, as if to test him.

"How could I? There's nobody in this world but you."

"I feel the same way." Christine stroked his face.

"Did you sleep with Miano?" Simmons said. That was gnawing at him.

"After my parents died? After I told you I'd never let him touch me again?" Christine said.

"Did you?"

"Greg, how could you even ask me? Absolutely not!"

The two were so engrossed with each other that they didn't notice the flight attendant rush to the cockpit. The copilot emerged and didn't miss another opportunity to glance at the beautiful American.

"Open the door," he said. "We just received a call. Some official business."

The attendant struggled with the handle and, with the copilot's assistance, opened the plane's door. They stepped aside for two policemen.

There was no hesitation. The cops knew who they wanted, and when they saw Simmons and Christine, they walked down the aisle and stood over them.

"Would you please come with us, Judge?" The larger of the officers said. He had on his solemn duty face. Firm. Excessively polite. Serious. "I'm Officer Garry and this here is Officer Vaughn."

"What is this about?"

"We don't want to embarrass you, Judge," Officer Vaughn said. They blocked anyone from moving in the aisle. Embarrass? Every passenger had dropped what they were reading. All other conversation ceased.

"You're both under arrest," Garry said.

"You're making a terrible mistake. One for which I'm going to hold you both personally responsible."

"Please, sir. We would rather not take you off the aircraft in handcuffs," Vaughn reasoned.

"Greg, what's happening? I thought I received immunity?" Christine clutched Simmons's arm.

"Manning! Don't worry, darling. We're going to make him look foolish again."

No handcuffs. Greg reached up for his carry-on bag, and Officer Garry helped him. They exited the plane, Garry leading the way and Vaughn trailing behind.

Seventy-four

The pizza parlor had been Ragazza's first stop when he was released from jail.

"It's got to look like a suicide or an accident," Ragazza said.

"Better a suicide," Jimmy Four Eyes said. "Accidents, they investigate too much. Always looking to see who's to blame. A suicide is better."

"You handle it any way you want."

"How am I getting paid?" Jimmy Four Eyes asked.

"The way you fucked up the golf course, and you're asking about pay?"

"That was an accident."

"Use the advance you got from Miano," Ragazza said.

"That ain't ethical," Jimmy said. "That hit was Carmine's contract."

"All right. Just do the job. You'll get your dough as soon as the judge gets back from Paris."

"Don't fuck with me, Rags." Jimmy narrowed his eyelids.

Riley was pondering the problem—accident or suicide—when a telephone call came from Riker's Island that made the problem academic.

"The boss said it's okay? . . . Yeah, Carmine, but it's a rush job . . . yeah I know they're leaving town. I know I owe you. . . . No, I'll work it out."

So now he had a dilemma. Jimmy Four Eyes Riley had just made a contract to hit the man who, through Ragazza, had hired him to hit the D.A.'s sister. The dilemma was easily resolved in his mind. By hitting Simmons first, he wouldn't have to perform the other contract. Maybe he'd just go over to her house one day and bang her. Who'd complain? Ragazza? The dead man?

The problem presented more of a challenge. Riley prided himself on innovation and preparation. He would visualize a situation and then, hypothetically, solve it. Thus, when the occasion arose, he would be prepared. It was like that English guy said about how they won all their wars—on the soccer field, or was it a cricket court? This was one problem he had prepared for—that could be put into quick operation. The question was how do you get a gun into an airline terminal? How do you safely get a gun in there, make the hit, and make a safe exit?

All it took was a few phone calls and Jimmy Four Eyes Riley was ready. His reputation had been tarnished by the golf course foul-up, but now it would be restored. The fact that his scheme required others did not bother him as much as the fact that it was raining. It was bad luck. Guns got wet, water caused distortion. All sorts of bad things happened in the rain. When he left the pizza shop, he tightened his Humphrey Bogart style trenchcoat. He sneezed. *Damned rain. It's giving me a cold.*

Seventy-five

Simmons and Christine were escorted by the police and walked down one of the airport's winding passageways. They turned the corner, and a man wearing a trenchcoat approached them.

Garry motioned for Simmons and Christine to stop. He fingered his 9mm pistol.

"Why haven't you read us our rights?" Simmons asked, as if that would change things.

Jimmy Four Eyes walked past them. He stopped. With a quick movement, he took Vaughn's pistol from its holster and aimed it at Simmons and Christine.

"Carmine sends his regards," Riley said. He emptied the pistol into their bodies.

With death both imminent and inevitable, Justice Gregory A. Simmons had performed the only selfless act of his life. He had attempted to shield her from the bullets, which pierced his body, went through him, and found her anyway. Simmons was spun around by the force of the bullets. He reached and hugged Christine; then they both fell. Riley fired, carefully making sure, as he had been instructed, that Christine was the last to die. The noise of the jet engines had muffled the shots. Didn't even need a silencer.

When his pistol was empty, Riley returned it to Vaughn's holster and extended both his hands straight out.

Garry handcuffed him. They led him away, one on each of his arms, holding onto him as though Riley had just been apprehended.

They walked quickly, but not too quickly. They rounded another bend in the passageway, now out of sight of the flight attendants, who were doubtless running to the crime scene. Like a charm. No witnesses except "police officers."

It was then that Barbara and Norman arrived. They had heard the noise but it was undefined. Suddenly, they found themselves confronted by police officers.

"Out of the way!" Vaughn barked.

"What happened?" Norman asked. He looked down at Garry's scuffed shoes.

"None of your business," Garry said.

Barbara and Norman moved to the side and continued on toward the plane.

Norman then did the inexplicable. He tripped Barbara and hastened her fall with a violent push.

"Hey!" Barbara yelled.

Norman liked hollow-point bullets. They would carom around in the body until they found bone to smash. There were no nice ways to wound someone. He fired several times, catching both "police officers." Garry got off a few shots, but they went wild. Not so with Norman's bullets—they hit Jimmy Four Eyes Riley squarely in the chest. The bullet severed his aorta and bounced into his lungs. Within seconds he—along with Garry and Vaughn—was dead.

"Uncle Norman? What have you done?"

Barbara was on her knees. Norman helped her up.

"I'm sorry, Barbara." Norman was still wary. They might still be able to shoot. He went up to them and kicked their guns away.

"My God, Norman. You've just killed two policemen!"

"Police officers don't wear scuffed shoes. They have to pass inspection when they start their tour."

"And based on that, you've just shot three men?"

"Nah, I also recognized one of them." Norman pointed to Garry. "He's no cop. He works for Miano. Besides, no cop ever handcuffs a prisoner with hands in the front."

"Norman, you're not even upset, are you?"

"Barbara, suppose one of those shots they fired had hit you?"

"I'd be upset," Barbara said. Was conscience that relative? Dependent upon the circumstances? Dependent upon whose ox was gored?

"Barbara, I'm afraid of what we may find down this passageway," Norman said.

He tried to restrain her but she brushed him aside.

"Don't be ridiculous, Norman."

A small crowd had gathered around the bodies. When Norman and Barbara arrived there, they pushed through the group.

Norman embraced Barbara. She began to cry, her hand moving to her mouth to stop the wailing sounds. Blood had spread around Simmons and Christine like a ghastly halo, as they lay on the floor, intertwined in death. Barbara just stood there, motionless, until Norman said, "Let's go." She took one last look. First David and now them. Violence seemed to be following them. Simmons and Christine were sprawled out like badly broken marionettes tossed on a scrap heap. "We have to go," Norman said.

"Why?"

"Because we can't do any good here."

"No, I mean, *why?*" Barbara said. She leaned heavily on Norman as they walked away.

It was odd how the mind worked. Barbara was grief-stricken and recoiling from the horror she had witnessed—yet her powers of observation were not affected. She stopped. "We have to go back!" Barbara said. Norman held her, but she broke away from him.

"Barbara, please."

"Leave me alone, Norman!" Barbara's voice was cold. She fought her way back through the crowd.

She gazed at them.

"Oh, my God, Uncle Norman. Don't you see?"

"See what?"

"She's not wearing any yellow clothing!"